VANITY KILLS

By

Erica Summers

More by Erica Summers

Books:
Bad God's Tower
Vanity Kills
Mantis

Short Stories:
"DERAILED" *(Amazon & Kindle Unlimited)*
"In the Blood of the Martyr" (Amazon & KU)
"Tines" (It Calls From Below)
"Take a Breath" (Anthology of Splatterpunk)
"The Mother" (Their Ghoulish Reputationg)
"Painted in Vermilion" (Air: Elemental Series)
"Sated" (Books of Horror Community Vol. 4)
"All the Same Color on the Inside" (Year Five Anthology)

Vanity Kills Trigger Warnings:
(This list contains spoilers)

Profanity
Homophobia
Consensual & Non-consensual sex
Blood & Gore
Harm to an animal (brief)
Self-harm & Suicidal thoughts

Dedications:

For the late Nic Wilder who inspired this story and Eddie Sampson who kept us all laughing until the day he died. I miss you both every day.

For Heather and Dave, I love you both so much.

For G, the red-headed beauty, who allowed a voyeuristic peek into severe body dysmorphia. I still think about your all-consuming relationship with Anna and Mia to this day.

For David Cronenberg, the man who inspired my love of body horror at a young age and continues to re-inspire me constantly.

And this is for those who don't understand how perfect you already are, scars and all. For those who sacrifice their health or life for outer beauty. For those that look in the mirror and see something other than what is there. And for those who stare into it, and see a hideous monster staring back... this book is for all of you too.

"Life, although it may only be an accumulation of anguish, is dear to me, and I will defend it."
— Mary Shelley, *Frankenstein*

"This is vanity: living to pretend, living to seem, living to appear. And this makes the soul restless."
-POPE FRANCIS

"Vanity kills. If the blast don't catch you, then the fallout will."
-ABC, *"Vanity Kills"*

VANITY KILLS

1

The menacing smell of death hangs thick in the air, hovering like a dense cloud of relentless mosquitoes in the hot July humidity. The hazy Louisiana sky looms vibrant and ominous overhead, as though tinged by the blessed smoke of a voodoo shaman.

There is fire. Licking its forked, heathen tongue up the side of an oak tree. Glittering in the squares of shattered glass, scattered among crunchy detritus and powdered dirt. The fractals reflect a million copies of the harrowing scene around them, like millions of microscopic television sets. There's a spray of pieces on the seat, dispersed unevenly in coagulating blood like clustered diamond flecks around leaky garnet stones.

Dark smoke billows from the sputtering engine of the silver SUV, belching thick plumes of blackened poison into the air, blooming out from beneath the crumpled hood.

The mechanical hisses and whirs of the once-growling engine are deafening amid the symphony of sounds in the southern wilderness. Birds and locusts gawk at the tragedy, watching the stillness of it all as reverent onlookers.

A horrific scream rips the air, reverberating like a megaphone off the miles of bone-straight pavement ahead. It's guttural, like something almost inhuman, but decidedly male.

The river of glass tinkles as his lacerated hands tremble their way across the seat. His eyes strain to focus. Fear sits thick in his gasping throat. A blood-smeared airbag is deployed over him like a burst bubble of gleaming white chewing gum, claustrophobically suffocating him with draped fabric. It's deflated over the bulge in his lap, like a cloth doorway to the fresh hell and years of nightmares that lie beneath. He weakly touches it, hands tremoring in utter shock.

His trembling fingers tangle in the lock of wet, dark hair beneath the folds of the spattered material. It's all become partly detached from the crushed human skull pinned between the bent steering column and his lap.

Her *skull.*

There's no one else's it could be, though he prayed to God that he was somehow wrong.

Please *God* let it be wrong.

The fleeting moments before the crash rush back like a boulder rolling downhill.

Picking up speed.

Smacking him in the face like a Mack truck.

He screams again, leaving every trace of his soul in the cry as it dissipates into the ether above the burgeoning eddy of gray smoke.

Pink spit dribbles down his gashed face and neck, scored with straight cuts from the exploded windshield. He writhes, unable to free his pinned lower half from the nightmare he's opened his eyes to.

The miserable nightmare he'd do anything to wake from.

But he didn't understand misery yet.

No, that *he would learn in the cruel years to come because in this moment, he cannot even begin to fathom the fallout and repercussions of one single moment of time.*

Lives altered forever from one careless over-correction.

He screams so loud that he chokes on a lungful of smoke, hacking up pink drool, sucking in snot and tears. He coughs again until he gags out the window, where he locks eyes with a panting dog.

He swears the mutt has a judgemental look in his eyes. And why shouldn't it? It's seen everything.

It scrutinizes him, the catahoula pup. Raising its young, curious face at the wreckage with its paws crossed, lounging calmly on its belly in the grass.

As if he had no part in this.

As if, for him, *everything will be just fine.*

As if, for him, *the world is* not *on fire.*

2

Jack LeBlanc sits upright, springing from his nightmare, gasping air in thick gulps and breaking down into a single heavy sob. He wipes the wetness trailing beneath his normal, hazel eye. The duct of the scarred one, sunken slightly deeper in his face by skin grafts that hug the curvature of his bones, hasn't been able to shed a tear in years.

Though the nightmarish recollection has recurred for years, it feels just as potent as the first time. A thick sheen of sweat forms on the unburned half of his face, which peeks out of the cowl of his sweat-drenched blue hoodie like some ethereal shade. The jacket is old and frayed near the cuffs and corners of the kangaroo pouch, but it's offered him seclusion and security for years. Despite his aversion to mirrors, he wouldn't even dream about walking around his own apartment with it on.

God forbid, he might catch a glimpse of himself in something reflective without it.

An audio file drones on through the tinny speakers of his laptop. A boring doctor prattles on, regurgitating medical information of a patient that Jack is supposed to be transcribing. He wipes the drool off his chin and eyes the open document on his laptop, barely even started.

He checks his phone, blood pressure still pounding in his scarred temples. "Son of a bitch."

It's not original.

It's just all he can think to drum up through the grogginess.

He frantically slams his laptop closed with a hand that is gnarled by healed burns, seamed by lines of pink between patches of skin whose tones don't match. *The hand of Frankenstein's monster,* he thinks.

He crams the device in his laptop bag, wrenches the handle on his rolling suitcase, locks the door and scurries out.

Once outside, he sighs, realizing that he's once again locked both his apartment and car keys inside.

3

"This little black pill has the potential to completely revolutionize healthcare and change lives." A single, glistening capsule is held in the air. Behind it is the smiling face of Nurse Eileen Tate. A rag-tag group of potential guinea pigs sit in rows of bland conference tables in front of her. Eager and hopeful. Hungry for a chance to earn some easy cash.

"By participating in this phase one clinical pharmaceutical trial, you could be instrumental in changing hundreds, if not *thousands* of lives, for the better." Her bright, feminine face is framed by cascading waves of brunette hair. Her tired eyes crinkle in the corners when she smiles. She seems enamored by the oval pinched between her fingertips.

Jack slinks into orientation, sweat still drying to the sides of his hood, with the thin outline of white from the salt on the edges.

He's paralyzed by the realization of his worst fear as he walks in: *he has everyone's full attention.*

He tells himself it's because he's late, but that baleful whisper in his head chants: *They can't stop staring. They'd pay good money to see a freak like you at the circus. You'd be the star attraction. They'd gladly shell out hard-earned dough to see the barbecued mess beneath your hood. It would satiate their sick appetites for entertainment to view, in broad daylight, the hideous demon you truly are.*

He's jostled from his abusive train of cruel thought by the fingerless-gloved hand fluttering through the air, vying for his attention.

It's a familiar face. One that quells his momentary anxieties enough for him to take another step inside. It's Mick. He recognizes the sly smile draped across his tan face, covered by a chest-length thatch of chestnut beard hair. His bright green tie-dyed shirt that says 'FUCK NAZIS' is enough to make him stand out all on its own.

"Yo, bruh!" Mick's Cajun accent is so thick, he's hard to comprehend. It comes through in nearly every word.

On Jack's way over to the empty spot beside Mick, a stunning blonde catches his eye. Her shining shoulder-length locks glint under the fluorescent ceiling panels of the hotel meeting room. She's seemingly perfect. *One thousand percent out of his league* in his mind, from her slender frame to the soft dimples seated in two supple cheeks. Her eyes are like two azure orbs beneath manicured brows the color of honey. He feels like they're staring straight through him, arresting him on the spot. He flashes a smile in her direction without thinking, positive she's not actually looking at him. *But she is.* Her eyes have locked with his and her sweet smile warms him like a campfire.

Mick yanks the hem of Jack's hoodie and he sits obediently. Like a dog.

Like a fucking dog.

"Where 'da hell you been?" The brash Cajun whispers.

"Passed out while I was transcribing. Locked my damned keys inside. Had to wait for an Uber." Mick laughs at his misfortune. *Classic Jack,* he thinks. "I thought you was gon' ditch me. Wouldn't that be somethin'. You ropin' me into 'dis an' 'den neva' show."

Jack flashes a look that says: *you know me better than that* and slinks down. He absentmindedly tugs the braided strings so the opening in his hood closes a bit, obscuring more of his burned face.

The surly twenty-something on the other side of Jack raises his hand. Eileen points to him. "Yes, sir?"

"Hi. *Alan.*" He gives a half-assed wave after introducing himself and then re-crosses his arms over his chest. A mop of black hair is draped dramatically across his pale, angular face in an emo-style swoop. Long in the front and short on one side. He's in black from head-to-toe. "Where are the rest of the volunteers?"

"You' lookin' at 'em." Mick interjects, carefree as always. "'Da *few,* 'da *proud,* 'da *guinea pigs.*"

A few people snicker.

"Yes, it seems this is it." She does a quick, silent headcount of the fifteen or so people peppered through the room. "My name is Eileen Tate. I'll be your nurse for the course of this trial. I'll be aiding your Principal Investigator in the coming weeks. He's a recipient of the ACCP Distinguished Investigator Award. He started out in biochemistry twenty-five years ago and then moved into oncology around twelve years ago.

Then, roughly seven years ago, he started developing the pharmaceutical you are here to test now. Over the course of his career, he's been a pivotal developmental part of three, large over-the-counter medications on the market today. The candidates who agree to the terms of the trial will meet him tomorrow for the surgical prep. Afterward, I will administer the first round of the medication."

She beams out over the audience of hopeful volunteers. "Right now, I'm going to hand out something called an *Informed Consent Form*. This packet lays out all of the pertinent information of the trial. Take a look. Read it thoroughly. Ask any questions you'd like, because by signing this, you agree to participate in the remainder of this three week trial."

As she passes forms around the room, Mick's gaze settles on a busty woman seated across from him. The colorful square plastic tag on her gaudy key ring reads: *Angie*. She's drop-dead gorgeous with mid-back length natural red hair, shiny and thick like rust-colored ocean waves. She grins back at him with a look that says she is trouble incarnate.

"Bruh, did I... die and go ta' Heaven?" Mick whacks at Jack with his knuckle. "Because I'm clearly in the presence of an angel."

Jack leans forward with a smirk and whispers. "Hate to break it to ya, buddy. I don't think that's where you'll be goin'."

"Aww man, fuck you." The Cajun jests, struggling to tear his eyes from her like they're attached with thick strips of Velcro. He motions to her. "Dibs on the ginger."

Instead, Jack looks past her at the trim, bald-by-choice black man sitting shoulder-to-shoulder with her.

"Interesting. I didn't think he was your type. Very *progressive* of you."

Mick shoots a fingerless-gloved middle finger at him.

Jack continues playfully instigating. "It's cool, man. Love who you love."

"*Pfft.*" Alan scoffs at their conversation, aggressively clearing his throat.

Jack and Mick turn to look at him.

Alan drums his fingers anxiously on the table. Scars writhe up his arms like thin, pink snakes, plain as day. Two deep now-healed gashes run from wrist-to-elbow on both forearms.

Jack shivers a little at the thought of someone voluntarily flaying their own arms open just to end their suffering. He imagines the level of misery that an act like that takes.

"Got a problem, *Gerard Way*?" Mick chirps.

"Nope, I'm great."

But he does have a problem. They can feel tension in the air.

"*Nice gloves.*" His tone is still salty.

"What can I say? Always a trend-setter." Mick's reply is light. He can't take this kid seriously.

"Find those in the trash at the gym?" The bitchy emo fires back, goading.

Mick grips the rubber wheels by his side and rolls out from beneath the table revealing the chair he's confined to. "Do I LOOK like I hang out at a *gym*, asshole?"

Alan feels a sudden pang of embarrassment at the sight of the wheelchair. His eyes dart.

But Mick's not done talking. "Awful ballsy for someone dressed like 'dey headed to a *Panic at the Disco* concert. You get a notch on ya' punch card every time you purchase an angst-ridden ensemble like 'dat at *Hot Topic*?"

Nurse Tate plops packets down in front of all three with a serious expression, one of an angry mother about to threaten three chaotic kids fighting in the back seat.

But Mick's already changed gears, flagging her down with the wave of a glove. "Angel, when we gettin' *paid* fa' 'dis?"

Tate stops in her tracks. "All participants will receive a check for the full amount after the conclusion of the trial. Fortunately for you, compensation is quite high for this trial as an incentive to join us versus the one starting up in Baton Rouge tomorrow. The allotment for this is $1400… per *week*."

A female applicant chimes in. "Wait, we're not getting paid for almost a month?"

"Three weeks, yes." Tate nods.

Another man in the back speaks up. "There's a LOT of stuff listed under potential side effects. Is this, like, *safe*?"

"Well," she laughs nervously, "the function of the trial is to prove that the drug *is* safe and effective and to determine what the potential side effects are. Once we complete this phase and submit our results, then we are able to get funding for a much larger trial of the same drug. Each of these is a step on the road to getting any medicine approved by the FDA for the general public."

"So, we have to sign forms saying that we understand… this could kill us?" Another asks, sounding distressed.

"I assure you, Obsidian has had *astounding* results in the animal trials–"

An irritated voice interrupts, "Nah, I'm out." He tosses down his packet and storms out. Several others quickly follow suit leaving with their luggage. Seven participants remain.

Tate pats a spot on the table up front and tries to mask her frustration with the sudden walk-out. "For those remaining, please drop your signed packets here when you're done. Then, if you have a car on the premises, grab one of these purple parking passes for your vehicle. Blurred vision is a possible side effect so, legally, we cannot allow you behind the wheel during the trial. They'll all be kept in the secured parking garage here on level 2. There's video surveillance and active lot guards, so there is no need to worry. The shuttle outside will take you all to your accommodations."

The handsome, black man next to the girl with the glimmering blue eyes speaks up, his voice effeminate and disappointed. "Oh, we aren't staying here in the hotel?"

"No, we have a full, state-of-the-art medical campus that is just a twenty minute bus ride down Airline, across the St. James Parish line. We have on-site testing equipment, full housing, and recreational accommodations there."

Eileen Tate's smile broadcasts total confidence to the remaining participants. "After all the paperwork is signed, you can bring your suitcases to the shuttle. I'm excited to show you where you'll be staying."

4

The shuttle coasts down Airline Highway next to the miles-long fingers of Bayou Conway, like watery claw marks dragged through the land. It flanks the vast expanse of lonely road peppered with local fauna and twisted cypress trees, their knobby knees jutting out of the murky brown water. Its rippling surface glints blinding, white reflections from the scorching summer sun overhead. Spanish moss crawls thick through the treetops along the desolate thoroughfare.

Jack watches a water moccasin slither through the murky brown liquid onto the bone-dry bank and lifts his head away from the rattling glass window. He scans the small bus at the other participants, wondering what their reasons for being there might be. Some seem obvious, like Alan with his wormy trails of self-mutilation. Others, like the girl with eyes like sapphire gemstones, remain a mystery.

She looks up, almost as if she can telepathically hear him thinking about her. She catches him staring. He wants to look away, wants to hide inside the cowl of his hoodie and tighten it until he looks like *South Park's* Kenny, mumbling and shrugging through a slit. But her gaze freezes him in place. Her soft smile is like the pause button on a remote, halting the world in its rotation.

He looks away after a full, single second that feels like a literal eternity, and lowers his hazel eyes to the floor. He doesn't feel like he deserves another moment of her attention. He re-affixes his stare back outside on the racing asphalt lines, noticing the area. Noticing how *sickeningly familiar* it all seems.

As if cursed to be reminded for eternity, it springs to the forefront of his mind. Somewhere around here, his whole life and future changed in the literal blink of weighted eyelids. Ones that fluttered with gratification. It still hangs over him like overpowering deja vu.

Somewhere near here, he'd ruined innocent lives.

Somewhere near here, he'd changed himself forever.

Changed so many others forever.

He blinks to keep the welling tear in his good eye at bay, closing his lids so long he misses the sun-faded cross wrapped in pink ribbon at the base of a gnarled tree trunk entirely. The blackened oak behind it bears a deep, horizontal gash.

No, Jack doesn't open them until the bus has long-turned down the dirt road on the left and he feels the fat wheels beneath him grind on the tiny grated bridge. It groans like it's not strong enough to hold such heft, but it holds. The horrendous *grrrrrrnnnnnn* sound is short-lived and the whistling driver's foot lands heavily on the gas pedal once again.

The shuttle jostles down the dirt road, winding through the narrow single-vehicle path, nearly overgrown by tall grass. Invasive wisteria, whose periwinkle blossoms have withered and died for the year, have left behind a spider web of insidious vines woven tightly through the trees overhead.

After a slow half-mile down the path, the thatched canopy of shade opens to an astonishing multi-building facility perched along a bulge in the bayou, water disappearing in both directions. Around the buildings sit wide-open acres of fresh-cut St. Augustine grass, dotted with evenly-spaced ornamental shrubs. The bus squeals to a halt in front of a large building in the middle, jostling everyone aboard.

The driver cranks the handle and the bus squeals as the door hydraulically opens. They pile out. Alan flashes an angered glare at the driver in the giant bulging mirror overhead from beneath his swooping black bangs. Chase follows behind him, tapping the driver on the shoulder, leaning in to whisper, "It ain't personal. He's been salty to everyone."

After struggling to get Mick back down the steps and into his chair, the participants follow Eileen down a grassy path to the picturesque two-story building at the end, seated feet from the water's edge. Tate beams proudly, scanning the property with eyes that are striking, even behind nerdy, blue wayfarer-frames.

"For those of you not from around here, this is the Blind River. It leads right into Bayou Conway." She points to the water. Its edges are thick with dense bio-diverse vegetation. Tufts of wild, local fauna contrast starkly, juxtaposed with short, manicured grass in the immediate area around the buildings.

An errant mullet jumps out of the water, careens through the humid air, and splashes back beneath the surface near a massive outcropping of lily pads adorned with vibrant, canary-yellow flowers. The waves from it gently undulate a thick throng of blooming water hyacinths.

"There's some excellent fishing down the way if anybody enjoys that sort of thing. Tons of bowfin and catfish in there. There are rods and tackle boxes in that small, green tool shed on the far right. There are also kayaks behind the shack on the far left of the property near the dock. And if you go beyond it a bit, there's a really lovely little shaded walking trail down there."

She claps her hands together and points. "This building to the right of the main house is the clinic. There's a small infirmary, the doctor's office and all of our hematological testing equipment. And upstairs, the doc actually lives there."

"I'd wanna live out here, too. This place is amazing," Chase chimes in, voice sweet, almost dainty. "It's so serene."

Alan violently smacks at a mosquito feasting on his neck. He grimaces, squinting hard to avoid the blistering sun as they follow Tate like ducklings to the large white building in the center.

Jack stares at the decrepit, battered, brown shack off to the left a stretch, the one with a rack contraption that stores the kayaks upside down behind it. Unlike the others on the property, all maintained and well-kept, the building on the end looks dilapidated, as if the roof might cave in at any moment. Two cracked windows sit in busted, wooden frames above a rotted porch missing boards. Jack sees something dark brush past the window.

It's *massive*. Eclipsing the entire window frame, it whooshes by.

He could swear the fleeting shadow had eyes, but they were far too large to be human.

""'Scuse me. Um, what's in there?" Jack points to the now-vacant window, scarred brows furrowed, the tough skin struggling to wrinkle.

"Nothing." Eileen scoffs, immediately turning her attention back to the central building. "That one hasn't been used in years. It's falling apart inside. The wood's rotted. Doc's been getting quotes to have it bulldozed. We ask that you stay clear of that one for safety and legal reasons. It's a liability."

"Something just moved in there." Jack tries to not sound alarmed. Though appearing empty now, he knew *something* was just there. Something too large to explain.

"Oh yeah, I don't doubt that. There's holes all over that thing. Part of the roof is caved in in the back. Critters make a home in it all the time."

"Bruh, this is *Louisiana*." Mick said it like *Loose-anna*. "Probably a whole *family* 'a coons or somethin' livin' in 'ere." His loosened brake falls and locks his wheels, stopping him in his tracks. He growls and tries to slam the stubborn lever back up with the heel of his hand, nearly dumping the wheelchair on its side with him in it. "Uhhh, little *help* here?!

Jack squats, examines the lever, and bangs his gnarled hand upward on the brake twice more to unlock it. "There, *cyborg,*" he teases, heaping his suitcase onto Mick's lap, atop the black duffel bag that's already on there. He grabs the handles on the back of the chair. "C'mon, Miss Daisy."

***

Tate turns on the lights as the patients assemble in the main, two-story building. "Welcome to your home-away-from-home. In that drawer over there, there's a ton of bug spray. The opossums keep the tick population down but the mosquitoes can be merciless, especially after a good rain. Over here are lighters and candles." She pulls out a drawer stuffed with tea lights and long wax sticks.

"The power here in the boonies can be a bit finicky. Lights go out, occasionally, but we have a manual backup generator and we can usually get the power back up shortly. Let's see, there's a big fridge in the main kitchen and a smaller one upstairs in the game room, both fully-stocked. Out back, there's a storage shed with extra toiletries, canned goods, first aid kit, all that good stuff."

"Oh!" Her voice echoes off the high ceilings and glass doors that provide a spectacular view of the bayou out back. She lifts a handful of notebooks from the spacious, main living room's table. "These are your patient journals. They're pretty self explanatory and easy to fill out. They must be completed every day with some sort of entry, even if you aren't experiencing any adverse side-effects or symptoms. These are important for the doctor to track everyone's progress. He has to submit these to the higher-ups later to get phase two approval, so these are *crucial*. Please, don't lose them and don't forget to make at least one daily entry. They'll be checked each morning before your next dose of the medication."

Tate points up to a security camera bolted into the corner of the room. It flickers its tiny red light, indicating they are all actively being surveilled. "There are cameras throughout the house for your protection as well as ours. Since the cabin is co-ed, legally, we have to have these in case there is any sort of harassment or slip-and-fall type accidents."

She grabbed a locking cash box from the kitchen counter and held it open, then lifted the black plastic insert. Tate went around the room. "As the packet stated, for privacy and social media blackout purposes, I need to collect everyone's cell phones." The participants reluctantly relinquished their phones, dropping them into the metal box with a *thump*. "Don't worry, though, you're still able to call out on the landline. We just ask that you don't discuss the details of the trial with anyone when you do so. Privacy at this stage is important, but we also don't want you to feel like you can't have contact with the outside world. Unfortunately, I have to mention that if you do discuss the details of the trial with anyone on the outside, it can jeopardize the testing and you can be subject to legal ramifications and fines, as well as terminated from the program, without pay. So, please keep personal calls to a minimum."

Jack's gaze drifts over to the corded phone by the glass sliding door. He wonders how long it's been since he's seen a landline in the wild.

Eileen clasps her eager hands, voice bubbly and excited. "Tomorrow, I will come get you for your individual admission appointments. There will be an intake evaluation and then the topical surgical procedure will take place right after clearance from the doc. I'll administer your first dose of the medication and you'll be free to enjoy the rest of your day."

She placed her hands on her curvy hips and rolled her shoulders back. "Y'all's rooms are upstairs. You can decide whose is whose. And just in case, I left a blank copy of the consent packet on the kitchen counter for reference."

The group nods through the awkward wrap-up. Tate takes a deep breath.

"Alright, I'm sure you're eager to settle in. I'll be next door, in the gray building, if y'all need me." Her tone erupts into excitement again. "Get some rest tonight."

She locks eyes with Jack and smiles. "Tomorrow, y'all are gonna make *history*!"

The way she says the final word is almost manic. Her excitement, while infectious for some, makes Jack feel uneasy. He's not sure if it's the sudden, unwanted eye contact or the nurse's inflection.

All he knows is her uplifting promise seems more like a threat.

5

Iris enters a modest, freshly-painted room, claiming it as her own with the plop of her suitcase on the bed. Below it lies a feminine bedspread decked out in rabbit outlines made of curled gold ribbons against a blush background. The walls are peppered with colorful store-bought canvas art depicting abstract bunnies in pastels. A vase full of fresh-cut wildflowers sits on the bedside table beside a lamp with brand new tea lights and a lighter scattered around its base.

The window sill is cluttered with decorative candle holders stuffed with tall, colorful wax sticks, like some sort of shrine to the sunshine outside. Iris traipses over to it and lifts the window to let some fresh air into the dwelling.

She spots a dog outside and smiles, admiring its multi-colored markings. He's mostly gray, peppered with various-sized black spots throughout. He stares up at her with blue eyes and a muzzle with golden-brown fur the color of drying mud.

"Awwww, hi, babyyyyyy!" She elongates the word.

The dog just sits, soaking in the sight of the overzealous newcomer waving from the second floor. She smiles at it like a loving mother would an infant.

She always wanted a catahoula.

6

Mick, Jack, Chase, and Iris congeal around a small table in the living room of the larger cabin, all chowing down on the home-cooked meal Fisher has made with the ingredients from the over-stocked fridge. A true Louisianan at heart, he bustles through the kitchen despite already putting enough food for an army displayed on the bar dividing the rooms.

Iris pushes up the sleeves of her knitted, pink shrug and reads aloud from her *Informed Consent* form.

"You're here to participate in a groundbreaking, phase one clinical trial. Nicknamed *Obsidian* due to the formula's color, this medication holds the potential to repair defects like cleft palettes, injuries, lesions, scars, stretch marks and surgical incisions with permanence and without the use of invasive plastic and reconstructive surgery. The drug is designed to target skin cells and musculature with recent cuts or abrasions. The medicine zones in on the traumatized tissue to facilitate ultra-rapid restoration in full."

"Can I see?" Chase extends a hand. Iris hands it over and returns to picking at the food on her paper plate, despite being stuffed to the gills.

Chase skims it. "God, Tate wasn't kidding. Did you guys see this? *Side effects may include, but are not limited to, fever, nausea, insomnia, aggression, stomach pain, blurred vision, depression, thoughts of suicide, hallucinations–*"

"Yeah, dude, the list goes on and on," Iris says, jabbing a small bite of pasta into her mouth.

"Why don' drugs ever give people any *positive* side effects?" Mick chimes in, his thick accent slurred by the liquid dinner he's swigging out of a duct-taped, plastic flask. It's a recycled Listerine bottle decorated with pirate skulls and swords. He takes a long drink and swallows hard, wincing from the burn of the cheap, bottom-shelf bourbon, the only kind he can *afford*. "Like, uh, fuckin'... *night vision*?"

"Or like, spontaneous orgasms." Iris fires back.

Mick bursts out in laughter. "Yeah, like 'dat."

"What about," Fisher thinks, anxious to join in the conversation, "the ability to see through people's clothing? Like *Superman*." He laughs, wiping his slender hands on a dish towel and throwing it down.

In the recliner nearby, Alan winces at the sound of the man's effeminate voice, batting around a crouton on his plate of salad.

"Not sure that would always be a good side effect," Mick hollers over his shoulder. "Guess it depends on if you can turn the affliction *off*."

"Of course you can't. Not any more than you can turn off, like, trouble breathing or a rash." Fisher's smile beams from the rectangular hole between the rooms.

Chase laughs and scans the room, glimpsing Alan staring at him from across the way. Alan darts his eyes away, back to the others.

"Speaking of wanting to see through people's clothes, where' 'dat other girl at? The little cutie who sat on the back of the bus with the gigantic," Mick motions to his chest with cupped hands. "What's her name?" He snaps his fingers weakly, struggling to recall it.

Jack speaks up, "I think her name's Angela."

"*Angie*! 'Das it." Mick shuts his eyes and moans at the thought of her, Jack shakes his head. "Walsh betta' watch out. If anyone's gon' be playin' doctor wit' her, it'll be *me*. Who knows? Maybe she' freaky. Maybe she' be down for a little *ROLL* play." He rolls back and forth in his chair, bouncing his eyebrows.

Iris throws her head back and laughs. As her giggles die down, she glances at Jack.

He can't force his eyes away from her. She's *captivating*. His heart beats faster. He's frozen like future roadkill in oncoming headlights. No one else in the room notices his world is standing still.

Alan's voice is like a quiet growl. "She's *so* outta your league, dude."

"Why?" Mick's on the defensive. "You don' think she could be attracted to a gorgeous guy like me jus' 'cause he' in a chair? I get my fair share, okay? Shit, I've pulled more tail than a slow kid at a petting zoo."

Alan scoffs, toying with his salad. Too chicken-shit to make eye contact with the person he's arguing with. "Hell, I'll bet you can't even get hard."

"'Ey, prick," Mick's loud. "The dick still *works*. Plus, on top a' 'dat I got a tongue and ten *magical* fingers 'dat *all* aim ta' please." The Cajun fakes as if he's playing air piano and flourishes the movement into a middle finger at Alan.

"Yeah, how *else* do you think he wore out the fingers on those gloves?" Jack jests, trying to lighten the mood. Trying to think about anything but those blue crystals shining their laser beams straight into his soul.

Iris bursts into laughter and Jack smiles, hanging his head to hide his mangled face.

Mick wheels around to face his friend. "Why motherfuckers always bustin' my balls about my gloves?"

"We're jealous." Jack tries not to laugh. "I wish *I* could afford to order from the *Ramirez Night Stalker Signature Collection.*"

Playful, Iris joins in. "You look like Judd Nelson in *Breakfast Club*." She pounds her fist in the air and now it's Jack's turn to chuckle like a child.

Mick's tone is brash. "Girl' wearin' a sweater when it's 90 degrees out and she' teasing *me* about fashion. *Cool.*"

The sarcasm cuts Iris to the bone. Her demeanor changes. No longer laughing, she moves her feet up to the cushions beside her with subtle shame.

Jack notices.

Fisher enters, setting a bowl of noodles down. Linguine with goat cheese, olive oil and cherry tomatoes. It's plated beautifully, like something straight from a restaurant billboard, but they are all too over-stuffed to portion off any. He sits in the seat across from Alan who flashes a fiery glance like a skittish animal, ready to bolt.

"You made more?!" Mick's voice rose an octave.

"Yeah," Fisher says bashfully. He's worried about how much attention he's already drawing to his eating habits but he feels a rush thinking about the purge that will follow later.

Iris holds up her empty plate. "Thank you for the meal. My compliments to the chef."

"Yeah, thank you. I feel like I've been livin' off soup and salad forever. This is a nice reprieve." Chase scans the faces around him again. Alan tosses his plate down on the squat table in front of them all with a grunt and half of the lettuce bounces onto the floor.

"Everything *okay*?" Chase closes his eyes, inhales deeply. He finds it irritating to already have to walk on eggshells with this guy.

"Sure," he says passive-aggressively and then firmly pinches his lips. "Just don't feel like getting eye-fucked by some knockoff *Ru Paul* while I'm eating." He nods at Chase casually.

The comment is like a bowling ball clattering against everyone in an instant.

Chase chuckles and squishes back into the L-shaped couch, placing his arms on the backrest. His designer shirt pulls tight over his rippled abdomen and he forces a phony smile at Alan. "It's all good, honey. I wasn't eye-banging you. You ain't my type. I like *good-looking* guys. So *relax*."

"Sure." Alan nods in disbelief.

"I pull hotter than you on my *worst night* at the clubs, sweetie." He drags out the words, punctuating them with a head tilt. It makes his foe cringe. "You know, fun fact. Studies show most men are homophobic due to their *own* latent homosexuality. In fact, I feel like I've seen you on *Grindr* before?"

"Yeah, *I'm* the gay one here, Fred Schneider." Alan scoffs and pushes his plate away.

"Oooh, a deep cut. I'm impressed you're a B52's fan." Chase pretends to fan himself.

"Fantasize all you want, just keep your glittery, little paws off me for the next three weeks and we'll be fine."

"Child, *please*, don't flatter yourself." Chase rolls his eyes as he says it, unable to hold his sassiness in.

Alan yanks up his can of soda with a splash and leaves the room, brushing past Angie as she makes her way down the stairs.

"Hey, I was jus' talkin' 'bout you." Mick has a charming, million-dollar grin plastered across his bearded face. He's eager to lighten the mood.

"Good things, I hope?"

He bounces his eyebrows. *"Very."* As she disappears into the kitchen to make a plate of food, he tugs a lighter out of his pocket and taps it on his leg, drumming through the awkward silence. He flicks it on and off out of pure boredom.

Jack tenses at the mere sound of the lighter striking, his hazel eyes locked hard on the flame. "*Mick.*"

Mick ignores his friend's quiet plea to stop, flicking the metal roller with a grating, repeated *shhhick.*

Chase leans back, lifts his white wine in the air. His index finger pops away from the glass and does a sweep around the table, pointing at everyone. "I can't tell what anyone's here for." He lowers his head at Jack. "Except you. *No offense.*"

Jack senses the attention from the other participants burning through the fabric like x-ray eyes, if only for a moment. He nods, but inside, he's crawling back into himself inch-by-inch, wishing his oversized jacket would swallow him whole so he could hide from the world forever.

Mick draws back another slug of shit-bourbon and wrestles up one loose pant-leg with a grunt. The limb beneath is atrophied, pale and thin. His knees are gnarled by two mounded craters like fleshy volcanoes in the soft tissue stretched across his kneecap. The area around it is like the skin of Frankenstein's monster, minus the neck bolts, marred by healed surgical incisions that crawl in multiple directions. "Got me a matching set of these bad boys by crossing the wrong Irish *asshole.*"

Chase winces, sucking in air with a hiss.

"Four surgeries and two near-death infections later, here I am." Mick drops his pant leg back down and flicks the bic again. "Gorgeous as eva'."

Fisher chimes in, next, trying to get his public speaking out of the way. He twists his scrawny arm at an awkward angle and shows off some thick, chunky wounds on his elbow and forearm. "Skateboard scars on this side," he twists the other arm in a similar fashion to show a long, narrow slice of pink up the back of his other arm, "asphalt up this one from a fight with my dad."

"Brutal." Chase shivers and turns to Angie. "What about you, miss-*thang*?"

Coy, she points to herself as if in disbelief that he is addressing her. Without missing a beat, she slides up the hem of her tank top to reveal a tight, muscular pelvic area with a long horizontal scar paralleling her lacy panty line.

"Looks like it hurt, mama. Want me to massage it for ya?" Mick bounces his eyebrows, hope glimmering in his soil-brown eyes.

"Pass," she replies without batting an eye, pulling her shirt back down and her skirt waistband up.

"You' not gon' wanna deprive yourself of 'dese magic fingers."

"My *husband* teaches MMA and jiu-jitsu." She sounds smug.

"Cool. He can watch if that's his thing. I don't mind an audience if the cuck wants a show."

"No, ew, in your *dreams*. I meant he could kick your ass." She almost laughs but bites her cheeks instead, staring forward to avoid his gaze.

"I don't think so. He gon' risk his rep' makin' it into the papers fa' pummelling a handicap? *Please, sha.*"

"Creep." She says it but doesn't mean it. She adores attention. She is eating it up. She misses people fawning over her like they did in high school.

"And *you*, beautiful?" Chase's voice is kind as he turns to Iris.

She freezes. Unable to speak, trying to find the words, she can't even clear her throat. She has no intention of sharing something so personal with a group of people she doesn't know.

Mick flicks the spool of his lighter again to kill the growing silence.

Jack sees how uncomfortable the question makes her. He erupts at Mick, drawing the focus from her with intention. "Jesus, dude! What the fuck do I keep saying?" He snatches the bic out of Mick's gloved hands and scolds him in front of everyone. "This isn't a fucking *toy*."

He shoves the lighter in his pocket and storms off into the kitchen. Through the rectangular cutout, he winks at her. She blushes and tries to display how grateful she is for the diversion.

"Fuckin' drama queen!" Mick hollers without bothering to turn his head. "Don't care, bruh. Fuckin' keep it. I'm outta bud anyway right now. I'll just have Ed bring me anotha' when he comes."

After a moment of tense silence, Fisher runs a hand through his black hair and exhales. "So, where's everybody from?"

7

Alive throughout the evening with the electrified buzz of new friendships, the once-bustling house is silent now. Jack sits at the wobbly, little desk in his room, lit only by the dim, bluish screen of his laptop. On it, a website displays step-by-step instructions on origami swan-making. Before him sits a rumpled pile of colorful construction paper. He is folding, deep in thought.

Creeeeak. A groaning plank of the hall floorboard sounds beneath the weight of a human. He jolts at the sudden noise, head whipping on a swivel, struggling to see past his hood, fabric stretched taut like horse blinders.

"Hey." A woman's voice. Cheerful and sweet. He's only known her a few hours but he feels like he would know her voice anywhere.

"Sorry. Didn't mean to scare you." Iris whispers through the darkness, pressing her petite body against the open door.

"It's alright. Caught me off-guard," he murmurs back.

"Can't sleep?"

"No. Had an impromptu nap before orientation." He tosses down the hot, folded mess of colorful paper. "Now I'm, like, wired for sound."

"Aww." She is stepping in now, pointing to his wonky swan. She looks around at his tiny menagerie of other paper creations already born of boredom and skills honed by years of being a recluse.

"I suck." Jack holds up an odd-looking creation that looks more like a giraffe.

"No, you don't." She shakes her head, blonde hair spilling around her face as she looks down at the floor, delving right into what she really came for. "I wanted to say thanks for what you did down there. Pulling the focus off me like that."

There's a long silence between them now. She grins, her dimples pitting her perfect cheeks. It's hard to tell because of the darkness, her coy face lit only by the half-moon glugging lazily in through the window, but he could *swear* she's blushing. He averts his shy gaze. Even in the darkness, she's making him feel bashful.

"I was about to take a walk down by the water. Care to join?"

"*Now*?" He looks outside, serious. The skeletal silhouettes of trees bursting with thick foliage sit like sooty ghosts against the hazy night sky.

"Scared of the dark? Don't worry. I'll protect you," she teases.

He snickers, barely offering a head-bob while staring back down at the folds of paper he's fumbling between knotty fingers. "If I was scared of the dark, why would I be sitting in it?"

"Touche." She smirks and turns toward the stairway. "Offers on the table if you want to come."

As he sits in the lateral stripes of moonlight streaming in through his blinds, he thinks about the odd truth of the matter. Since his disfigurement, the darkness felt like his one *true* friend for offering him the reliable gift of obscurity, allowing him, and his deformities, to disappear.

***

Iris and Jack walk down a dirt trail near the bayou's edge, their path lit only by the moon. The bayou has come to life. The edge of the swamp reverberates, full of animal activity. Frogs croak over each other from soggy spots around the marsh. Bugs chirp deafening mating songs. Ravenous opossums rustle through the trees and underbrush, tunneling their gray, almond-shaped bodies through the detritus to feed on snakes and carrion. A beady-eyed raccoon's chitter rings out across the stilled waters.

"You and Mick know each other outside of here, I take it?"

"Yeah. Been friends a long time. Couple years. I'd take a bullet for that cranky bastard. Hell, I've almost *had to* a few times. The yammering *coonass* doesn't know when to shut his mouth sometimes."

"How'd you meet?" Iris looks at him.

He feels her eyes burning into him through the darkness. He keeps his own fixated on the grass. "Rehab."

Iris feels a moment of panic, nearly stopping in her tracks. She wonders how the hell she's managed to get herself into a situation like this. *Again*. With a total stranger. In seclusion. With no weapon. No phone.

She clears her throat, pressing past the fear. "Like AA… or NA?" She's fishing.

Jack's gravely serious. He takes a long time to answer. "It was… *sex addiction*, actually."

Iris's eyes bulge. Without thinking, she slowly veers away from him, spreading distance between them on the worn grass path, unable to make eye contact. Her hands tremble. She tries to lie to herself and say that it's from the chill in the air but it's still sweltering, even *without* being bundled in an angora sweater.

Jack laughs loudly, doubling over at the waist, breaking her from her anxiety spiral.

"You should see your face right now. I'm *kidding*. I *promise*."

He laughs again, staring back down at the path. Missing her reaction completely. She's not fully relieved yet.

"We *did* meet in rehab." He giggles. "But, like, as in *physical therapy.*"

Iris releases the breath she's been holding for too long, chuckling nervously. "Oh. You *got* me."

"Yeah." He presses forward again. "We both had our... injuries right around the same time and we did PT at the same facility. Been buds ever since."

They come to a rickety, wooden fence that starts to line the path. He sets his forearms on the top post and leans onto it, staring out at the bayou.

Iris joins him, doing the same but from a distance. She stares at the sky.

Jack can't keep his eyes off of her, stealing glances every moment he feels she won't notice. Though he would never touch her, could never initiate contact like that, it didn't stop him from longing for it. Longing for that intimacy.

Touch.

It had been *years* since anyone had touched him. And years since he'd touched them.

Except the doctors. Gloved hands and tweezers and scalpels prodding and palpating, checking scar tissue.

He was once handsome, having his pick of attractive females in high school and college. With his chiseled jaw, hardened like it was carved from stone, galactic, hazel eyes with rings of gold in the centers, and an effortless five o'clock shadow that made him look like a walking cologne ad, the hardest thing he had to deal with was fighting off temptations.

Now, he is a creature of the shadows. Like Nosferatu if he'd been burned to death by rays of sunlight. As he fidgets with his hands, slipping his fingertips along the smooth, taut scars, he knows that those days are just a sad, blurring recollection of better times long gone.

She notices his glances in her periphery though. Just about every one of them. Normally, the attention would make her more squeamish, but there's something in his softened expression that makes Jack seem *kind*.

He finally looks at her, dark eyes huge and glinting in the moonlight like a nocturnal animal. "God, I hope this doesn't make the next few weeks awkward, but I really just gotta say... you're absolutely *gorgeous*."

She almost sounds irritated by the admission, scoffing. "*Sthaaaaap.*"

"No, ever since Chase mentioned it at dinner, I've been racking my mind. I keep thinking, he's right. What could *you possibly* be in this thing for?"

Her smile fades. The tone of her voice makes it clear that she's trying hard to stay composed.

"It's the reminders, you know? I... want to look in the mirror and feel *normal* again."

"Jesus, you're..." he struggles with the word, finally muttering it, "*perfect*. I don't see a single thing wrong with you."

"*Stop*." Her order cuts the air like a knife. Jack looks as if he's just been slapped, eyes wide with confusion. She bows her head, ashamed, and turns. "Sorry." After a moment of looking glum and defeated, she stares up at the sky. She changes the subject, hoping to get beyond the awkwardness of the moment.

"You want to know my favorite part about living in Louisiana? Sounds weird but, it's *that*." She points up. "The sky is dark *violet*. But only *here*. I've been all over the country. Been to *other* countries. Never seen a purple sky like the one here."

"It's probably pollution." He tries to lighten the mood. "You know, from all the industrial work.

"Probably." She laughs, still staring up. "Still, it's so unique."

Jack tightens his hood strings a bit, careful to not expose too much of his injured skin, even in the darkened veil of night.

After a silence that's long –painfully long– Iris speaks again. There's a note of bravery in her voice. Like she's facing her fears. "You wanna know what I'm here for?"

He shakes his head solemnly. "I feel like I've already made you uncomfortable enough." He laughs a little. It's genuine and apologetic, she can tell. Hearing it soothes her.

"I haven't shown anyone this in a long time."

She timidly tugs her angora sweater over her head, turning her back to him. Jack holds out a charred hand, wanting to stop her but he can't find the words.

A stripe of ghostly moonlight through the trees reveals a set of scars that trail from her shoulder down her scapula, dipping just below the edge of her strappy, gray camisole near the top of her rib cage.

It's a word. Four capital letters, crudely carved. Almost illegible. But not illegible *enough*.

S.L.U.T.

Four letters that tossed a young woman into a violent whirlwind of self-loathing and fear.

"I was leaving work one night," she explains...

8

Seven years ago, that October night, was frosty. Screeching owls hunted prey in the overgrowth near the edge of the Wayne's Wing World *parking lot, flapping powerful wings into the evergreen foliage.*

Iris tugged tightly at the strap on her purse, unnerved by the other hooting and hollering that arose from beneath the overhead parking lot lights. Cackles and caws that belted from slurring human mouths, drunk on $10 pitchers of heady IPAs. Mouths that reeked of buffalo sauce and hops. The sleepy little town of Micanopy seemed to spring to life at night, mostly due to the new Bare-All strip-club down the block. Floridians from other parts of the state would flock there on a Friday night, chowing down on chili-cheese tots and sub-par burgers made by a lousy line-cook who only got the job because his uncle, Wayne, owned the joint. The pimply-faced prick made sure everyone knew he was white-trash royalty, too. The kid seemed untouchable.

Her shift was over and she couldn't wait to get out of the waist-cinching pantyhose beneath shorts so tight she could almost taste them. Her push-up bra and ultra-clingy Wing World *tank top were equally oppressive.*

Backwoods Hooters, that's what the local Floridians called it.

Some of the patrons were friendly enough, but after a decade of living there Iris felt like Central Florida was filled with the scourge of

America. It was all either dying snowbirds from New York coming down to "God's Waiting Room" to pass their remaining time, or it was 20 to 50-year-olds, with missing teeth, who all have lived on food stamps and yet seem to be vocal about how much they hate people who are on food stamps.

Tonight was mostly the latter. Her two and four-tops all seemed to be middle-aged males. Ones who would get itchy if asked to back up their opinions with facts during a raging, political argument. Ones who brag about watching MMA since the days of Randy "The Natural" Couture and "The Iceman," Chuck Liddell. Ones who have taken a couple lessons in jujitsu and feel like they know enough to teach it.

The fights were on that night, and one of her tables had been particularly rowdy. One man, in a mesh trucker's hat and a black t-shirt with a gaudy silver cross and flourishes all over it, pounded the table with a closed fist about the rareness of his burger, shouting, "I ordered medium-well," like an ape, if apes were dumb.

She didn't have the heart to tell them that the line cook only knew how to make them rare. Eventually, that kid was gonna kill somebody.

His friend sat there, boring her with stories about how they were visiting Florida for the first time and how the women were as pretty as everyone always said they were, including her. The dumb ape sat in silence, eyeing her like a thick hunk of steak in a deli-counter window. Sizing up every inch of her, gawking rudely. Calling her Iris, over and over. Making her wish she didn't have to wear a name tag. He invited her back to their hotel to "party." She declined. They said that a girl that worked in a place like that must be down to have a little fun every now and again.

It didn't bother her. That's really what they were selling at Wayne's, in her opinion. It certainly wasn't a decent burger and the wings tasted like shit. Nope, a tease of good ol' tits and ass was the real hot ticket item. The hint of sexuality, but without the expense of the full nude girls lap-dancing at the Bare-All around the corner. Though, just like the strip club, there was at least one person a week who thought they could tip enough to get a blowjob from their grateful, small-town waitress.

For Iris, the job was a means to an end. At 20, she was close to finally having enough to move to New Orleans, a dream she'd held tightly to since she was just a girl who loved to doodle. After taking a family vacation to the French Quarter and seeing all of the galleries full of paintings and sculptures, she knew it was where she needed to be. She estimated that by spring she'd have enough to cover the exorbitant costs and she'd be free of the Floridian cesspool she'd been raised in.

Approaching her sedan, she rifled around through her purse, sifting through damp wads of singles left as tips from her shift, trying to find her car keys. One of the rowdy men, the dumb ape from her dinner shift with the lead fists, rounded the corner of the back of the building and stopped in his tracks when he saw her. His friend joined him by his side, inebriated.

"Well, now. If it isn't the best wing-woman in all a' Micanopy," the dumb ape mused, quickly strolling toward her vehicle. She rolled her eyes, wishing she could just drive away, still sifting through the contents of her bag for the jingling set. Coming up empty with every pass.

Before she knew it, they were flanking her, pressed against the sides of her Toyota, inches from her. The ape's friend ran a finger up the goose-flesh on her arm, damp with the evening's humidity. She jolted away as if his touch were electric.

"C'mon, guys. I'm not in the mood for company so, please, just leave me alone." Her voice stayed calm but, inside, her heart was pounding like a timpani drum. She pivoted from searching for her keys to looking for something that might offer protection from them. There was nothing more than chap-stick, Wendy's napkins, money and sanitizer.

Things seemed to turn sour without much ado. In a moment, the friend had snatched her up by the arm, his grip tight and painful. The dumb ape wedged his knee between her pantyhose-covered thighs and sidled up next to her like they were dancing intimately. She fought to drive her knee up into his balls but he squeezed her thigh with his own thick ones, strong and flexed like a footballer. Knowing this was going south fast, she struggled, tried to scream, "fire" because she'd heard people respond to that, while they'll often turn the other cheek and keep walking if you cry "rape!"

"Now, c'mon. That ain't nice," the ape said.

His friend snatched her up with a fist by her long blonde hair, using it to wrench her neck at an awkward angle and moved his meat hook from her bicep up, clamping it over her nose and mouth. His broad hand covered both, cutting off her air supply completely. He giggled as he pinched her nose, hearing the muffled sound of her screams in his palm.

"That tickles. C'mon now." He neared her ear. "We can do this the hard way or the easy way."

With that, he let her go and she screamed right into the face of the dumb ape. In a flash, he whipped his balled-up fist across her face, with an outstretched arm, and her tiny frame dropped to the ground like a sack of rocks.

She heard the friend giggle again as the ape snatched her up by the hair and yanked her to the other side of the car, where the wheels met grass and woods beyond the lot. He smashed her face down into the grass with the pressure of something mechanical. He was more fit than she'd even imagined when he was pounding those vicious paws into the clumsy table. Suddenly, he was using them on her and her strength proved to be no match.

His friend flicked out his pocket knife and they attacked in another flurry of movement, pain searing through her like flashes of lightning. She felt him jab the small blade in the ankles of the left leg of her pantyhose and rip a hard, straight line to the bottom of her ass, sawing through the material of her painted-on shorts as she cried into the dirt, begging them to stop.

The ape kept a lookout as his friend violated her, forcing her head into the dirt with his knee and wrenching her arms behind her upper back, pressing so hard she feared he would dislocate them from the sockets. His friend struggled to bury himself in her squirming body at her flattened angle, and fortunately didn't last long once inside. As he wiped his hands clean on her shorn shorts and leaned back, he laughed, "You're up, bud."

The ape replied, still wrenching her arms though she laid still, "Dude, I fucking know where your cock has been. I wouldn't take your sloppy seconds for anything."

After a moment of thought, he piped up again. "Trade you. Gimme the knife. I won't fuck her but I'll leave this little cock-tease something to remember me by, nonetheless."

The friend tucked his dick back into his pants and zipped up. He plopped the Swiss army knife onto the shredded seat of her bloodied once-white shorts and grabbed her wrists. With a smile he said, "What are you gonna do?"

The ape just smiled. He knew exactly what he wanted to do.

He wanted to carve.

9

Jack is silent as Iris finishes her regalement, shying away from the more vivid details and exposing her marred scapula to him beneath the moonlight.

"They left me with this *memento*. Even with the rape kit, nothing ever came of it. Police never caught 'em. They're still out there, I'm sure. *Free*. They probably don't even think about it." She chews her lip and looks up at him. "But *I* do. Every day."

"I'm so sorry," he says, but he's more astounded than anything. He hears strength in her words and the power she wields, as she faces her own darkness head-on. He wishes he could talk about his own traumas with such candor. Instead, he's held captive by them. Cursed to keep them under wraps. Speaking of them only reminds him of what he's done.

All he's taken from this world.

She pulls up her angora sweater, hiding the letters carved into her shoulder blade like teen's initials in the trunk of a tree. Covering her *shame*.

Covering the marks of the beasts.

Jack soaks in that for a moment. "You wish you could look in the mirror and just feel normal again. I wish that, too. Wish I didn't have to wake up every day and remember all over again that I'm a ..." he wants to growl the word *fucking* but pauses, curbing his tongue, and utters, "monster."

She manages a weak smile at him, edging closer to his portion of the fence line. "No. I can already tell. You're no monster."

He scoffs, intending for it to come off like a laugh, but it doesn't. "You don't know me. I don't just *look* like a monster, Iris. I *am* a monster." He opens his mouth to speak, but winces instead, stifling tears.

"You seem like a nice guy."

"You don't know what I've *done*."

She searches for something to twist the conversation into something lighter, more positive. "You're still alive. That's what I tell myself. That has to count for something, right?"

Jack is losing the battle against his tears now. They're hot and fat, rolling between the numb grafts that make up the bulk of his face, dripping down the seams like water filling a dry bed, pooling at the dimpled flesh above the edge of his lips. Those words make him feel angry at *himself*.

"Oh, yeah." His sarcasm leeches through every word. "And *what a life* this turned out to be."

"I'm sorry. I wasn't trying to–"

Jack sniffles, instantly regretting the cold comment. He interrupts her, apologetic. "No. I'm sorry." He looks up at her, his eyes wet and glittery beneath the plum sky. "I never should have come here. I don't belong here. I don't deserve to be fixed."

"Yes, you do." She whispers as if it's preposterous. "Whatever you did, you don't deserve… this." She motions weakly to him. "You don't deserve to feel like this. No one does."

After an awkward silence, punctuated by the vibrating screech of a baby raccoon far beyond the fence, they walk back to the cabins.

The night seems louder than ever now.

10

DAY ONE OF TRIAL

Patient Journal Entry provided by the St. James Parish Police Department.
Evidence Item #SJPD-11289C
Criminal Case #: 7-23-mu-187462-OB
Translated to digital transcript by Mary J. Stearns

Subject Name: Chase ▮
Date: 6/27/▮
Written Journal Entry: *I'm not really sure how to write one of these things. The instructions were kinda vague. So I guess I'll just do my best.*

I'm feeling fine physically this morning but I haven't started any treatments yet either.

I'm anxious about the procedure this afternoon though. The packet says that the doctor has to cut and score (when I hear that I think of someone running sharpened cowboy spurs over my skin like they're cutting a pizza) our old wounds open for the drug to work. I'm grateful mine is just a small hernia scar on my belly. Some of these people have big ass scars so I know they are gonna be in for a world of hurt for the next few weeks.

Time Symptom Started: N/A
Time Symptom Cleared: N/A
Location on Body: N/A
Severity: N/A

11

"Mister… um," Tate sweeps her brown hair from her face to get a better view of the small name on her clipboard, "*LeBlanc.*"

Jack stands with hesitancy, rising up from the couch. He smooths out his hoodie as he approaches.

"Jack, right?" She confirms with a smile. He nods, almost imperceptibly.

"Knock 'em dead, kid." Chase hollers, as if they are already old friends. "You got this. Ain't nothin' but a piece a' cake, brother."

LeBlanc nods appreciatively at him. The nurse motions for him to follow her out the front door and he does.

As they make their way across the lawn to the next building, Jack's face grows stoic, blood pressure pounding in his head beneath the southern beating sun blasting down on his cotton hood.

"Excited?" Eileen smiles, keeping her brisk pace.

"I will be if it works."

"*It works.*" She utters with total confidence, paired with a gorgeous grin. "Don't be nervous."

But he is. No pep-talk will change that.

As Jack crosses the threshold into the building, he shivers at the drastic, artificial change in temperatures. Inside, the main room is wide open and painted a soothing slate blue. The main focal piece of the room is an exam table, the kind you'd see in a family practitioner's office. It sits in the middle with its pneumatic back arched up like a recliner, coated in a thin sheet of paper stemming from a roll in the back. The edges of the right-half of the tidy room are filled with scientific devices; thermal centrifuges, microscopes, and multiple flat-screen monitors joined in the middle by a massive printer. The back wall has a light-mat with clipped-up x-rays of Mick's drilled-through kneecaps illuminated. The floors are spotless, checkered gray and light blue to match the exam table and wall paint, to give a cohesive, sterile look to the place.

"Doc, I've got LeBlanc here." Tate says to, seemingly, no one, leading him through the doorway in the back.

"Excellent, send him back please." The male voice finally answers back as they are rounding the corner into his office.

Jack's heart nearly falls out of his chest when he sees the man.

They know each other.

All too well.

Jack is stunned. Frozen in the doorway. He wants to flee but Tate is behind him, like a sheep herder corralling him into the room.

"Is this," he's shaking so violently he can't even get the words out without stuttering, "i-is this some kind of fucking joke?"

There is a pause before the seated doctor takes off his glasses and folds them into the breast pocket of his white lab-coat. He leans back in his chair. His face is time-worn and fatherly. His graying hair is thick and full, trimmed recently, his eyes are deeply ringed with thin streaks, depicting the harsh cruelty of father time.

He's aged exponentially in the years since their eyes last met.

Jack's anxiety is through the roof. He wants to cry just looking at the old man.

"I assure you, Mr. LeBlanc, this is not a joke." His voice is serious and dry, but something about him seems soft. He raises his craggy hands like someone being robbed. Like he's about to say: *Just put the gun down. No one has to die.*

"What is this?!" Drool is forming on his tense lips, his jaw clamped tight. He looks like he's about to erupt.

"This is a trial."

Tate watches the scene closely, her brunette curls bobbing as she swishes her eyes from one man to the other. She pats Jack on the shoulder and he flinches like she just punched him. "Mr. LeBlanc, please, just have a seat and hear him out." Her voice is calming, but Jack just can't fully comprehend the man before him.

"This is so embarrassing." Tears flood his eyes as all foolish hopes of normalcy vanish from his mind. He can't stomach the face before him. He sniffles, choking back a wave of emotion. "I didn't *know*." His hands shake in his lap. The sudden feeling that he's in trouble washes over him.

"*I knew*." A soft smile spreads onto Walsh's face and his tone shifts to caring. "I *recommended* you for this."

Jack is speechless at the admission. His eyes finally drift up to Walsh's, searching for some level of comprehension in this mess.

The old man continues, "Dr. Lauden in Baton Rouge has a *massive* anti-aging study going on. It's been *impossible* to gather enough volunteers for this and we need damaged tissue. The more serious the initial disfigurement, the better the results will look to the board. And, well," he trails off, knowing Jack catches onto what he's inferring. "I'm an old colleague of your regular practitioner, Dr. Hounsman. A few weeks ago, I asked him to put in a good word about this trial with you."

Jack's voice turns venomous. "You... *what*?"

"I'm going to level with you, Jack. I'm desperate here. The phases of these trials are lengthy. There's so much red-fucking-tape, excuse my language, and I'm getting old. I want to see Obsidian change lives while I'm still *here*. I knew that, despite my *issues* with you, the extensive amount of tissue damage you suffered, and all the grafting, would make you the absolute *ideal* candidate for this trial."

"You can't *possibly* be serious." He scoots to the edge of his leather seat, one that matches the upholstery of the exam table in the main room almost exactly. "Why would I ever–"

Dr. Walsh cuts him off with a holler, "Lauden's got me over a barrel! I had to try. I'm already scraping this together as it is, self-funding this damned thing out of the legal settlement."

More like blood money, Jack thinks.

"Without the minimum required volunteers, this all falls apart. Years of work–"

"Absolutely not. You tricked me into coming here!" Jack growls, starts to stand. Walsh does the same, hand outstretched and splayed in a panic.

"Mr. LeBlanc, please just–"

"It's *Jack*, alright?" He screams, pounding a scarred fist on the oak desk, forcing the files and papers to jump. "You didn't have any problem calling me Jack on the stand. So don't bother being formal *now*."

"Jack," he obliges, taking a breath to bring the tone of the heated conversation back down to a calmer level, "your hesitation is noted and *understandable*. I never meant to trick you. Frankly, if I saw myself sitting here, I'd want to walk out, too, okay? I get that. But here's what I'm prepared to offer you. After the procedure today, we won't have to see each other outside of the daily exams. They're fast. You're in, you're out. *Boom.* Done for the day. Just a mutually-beneficial interaction."

Jack starts to stand again. "I'm out of here."

"I'll double your pay if you stay."

"No way. This is... crazy."

Jack is brushing past Tate when Walsh hollers something that makes him stop in his tracks, eclipsing the doorway.

"I can make *sure* that you're not a control patient!"

Silence.

No one moves.

He continues, pleading calmly. "It's not a double-blind study."

Interest piqued, Jack turns around to face the old man. "Does that mean… what I think it does?"

"It means," he sounds breathless, standing to address Jack respectfully, "It means you *won't* be receiving the placebo. You won't be wasting your time. I can *fix* you."

The last six words mean more than a million dollars to Jack. The very idea that he can be fixed *at all* brings a glimmer of hope to his hardened heart. Even though he doesn't believe the words Walsh is saying…

He *wants* to.

More than anything.

"It probably doesn't even work." He sounds distrustful.

The look in Walsh's eyes changes in an instant. Jack sees it. Walsh is truly excited, giddy even. "Oh, it *works*. Trust me." He starts to come around the desk, approaching Jack with newfound excitement. "Think about the *good* this could do! Think of this as a chance to *restore,* to give something positive to the world that you've taken so much from."

The power of what he's saying is like a waterfall, pounding down on Jack. The old man is playing into his guilt and it's working.

After a moment, he opens his mouth again, this time with hope and excitement, "Jack, this is finally your chance to give something major *back*. To redeem yourself." He grits his teeth as if the words pain him. He relaxes and smiles again, his light-colored eyes locked, unblinking, onto Jack's. "This is an opportunity for *balance* and *equilibrium*."

Though Jack wants to run so far and fast that he forgets this place exists, those words cut straight to his soul. The only thing he wants *more* than to be away from Walsh right now, to be hiding in his apartment, is to make things *right*. To make that fateful day that changed so many lives hold meaning. To change the horrors he could never have before imagined, into a positive act of selflessness.

Still shaking, Jack lowers himself back into the blue chair, gaze still locked on Walsh. Finally, he looks down at the floor, the cowl of his hoodie engulfing his head like a hungry blue whale.

Walsh slides some paperwork across the table and clears his throat. "Before we begin, I need you to fill out some standard surgical forms so I know all allergies and family history to clear you for the procedure."

Jack pulls them closer to read them, blinking through the tears flowing from his unmarred duct. He raises his head, stares at Walsh like a child, "Do you have a pen?"

A pleasant smile spreads across Walsh's wrinkled face and he nods, plucking one from beside the pile of stacked patient journals and sliding it carefully across the glossy finish of the desk toward him.

12

Though he knew what the consent forms mentioned about the procedure, they were just words on a page. Things were always so different in reality.

As Jack tried his best to relax back into the clinician's chair, the situation he found himself in drifted into the surreal. A man whom he feared, and more importantly, one who hated *him,* hovered over his exposed torso, stripped of his shirt, pants, and all-too-comforting blue hoodie. Bare to the world. Laid bare to a person who he knew, deep down, wanted him dead. A man who said so, years ago, directly to his face. Spitting those words, bleary-eyed and in pain.

Now he had the opportunity to make Jack feel pain, too, albeit, in a way that would *heal.* Unlike his own.

Walsh's bristled chin, covered in salt-and-pepper stubble, undulated in waves beneath the angered clenching of his jaw as he prepped Jack. Finally, he spoke.

"Eileen, can you roll over the nitrous and the tray table with the gauze pads, please?"

"Certainly, Dr. Walsh."

The way she said his name was respectful. Eager.

In a flash, she has them both by the chair.

"Go ahead and administer the first dose, if you would." He motions to the locked safe on his desk. "He gets bottle A." He glances back at Jack and injects. "Non-placebo."

Though it should, his wink doesn't put Jack at ease.

"Who gets the placebo?" Jack's voice is almost imperceptible.

Tate chimes in, "while it's not a double-blind study for us, I'm afraid we cannot give out medical information for the other participants in the trial. We can only discuss *yours* with you. What matters is that *you won't.*"

She offers up two, tiny, paper cups. One has a singular, shiny, oblong black pill at the bottom. The second is filled with an ounce of water. He hesitantly pops the oval into his mouth and holds up the cup.

"*Nostrovia.*" He mutters, cheering her with the second cup before washing the pill down with it.

Walsh speaks up over the rushing water as he scours his hands with a soapy scrub brush. "Obsidian is formulated to leave all healthy or healed tissue intact; therefore, any areas we wish to target will need to be surgically re-opened or scored. Basically, we cannot heal what isn't injured. I got the idea from cancer itself, oddly enough. You see, your body has these things called T-cells, or T-lymphocytes. When you get hurt or sick, and they're working correctly, those cells come to the rescue and start fixing wounds and aiding the human immune system until repaired. But, once in a while, those T-cells won't turn off. They just keep going until they wreak havoc and develop abnormalities and tumors. Some start attacking the skin. Then you've got cancer."

He turns the water off with his wrist and runs his hands under the Dyson blower. The neon-blue lights up his aging hands. He pulls them away and stares at Jack, pulling a set of fresh gloves over them. His eyes lock on Jack like lasers and he speaks in a tone that is gravely serious. "When something tries too hard to heal, and doesn't know quite where to stop, it can be a very bad thing, you see."

Jack nods as if he understands, but he's not sure he does.

"Disastrous results." Walsh adds, with a tense nod. "Well, what I've developed here is something like artificial T-cells. Only these know *exactly* when to stop. When I injure the old tissue, it will attack with a vengeance, healing the tissue until it's fixed, better and faster than your body ever could on its own."

"How does it know when to stop?" His eyes have grown large, like a deer, as Walsh tugs down a circular overhead light, illuminating the scars scrawled across Jack's torso like wavy desert terrain.

Walsh laughs. "Now that requires a more complicated answer but I'm afraid its time to get started. This procedure is going to take a little while. Due to the severity of your burns, I would like to offer you the option of nitrous oxide. It's what dentists use to put you out for a procedure. I think it's the best call for the pain because the topical is still going to be awful with this severity. You'll feel a little groggy after, but—"

"I'll do it." Jack nodded and held his hand out for the nitrous mask. Walsh hands it over and Tate helps him seat it securely over his mouth.

As Walsh turns it on, he leans in and speaks over the hiss of the excreting gas. "There is going to be *some* discomfort after the procedure, but I'll do everything I can to keep that as minimal as possible."

Jack nods but he notices Walsh isn't looking at him. Not quite. He's staring through him. For just a moment, before Jack drifts off into hazy nothingness, he gazes into the old man's serious eyes. Eyes that, before today, he hoped he'd never see again for the rest of his life. In them, he did not see optimistic hope or the dream of creating a better future for the world.

No.

Instead, the last thing he sees before going under is fueled hatred, burning brighter than the fire he'd once been swallowed by.

13

Kate was beside him. She was healthy.

And alive.

She smiled. He reached across the upholstered chasm between them and touched her face. She felt the stress of the family dinner radiate from him. His jaw tensed like a rock. His fingers went back to gripping the steering wheel, locking hard at ten-and-two.

She caressed his inner thigh and he stared forward, unable to think of anything except the disdain he held for his new in-laws. Inheriting them was the only downside to asking her to share her life with him. The snarky comments Kate's decrepit father made replayed in his head. Especially, his lecture about how a shrimping boats was a terrible investment for his son-in-law to have made. He spoke of how the job wouldn't pay enough. BP oil spills. Polar caps melting. Shoreline erosion. Rising water temperatures and blah-fucking-blah. Droning on as if he knew every damned thing. Sewing seeds of poisonous doubt.

And Kate's mother – the cunt – *had something shitty to say about every petty-fucking-thing from the clothes he wore to the immediate lack of grandchildren.*

Tick-tock-tick-tock. Time, she's up, Kate. Where's my fucking grand-baby?

His knuckles whitened as the conversation rehashed in his head, along with all the clever retorts he only wished he'd thought of in the moment.

Kate slid her hand further, stroking him through the fabric of his jeans. He felt a tingle, a pulsing that grew as he felt the vibrations from the metal teeth as his zipper lowered. His stiff cock throbbed when he saw her lower her head to his lap, flashing him that sly little grin in the rear-view that she always gave when they were about to fuck.

He stared out at the brilliantly-colored sunset, one that painted the sky a blend of moody magenta, tangerine, and hot pink.

The ancient silver SUV rattled down the gravel path, overhung by thick southern foliage, lined on both sides by dry brush. He felt Kate take him in her warm mouth, felt the pressure and resistance from the soft tissue in the back of her throat as she slid all the way down until she physically couldn't take any more without choking. He felt a drug-like rush of ecstasy pulse through every vein in his body, head light from the sudden blood rush.

He glimpsed his own eyes fluttering with pleasure in the mirror. They struggled to stay open. His lips parted with a gentle moan, one that drowned out the noise of the wet strokes below. He snaked his fingers through her raven-black hair and gripped it softly, guiding her head down further, diving deeper.

Suddenly, a dog raced into the road – that goddamned catahoula. *Kate's head still bobbed as she struggled to take more of him inside of her in the cramped space.*

"Shit!" It was all he could mutter in the moment that changed his life.

He whipped the wheel to avoid the mutt, over-correcting wildly.

The tree came fast. Almost out of nowhere. Unavoidable.

He hit it square-on without ever having tapped the brake. Without even having the time to employ a knee-jerk reaction. The thick trunk of the oak didn't even seem to rock at the crushing force of all the twisted metal forced upon it.

He swore he heard a scream, echoing through the otherwise-silent backwoods. The noise the impact made was something he can never forget, no matter how much he wants to. It is a sound that will snap him from the comfort of sleep for years to come.

He was discombobulated, fumbling blood-caked hands through a sea of gleaming, white airbag. He heard the trickle of broken glass, like some million-shard waterfall, as he dug below to unearth the hellish nightmare.

A few yards away, the catahoula watched from a patch of scorching dirt, staring with judgemental eyes. As if the dog could say through telepathy, "I dare you to look in your lap, you prick."

He did look down. He wished he hadn't.

There's hair in his lap.

Raven-black. On a head that was no longer moving.

What was left of his wife's skull was a mangled, bloody mess. He felt a death-twitch in her throat which was still wrapped around him like a starving python swallowing thick prey. But he couldn't move her. She was fused to him by the *crushed-in dashboard, skull pinned in place by the wheel.*

He tried to pull her up, tried to inhale through the tears and shaken panic to get her head on the right side of the wheel. To get her clamped teeth off of the base of his cock.

But she was still.

It was a stillness like something irreversibly-inanimate. A thing. *No longer a person. He felt blood rush down her face and swore he felt an eye, no longer in the bony socket where it was supposed to be. No longer inside of her head.*

He stared out the window and erupted in the scream of all screams, a noise he didn't think himself capable of.

A scream that woke him from his nitrous-induced slumber...

14

"We're all done, Mr. LeBlanc." He feels the smooth skin of Tate's palm caressing the back of his unblemished hand. He can't see her, but he can hear her. "You were screaming. It's okay. You're okay." Her inflection is zen-like, like a yoga instructor. "I know you're probably feeling pretty groggy right now, so just relax. The procedure was a success. The doc bandaged you up really well. Everything went smoothly. You're going to be pretty sore but as soon as you're feeling well enough to stand, I'll take you back to the house."

He nods, making her out through the blurred vision in his unbandaged eye. He tries to utter something but his tongue feels lazy, and he knows it will just come out as gibberish, so he stops.

"He had to get pretty close to your eye so for a day or two he wanted to keep the whole eye bandaged. There is a printout of special shower instructions that I'm going to leave in your room that you'll need to adhere to for the next two or three days, until the injuries sufficiently scab over. But it'll be over before you know it."

15

"You're in great hands," Tate says reassuringly as she guides Jack to a cushion on the couch in the main room. "Walsh is a miracle worker. I've known him a long time. My mother was a volunteer in one of his oncology trials about twelve years ago. The doc, he cured her cancer. Stage four. *Complete* remission. We got another seven years with her because of it." She strains to set him down safely and stands back up. "She passed away from pneumonia a few years back."

"What kinda cancer did she have?" Mick asks bluntly.

"Adenocarcinoma," she says, adding for clarification, "*colo-rectal.*"

She watches Jack strain to sit. The majority of his face is wrapped in bandages and he winces a little at the discomfort as he settles in.

Mick taps Jack on the knee with the back of his gloved hand. "Hey *Invisible Man,* promise me you'll put two between my eyes if my chocolate starfish ever revolts and tries to eat my body."

Jack's snicker turns into a painful hiss as he relaxes into the seat.

"Ms. Iris, I believe you're the last one, hun." Tate smiles. Iris stands and joins her, never taking her eyes off Jack.

"You guys know the drill by now. I'll be next door if you need anything. I'll come back tonight to check everyone's vitals, freshen any bandages and administer more pain medication if anyone requires any. Make sure you guys write your journal entry for today, even if it just says 'nothing new to report.'"

Mick salutes her. "Aye-aye, cap'n. 'Da mummy over here's in good hands. Don' you worry ya' pretty lil' head, *sha*."

16

Fisher stares into the mirror, inspecting the bandage on his elbow. He brushes a tattooed hand over it, tamping his fingers against the plastic exterior. He stares at his reflection and fluffs a spike of thinning, styled hair so that it looks fuller around his gaunt face. His body is bone thin and bird-like. His fragile figure doesn't have an ounce of fat to spare. He glances over his skin, no longer seeing the individual tattoos that grace the majority of its surface, crawling up his neck to his jawline like black, blooming watercolor paint splotches.

He lifts his shirt to examine his dwindling waistline and wonders how many more meals he can miss without the others noticing. Wonders if maybe he should make a big show of something he won't mind tasting twice and then excuse himself to scurry off and purge. He runs his hands along his ribs, feeling them like a xylophone beneath the thin barrier of skin, and smiles lovingly at his emaciated form before flicking off the light and heading out.

In the main room, several of the others have gathered, chatting among themselves. Fisher plops down on the couch beside Chase and stares across at the perpendicular couch. It seems like Alan is staring right at him, glaring with unblinking, hateful eyes. Fisher cocks a brow.

"Something I can help you with?"

At the sound of his voice, Alan whips his eyes to the opposite side of the room and it is then that he realizes Fisher hadn't been the target he was locked onto. It was Chase.

Ignoring the interaction, Angie pulls her long locks to her milky cleavage and looks at Mick.

He waves his hands in a black fabric flurry. "I ain't got all day, sweetheart. What it gon' be?"

"Dare," she sighs, "I guess."

He claps his hands together in excitement, rubbing the fabric together as if he has some dastardly plan in mind. "Eitha' ten push-ups, facin' me, or fi'teen jumpin' jacks."

Iris swats him with a pillow, laughing. "You're a pig."

"She said *dare*. I gave her a simple dare. C'mon now." He crosses his arms.

Angie's cheeks turn red. "I'll do you one better." She stands, tugs her tight tank top down, revealing even more skin and smooths her short skirt. She stands in the middle of the gathering area and proceeds to do fifteen jumping jacks, kicking her feet wide, bountiful breasts bouncing. She punctuates the end of the final one by dropping straight to the ground in a full split. Everyone cheers.

Mick clutches at his heart comically and then fans himself. He claps hard as she stands, proud of herself.

"Cheer captain, y'all. Three years." Angie bows deeply and her red hair fans in a wildly colorful display.

"Well done, girl. Well done, indeed. Yo' turn." Mick can't stop clapping, impressed that she went the extra mile to show off instead of bowing out shyly.

Angie looks around the room and stops at Fisher. "Ahh, you haven't gone yet. F-man, truth or dare?"

"Dare. All day, baby."

She thinks for a moment and perches on the couch near Mick. "I dare you," Angie looks around, "to show us the weirdest thing you can do with your body."

He scoffs. "Pffft, shit. I thought it was gonna be something hard." He stands in the middle of the groups and wrenches his wrists backwards and forwards far beyond where they should go. Some of them wince and groan, but he's not done yet. He hooks his hands together behind his back and wriggles both elbows into wildly opposing angles, crinkling the taped-on bandages covering his elbows and forearms.

"Eww, that double-jointed shit freaks me out!" Angie covers her eyes and shivers visibly at the grotesque, but painless, sight.

He stares down at his feet and pops his knees backward like some sort of alien being.

"Oh, hell no." Chase cries out, looking away, physically affected by the hyperextension of the joints. Fisher squirms until they snap back outward like a normal human knee.

"I think I'mma barf, dude." Mick exclaims, staring off into the distance, dazed.

"Shit, that's nothing. Wanna see something wild as hell?"

No one answers. Fisher, grinning, pulls off his shirt revealing his undernourished torso, pale white beneath the overhead hanging fixture.

"What, you got a third nipple or sum'n?" Mick still doesn't want to look.

"Naw, I want to introduce y'all to my brother." Fisher cups a hand under his right pectoralis and tugs on the muscle revealing several strange, hardened lumps beneath his skin with a stretch mark outline defining a soft edge. "His name is Hector."

"What am I… what am I looking at here?" Iris tilts her head sideways.

"What is that? Looks like a tumor," Alan adds with all the charm of a used toilet brush.

"It's called a parasitic twin. He's my little bro. My body absorbed most of him in the womb. See that?" He pokes at a fleshy lump divided by a straight indention. "That's his eye." He pokes at the nub beside it. "There's his little nose–"

"Alright, I officially hate this fuckin' game." Mick says rolling off with a dazed look on his face.

"Why isn't it bandaged?" Angie seems totally confused.

"What do you mean?" Fisher is being genuine. "*He's* not why I'm here. I told y'all what I'm here for."

"Oh, I just figured if this stuff works, why wouldn't you want to heal it all?" Her voice is quiet now.

"Because," he looks around and then back at her, "just because you *can* change something, doesn't mean you *should*. That's why all these people are out here fucking their face up with plastic surgery in the pursuit of perfection, making themselves look like bizarre walking-nightmares. Hell, I don't even *recognize* Renee Zellweger any more." He chuckles. "Sometimes those are the things that make you unique. These all tell a story. The shit on my arms, it's just shredded canvas, accidents. To me, they don't mean anything, so if I can get paid for letting them fuck around with that stuff, fine. Cool. Can't hardly bend my arms 'cuz that shit is so tight from the damage. But this," He pokes his chest hard enough that the release leaves a little white fingerprint in his already pale skin, "this is part of who I am. Something that makes me unique. People are so obsessed with looking the same. *Normal.* I don't give a fuck about looking normal. Some people put form over function and they annihilate everything that makes them unique. I don't know about y'all, but I don't want to look like some mass-produced Ken doll."

After a long silence, with nothing more to add to his tirade, Angie looks up at him. "It's your turn to pick the next person."

"Oh, uh, Iris, I guess."

She sits back in her seat and smiles. "Truth."

Mick hollers, "Aww, I fuckin' knew it! Lame!"

17

Iris shoves open her door with her right hand, a small bowl of rocky road ice cream in her left. She flips the light switch on to see an origami flower in the shape of a Siberian Iris on her bed, made out of purple construction paper.

***

Iris knocks lightly on his open door, fidgeting with the symmetrically-folded flower.

Jack is hard at work on a fleet of various-color origami boats. He turns and grants her his full, groggy attention. The whole left side of his face and neck are swathed in gleaming white bandages, secured with straight runs of medical tape. A similar wrap covers his left hand, a small amount of blood stippling through to the outside. The edges disappear beneath his clothing.

"It's beautiful." She looks down at the paper flower twirling between her fingertips. She tucks the taped-on paper stem of it behind her ear.

"I went for a walk this morning to try to hunt down a *real* one," his voice is repentant, "but all I ended up finding was poison ivy and some weird brown bug the size of a golf ball, so I had to improvise."

"Awww." She smiles, then it fades. She rubs something on the floor with her socked toe. She thinks about how long he was in Walsh's clinic and wants to ask about it, but feels strange bringing it up. Instead, she plucks the flower out from behind her ear and holds it up. "Well… Sweet dreams."

He smiles and nods, "Yeah, you too." He watches her walk away and grins for a moment before turning back to folding more paper with his bandaged hands.

18

Mick rolls through the living room of the larger cabin, the one he's staying in. Moonlight slices through the window blinds patterning his cheeks with uniform, blue slivers. All is quiet in the main area. Everyone's settled in their rooms for the evening.

He drags the landline phone off the cradle, examines it for a minute. He hasn't seen a real phone in God-knows-how-long. He dials and fishes a glove-full of candies out of the pockets of his corduroys, ones he pilfered from a jar in the kitchen. As the person on the other end answers, he pops one into the air and catches it in his mouth.

"Hey, man. It's Mick." He utters through sloppy chews.

The other voice is frantic, *furious*.

He tries to calm him down. "No, man. I can't. I asked. Hell, I begged. I don't get paid 'til after the trial."

Another long pause.

From the squeaky echo of the other voice, it's obvious he's getting his ass chewed by another male.

"You have ta' give me a grace period or *somethin'*. He wouldn't gimme any of the money upfront! I jus' said 'dat! It's three weeks. You can *wait* three weeks."

Mick listens to the man's response intently, reddening skin crawling up his cheeks as his blood pressure rises. He finally responds again, livid. Yelling now, talking over the other person.

"I'm in a goddamn *chair*! You think I'm raking dough on disability? I ain't exactly wiping my crippled ass with hundreds. I'm letting these assholes use my body like a fuckin' lab rat just to pay y– *What*?! *Cut me a fucking break.*"

Silence. *The calm before the storm.*

"No! You know what, fine. Shove that place up your ass, you goddamn *slum lord,* piecea' *shit*!"

Mick slams the phone down several times and tosses the cradle onto the floor. It smashes into the hardwood with a ringing *DING!*

19

DAY TWO OF TRIAL

Patient Journal Entry provided by the St. James Parish Police Department.
Evidence Item #SJPD-11288C
Criminal Case #: 7-23-mu-187462-OB
Translated to digital transcript by Mary J. Stearns

Subject Name: Iris ▉
Date: 6/28/▉

Written Journal Entry: *This morning I feel hopeful. I guess that's not exactly what this form is for but it is called a journal, after all. The site where my incisions were made is tender this morning, as I would expect it to be.*

I slept pretty rough because I can't roll over onto my right side. I also had a nightmare about the night I was attacked. I'm not sure if that's a side-effect of the medication so I'm mentioning it just in case.

I don't want to sound like a big baby but I suppose this is a private journal so I should be honest. Emotionally, the procedure was a bit traumatic for me. It didn't just feel like my wounds were literally being opened up. It felt metaphorical too.

Yesterday's incisions made me wish I had better access to therapists in the years since I was attacked. I could've really gone for a zoom call with my regular one in NOLA yesterday.

Time Symptom Started: Middle of the night.
Time Symptom Cleared: When I woke up.
Location on Body: Mind.
Severity: Not severe.

20

Chase leans over the edge of the wrap-around balcony railing, enjoying sunrise on the nearby water with a steaming cup of coffee. A pelican and her offspring splash playfully in the murky brown liquid nearby. He watches it with the intensity of a riveting television finale.

A man approaches. His untied boots drag through the thick grass of the property with a hiss. He's a fiery ginger with a short shock of hair and a far-too-scrawny frame for his height. Chase can see his ribs jutting out through the low cuts in his homemade tank top, which appears to once have been a t-shirt. On the worn apparel, a bald eagle clutches a weathered American flag. A cigarette hangs out of his pursed lips. One with an ash a mile long.

He nods up at Chase. "'Sup? Mick around?"

After a moment of sizing up the emaciated guest, he takes a longer sip of the piping hot liquid and nods. "Yeah, he's rollin' around here somewhere. Might be getting his little morning checkup right now."

"Can you tell him Eddie's here to see him?"

Chase beckons him with a nod toward the house. "Come on up and tell him yourself. We won't bite."

21

Walsh takes a blood pressure reading on Mick. But Mick is entranced by a large flat screen monitor on the far side of the doctor's L-shaped desk. On it, the checkered black and white squares show a live security feed of various areas throughout the cabins.

"You *do* realize the whole Big Brother security camera thing is super creepy, right?" The Cajun twang strikes Walsh as humorous and he looks over his shoulder at the feed.

"I don't even watch it. They made me put it in. In order to afford to host this trial, I had to do it outside of a commercial facility. But in doing that, the legal team said a multi-camera system was non-negotiable for liability reasons."

"Is there one in Angie's room?" Mick sounds hopeful. He leans forward to get a better look at the monitor over the doctor's shoulder. Walsh frowns. He releases the blood pressure cuff and bashes a knobby finger against the power button, turning the security feed black.

"Alright, Mr. Adams, everything looks good here. Vitals are excellent. No sign of infection in the scored wounds. So, it is time for your daily dose." Walsh pulls the set of retractable keys from his belt loop and unlocks the pharmaceutical vault, a small, cream-colored desk safe.

Mick watches Walsh interact with the safe, with a far-more riveted intensity than he'd used on the security feed. His curiosity was piqued.

Walsh uncaps a carefully-chosen bottle, notates something on his legal pad, and pours two pills into a disposable paper cup. He hands them to Mick, along with a cone-shaped cup of cold liquid from the small water cooler in the corner.

Mick toasts him. "Bottom's up!"

He swallows the pills with a grin.

22

"How are you this morning?" Iris sounds chipper.

"Meh." Angie shrugs, tosses a handful of her red hair over the shoulder of her terrycloth robe and takes the spot at the second bathroom sink next to Iris. She pulls the mauve lipstick out of her bag and starts to apply it in the mirror. "Slept for shit."

"Missin' your hubby?"

There is a pause. Angie frowns and then speaks quietly. "He and I split a few months ago."

"No!" Iris gasps, matching her tone to Angie's, as if they are sharing secrets. "Why?! Are--are you okay?"

"Yeah, I'm fine. It's just pretty fucked up." Her shoulders slump.

"Wanna talk about it?"

"Nah." Angie says quickly and then wiggles a little in her spot, "okay, *yeah*. I don't have a lot of girlfriends."

"Me either."

"This *has* to stay between us. Promise?"

"Swear on my life, girl."

"Well," Angie pauses, "last year, I was pregnant."

Iris gasps.

Angie holds a hand out to stop her in place. "Don't get excited. Eight months in the oven she died." She rubs the scar on her belly through her robe.

"Oh my *God*! I'm so sorry."

"I still had to deliver her and everything. Her name was Alexa. Or, it was *gonna* be--"

Just as Iris is contemplating how ridiculous it is to name a child after a common, electronic device, she realizes Angie has stopped applying her makeup. She is now fanning her scrunched face, trying not to burst into tears.

Iris puts her contouring brush down and hugs the near-stranger tightly. Angie squeezes her eyes, blinking tears into Iris's blonde hair and then wiping them away apologetically as she retreats. She sniffles. "I'm sorry."

"No! Don't be."

"So," she sniffles hard again and turns back to the mirror, brushing eyeshadow onto her reddened eyes, "the doctors gave me an emergency C-section and we had her cremated. I healed up. Thought everything was hunky-dory, and then after we had some therapy and time to process and grieve, Mack and I started trying to get pregnant again. So we are fucking and fucking and just going at it like goddamned rabbits. *Nothing. Nada.* So we go to the doctor and he runs some tests. Comes back a little while later and says that I am, quote, 'unlikely to bear children ever again.'"

"Oh *no*!"

"Mack couldn't handle it. Said he always wanted a family and that me being barren was a fucking deal-breaker." She shakes her head and presses her palm to her forehead, hard enough to leave a white pressure streak when she pulls it away. "We were married, for God's sake," she scoffs. "It wasn't in sickness and health, for richer or poorer, *but only if you can calve out children, you know?"*

"He didn't want to adopt?"

"He didn't want to adopt. He didn't want to surrogate. He didn't want to keep trying. He filed the divorce papers and conveniently, two weeks later, moved in with some little young thing that works at the gym where he trains. Bitch has wide hips and an underbite. Hideous little thing. But he probably doesn't care. Just wants a goddamned incubator."

"I swear, I will never understand men."

"No shit. Same. Serves me right. He was trash anyway. I met him at a trashy little bar. He bought me some *Cuervo*. We had a WILD, long night back at his place. Girl," she holds a hand out for emphasis, "I can *fuuuuuuuck* on some tequila. You get a little 'a that gold in me and I turn into an animal."

Mick rolls up outside of the bathroom in the empty corridor. He's not there with the intention of eavesdropping. Instead, he's a man on a mission, sitting patiently in the darkened hall waiting for the women to vacate.

Angie leans in to pencil in her thin eyebrows so they're bolder, more striking. "I see you talking to that Jack guy a lot."

"Yeah, he's nice."

"Someone's gotta say it so it might as well be me, but you could do so much better than some Freddy Kreuger-lookin' dude. 'Specially with *that* body."

"Nah, it's not like that," she lies. She has no intention of involving an unfamiliar person in her private business. "We're just hanging out. Passing the time in this place. He's... interesting. Little bit mysterious."

"How'd he get all," Angie motions to her face, "extra *crispy* like that?"

The crass joke makes Iris want to storm out but she plays it cool. In the hall, the comment makes Mick grind his molars.

"I honestly don't know."

"Well, if you just wanna get laid, that man'd be easy pickin's." She sighs loudly, the sound rife with frustration. She leans her face toward the glass to swipe on a thick coating of mascara. "I'm climbin' the walls, too. Been a dry spell since Mack. It's been months."

"I think Mick has a bit of a crush on you."

Mick listens closer, nearly pressing his ear to the crack in the door.

"The *wheelchair* dude?" Her tone is incredulous but after a pause, she shrugs. "Yeah, he's cute. Too bad he's crippled as fuck. If *not*, he'd be fire. Always had a thing for Cajun boys. I don't even know how that would *work*. Like, *physically*." She smacks her lips together, dumps her makeup back in her bag, and starts to exit.

Mick shoots backwards down the hall, rolling quickly, so as not to get caught.

"What do you think?" She shows off her face from every angle.

"I think you look beautiful." She smiles.

"You look cute, too. *I'd* do you. Hell, I'm getting horny enough–"

Iris holds a hand up to halt Angie. "Flattered. But, unfortunately, I'm straight."

Angie winks, flashing a glimpse of the earthy, brown tones on her lid. "So is spaghetti 'til it's wet, girl."

She elbows Iris and leaves, her humored chuckle trailing close behind. Iris catches a glimpse of herself in the countertop mirror, magnified. Flaws and all. She touches the bandage over her scar, almost as if she can feel the words burning through the gauze and tape. Her smile dwindles and she packs up the little makeup she has and leaves the bathroom, too.

Mick rolls out slowly from the darkened bedroom door frame at the end of the hall. As the girls turn the corner into the main living space, both totally oblivious to his presence, he rolls into the bathroom and searches all the cabinets and drawers within his limited reach until he finds what he was lurking around for:

Bingo.

Two stray bobby pins.

23

Mick's voice is full of life as he loudly exclaims, "*Eddie*! *My* man!"

Eddie pops his bony body off the dated, cushy couch and holds his arm way out for a hard, stinging low-five. "There you are. Been wanderin' 'round like an idiot askin' all these fools where I can find some ugly, handicapped numb-nuts 'round here." Eddie's southern twang is just as thick as Mick's. "The description musta worked cuz they all pointed me ta' you."

Mick wheels quickly up to Eddie and they slap hands with a resounding *thwack*.

"So... *this* is the place, huh? *Swanky*!"

"Bruh... You should see what dey's *payin'* us to sit on our ass all day."

"What's new about that? You sit on your ass all day."

Mick flips Eddie off and smiles. "But I don' get paid to do it."

"Got you a little present." Eddie suddenly springs to life, pulls a fat joint out of his pocket. Mick takes it with a smile.

"Oh, you beautiful soul." He places it between his lips to free up his hands and speaks around it, swinging his head to instruct Eddie to follow. "C'mon. I need your help wit' somethin'."

As always, Eddie follows blindly with a cheerful expression splattered across his sinewy, pale face.

***

Eddie is peeking through a cracked door, eyeing the hallway. He whispers. "Would you *hurry up*? You know I hate bein' lookout!" He scoffs angrily. "Hated this shit when we was kids. Hate it more now. Why I always gotta be lookout, huh?"

"Its hard to lean in the chair, bitch. Stop whining. Jus' chill." Mick has a stripped bobby pin jammed inside the lock on the medicinal safe and he's fumbling with a second. "I got this. Jack locks himself outta his apartment at least once a week. You think that motherfucker's got locksmith money? No. He comes to ol' Mick on bended knee."

"'Dis kinda shit makes me fuckin' itchy."

"Stop being a drama queen. You on the rag? Starting to sound like a little bitch." He jiggles both pins, rattling the safe audibly. "I almost...."

"Yeah, yeah." Eddie is not amused.

"Oh!" Mick whips out one of the pins and points it at Eddie, punctuating what he's saying by jabbing it at him. "'Fore I forget, I need you to get me a bottle of tequila."

"Ew, shit's nasty. Since when do you drink that swill? You' a die-hard bourbon fan, bruh."

Eddie picks the drippings off a melted candle near the door, no longer looking through the crack.

"It's not for me."

"*Oh*. Top shelf?"

"*Fuck no!*" Mick's insulted. Eddie knows his painfully-cheap self better than that. "*Bottom* shelf. Like, so bottom it's on the floor. We're talkin' large quantity, in-the-plastic-bottle-cheap. Put it on my tab."

"Everything's always on your *tab*. When you gon' *pay* that tab, son?"

The lock *clicks*. The small desk-safe creaks open.

"*Jackpot*!" Mick grins from ear-to-ear.

Eddie peers over his shoulder at the metal container's contents.

Mick plucks out bottles of labeled pills. He holds up a bottle of painkillers, tosses them to Eddie. It's loud, like a maraca.

"Shhh! Keep it down. You wanna get caught?"

Mick scoffs, his voice casual as he does a hushed, verbal inventory. "We got pain killers. Looks like… *vikes*. What do those go for?"

"Vicodin's about five bucks a pop. Oxys, on the other hand, I can move that hillbilly heroin for $15 a pill.

"What about these? They're muscle relaxers."

"Shit, these only go for, like, $3."

Mick hands him a handful of muscle relaxers anyway. Eddie looks confused. "Three dollars is three dollars, *innit*? Can you move 'em?"

Eddie rolls his eyes, sullen. "Of course."

"Maybe I can get more. Maybe I could fake somethin' and see if Kevorkian can write me a script."

"See if you can get any *Addys* or *Rids*. I got one rich-bitch uptown, Kelly. She'll buy five damn bottles of Ritalin in one shot. This cunt needs uppers like I need a hole in the head, but her cash spends the same as everyone else's. Plus, ain't hard to fake ADHD." Eddie reaches in and grabs one of the trial bottles. "The hell's a *placebo*?"

"*Dafuq* they teach you in school, dummy? You ain't neva' heard'a no placebo before? Dey sugar pills."

Eddie stares at him, hard, trying to understand.

Mick rolls his neck, frustrated. "One patient is getting the fuckin' sugar pills. Everyone else is getting the real drug."

Eddie's thin face turns sour. "That's *bullshit*."

"Why's that bullshit?"

"That means one of you's here wastin' time!"

"Yeah, and getting *paid* for the privilege!"

"But if that shit really *works*, that means someone just got all cut up for no reason." He points to Mick's bandaged knees below the line of his shorts.

His legs are frail and pale, atrophied from a lack of use. He squints, still trying to follow the logic.

"That means they get all new scars and they get to watch everyone else heal in front of 'em. That's kinda fucked up. I mean, what if it's *you*?"

Mick wants to object but realizes Eddie has a point.

"Fuck."

"Or what if it's *Jack*? You know that motherfucker never gon' get laid looking like a deep-fried chicken nugget."

"Well, when you put it like that… yeah, it sounds kinda shitty. But what 'da fuck am I supposed to do about it, Ed?

"We're standing here, ain't we? *Unsupervised.*" Eddie rubs his hands together playfully. "How about a little prescription roulette? We mix all the pills up. Divvy 'em back into the bottles. Then *all* y'all got the same random chance at gettin' the real ones."

"Sometimes, Eddie," Mick shakes his head, beard brushing against his death metal t-shirt with a squirrelly age-cracked logo almost no one can read. "I can't tell if you're a genius or a moron."

Eddie stares at him innocently.

"But I see your point. Fuck it." Mick shrugs and grabs both bottles.

Eddie holds out the bottom of his t-shirt and looks around. Mick dumps the contents of both bottles onto the belly of his shirt, swirls them against the American flag, and starts shoving the mixed lot back into bottles.

He drops one. It goes bouncing across the floor. After a second of half-assed looking, they divert their focus back to the bottles. Mick doesn't care to hunt the stray down.

Thunk, thunk, thunk.

Footsteps down the hall.

"Shit!" Mick whispers.

The men are in a full scramble now, jittery and shaking. Eddie replaces the caps and shoves the bottles back into the vault.

As Mick closes up the safe, jostling the door to make sure the locking mechanism closes, Eddie whispers proudly…

"We' done a *good* thing."

24

DAY THREE OF TRIAL

Patient Journal Entry provided by the St. James Parish Police Department.
Evidence Item #SJPD-11288C
Criminal Case #: 7-23-mu-187462-OB
Translated to digital transcript by Mary J. Stearns

Subject Name: Fisher ▮▮▮▮▮▮▮▮
Date: 6/30/▮▮▮▮▮▮▮▮
Written Journal Entry: *This place is boring af. Can we please get some video games or magazines? Or what about some more gym equipment beyond the exercise bike? I'm already turning into veal in here.*

Had a headache for a bit this morning but then I drank some coffee and it went away. Think it was just from a lack of caffeine.

Time Symptom Started: Morning
Time Symptom Cleared: About 20 minutes after I drank some (terrible) coffee. (Can we get some better coffee, btw? This store-brand stuff tastes like dirty dishwater.)
Location on Body: Head (duh)
Severity: Mildly annoying. Like this journal.

25

Alan sits in a plastic chaise lounge chair on the unkempt edge of the boggy Blind River. A turtle suns on a floating log in the water nearby, staring at him with a frowning, cranky face, much like his own. He closes his eyes beneath his dark sunglasses, feeling the heat of the day caress his face like a mobster's blowtorch. He tries to remember why he's doing the trial at all.

After all, he likes his scars.

It's others who don't. It's *always* been others.

He recalls vividly the judgemental stares he'd get during job interviews for shitty food service jobs viewing him as a poor investment of time. Or the students in his high-school A&P class glancing from the flayed body in the morgue on the field trip, back to his forearms, no doubt noting similarities between his pale, carved flesh and the cadaver's. He remembers shaking his ex's father's hand the first time Alan met him and watching the old man's eyes lock onto his wormy traces of agony, deciding then-and-there that he wasn't good enough for his baby girl.

It didn't matter though. *Fuck 'em.* That relationship didn't last long. None ever seemed to span more than a couple of months. Either Alan would get bored or the woman would get sick of his ever-present scowl.

Afterward, he'd always be right back where he started, feeling the cold rush of excitement as he dismantled his handle from the razor's blades and buzzing at the excuse to ease the numbness with bloodshed.

The turtle dives into the murky swamp, alarmed by the presence of another. Alan hears the rustle of the tall grass behind him, and the squeak of folding lawn chairs, accompanied by the low rumble of conversation approaching.

He turns to look, grimace prepped-and-ready to greet the newcomers, and his eyes lock on the duo trudging over. Angie waves and the colorful towels draped over her arms flutter in the breeze-less air. But he can only see Chase behind her, making reluctant eye-contact with Alan as he approaches.

"Hope you don't mind some company. It's such a nice day we thought we'd get a little sun on the dock," Angie says, but doesn't actually care about the response. It doesn't matter anyway. Alan's eyes hold fast to Chase's toned, brown form. Sweat is already forming on his pecs and starting to race down his rippled abdomen like a seductive finger, stopping at the line of his blue swim trunks that rest just below the clean patch of gauze taped over his appendix incision.

Alan returns his gaze to the floating stump and Chase breezes past with a folding chair, setting it on the dock and motioning for Angie to sit.

Alan tries his best to keep from glancing at Chase, who sits on the edge of the dock on a folded towel with his feet in the water, staring out at the small schools of fish below. He's right in Alan's field of vision, pulling his attention every few seconds. His darting eyes flit behind the dark shield of his glasses until, finally, he sighs deeply and trudges back toward the patient house in an angry huff.

"What the hell is that dude's problem?" Angie asks, watching Alan make his way back across the grass.

But Chase just watches him leave with a quiet grace.

26

Mick finishes doodling something on a piece of paper with a permanent marker he found in the kitchen. The crude drawing depicts a man in a wheelchair, wearing a t-shirt with a *Nine-Inch Nails* logo on it, playing cards with another male stick figure sitting on the bed nearby. He smiles, thinking about how comical it is going to be when Walsh looks at his video feed to see the drawing taped in front of the overhead camera in his room.

But for now, it goes on the wall. He scotch tapes it with pride, right to the satin finish of the new latex paint-job on the walls, among the others depicting the wheelchair man in various, humorous situations, ready to swap out at a moments notice, offering him both privacy and the simple satisfaction of an innocent prank.

Wheeling himself back, he eyes all of his creations, born out of the hours of boredom, taped to the lower half of the walls as high as he can reach from the chair like an art gallery for little people. The top half of the room is bare, a gentle, frustrating reminder that although he was once 6-foot-four, now he can't tape something up over five feet high.

He caps the marker and lobs it onto his desk. It rolls off onto the floor and he sighs, knowing he can make Ed fish it out for him later at some point.

He rolls toward his bed, eyeing the handle of the revolver sticking out of the open side flap. He smiles, lifting it carefully to double check that the safety is still on after having been jostled in his bag. His old, trusty .38. *Don't leave home without it*, he thinks with a snicker. He holds it toward the window, arms extended, and watches a large bird fly through the treetops outside through the sights.

"*Pow.*" He makes the sound quietly with his lips, as if whispering to the bird like Clint Eastwood, eyes squinted. He spins it on his gloved finger and pretends to holster it in the void next to his wheel.

27

DAY SEVEN OF THE TRIAL

Patient Journal Entry provided by the St. James Parish Police Department.
Evidence Item #SJPD-11288C
Criminal Case #: 7-23-mu-187462-OB
Translated to digital transcript by Mary J. Stearns
Subject Name: Angie █████████
Date: 7/04/████████
Written Journal Entry: *I got up and made breakfast and I felt fine. No fever or headache or nausea. Nothing that was mentioned in the entry packet you gave us.*

I did, however, peel back the bandage on my thigh this morning after showering to see how my dog bite is healing and I noticed something weird. The incision itself seems to have healed almost completely (which is the fastest I feel like I've ever healed from anything, so thank you! This medicine really does work!) but beneath the incision site, I noticed I could feel some bumps beneath the skin. They're tiny. And very hard. They feel like three or four small necklace beads under there. Is that normal?

Time Symptom Started: This morning. 7/4
Time Symptom Cleared:
Location on Body: Upper thigh, beneath where incision scar used to be.
Severity:

28

Fisher pops a hot plate of bacon down at the end of the table between he and Jack. Jack stares at the heavenly, greased meat. The sound of the sizzle brings him right back to that awful moment in time when the meat being cooked was his own. He shivers, despite being swathed in layers. He tears his gaze away from the pork and rests it on a cooling stack of pancakes, watching the slow waterfall of butter pour off the side.

"Alright, y'all." Fisher points at the plates. "You got your grits, scrambled eggs, sunny-side-up eggs, flapjacks, avocado toast, and, of course, bacon." He sits. The large, frayed tear in the knees of his distressed jeans spreads like a cervix giving birth to the hair-covered cartilaginous joints beneath.

Angie shovels some eggs onto a plate and passes it to Iris. Chase takes some cheesy grits. The plates go around in a flurry and utensils clatter against the china until everyone is finished.

"I think we should say grace," Alan utters, voice nearly baritone and sedate.

Chase snickers.

Alan's black hair catches air as he whips his head. His lips are pursed tight. The sinew in his neck stretches as he presses his molars together. "Something funny?"

"Just you pretending to be religious is all." Chase stares forward at nothing, not daring to make eye contact with the angry man beside him. His black fingers are steepled in front of him, gold rings shimmering in the morning sun pouring in through the panoramic windows wrapping around the dining room.

"I'm not pretending." Alan tries to soften his tone, barely speaking up, struggling hard to control his explosive anger. It's always been a problem for him and he feels the heat rushing across his face. Has been, ever since Chase laughed.

"You alleged Christians *never* think you are. Always picking and choosing the parts of it all that suit you and abandoning the rest."

"Well, the bible's got a lot to say about your kind." His words are cold. Everyone at the table is tense, hoping the confrontation won't persist.

"Yeah, yeah. You wanna quote your precious fuckin' Leviticus to me now?"

Alan tosses his fork back to his plate with a clatter and he runs his tongue on the inside of his closed mouth, tight with frustration. He leans back in his chair and crosses his arms. "You don't like it. I'd be pissed, too, if I knew I was going to Hell."

"Ha!" Chase rolls his eyes dramatically at Alan.

"Guys," Fisher holds his hands out flat in the air, avoiding eye contact with either of them like an impartial referee. "C'mon. Let's just eat."

"Nah. Depeche Mode over here wants to school y'all in Leviticus." Chase throws his hands up in the air. "C'mon now. Tell us what Leviticus says about my kind."

Silence.

"Awww, don't get shy on me now, Hot Topic." Chase runs a shaking hand across his shiny head, a nervous tic he displays in moments of stress. "You fake-ass zealots may look different, but y'all are the same predictable-ass broken record. Know what Leviticus actually says? 'Cause I can tell ya. It says: *A man shall not lie with another man as he does a woman.* You know what other dumb shit Leviticus forbids? Having your hair unkempt," Chase points to Alan's shaggy hair with a flourish, "tearing your clothing, bearing a grudge, and mixing fucking *fabrics*, for God's sake! Picking and choosing the parts of religion that *suit you* doesn't make you pious, it makes you a *hypocrite*."

Alan shoves the chair out with a groan, snatches up his plate full of food, and storms out the front door. They can see the mottled silhouette of him through the decorative glass windows as he plops onto a bench swing hanging on the front wrap-around porch. No one speaks.

Chase grabs his fork and angrily starts digging into his grits, shoving angry forkfuls into his mouth.

Fisher groans, leaning back in his chair, draping one tattooed arm over the wooden back of it. His gray eyes pierce Chase and he calmly speaks with an upward nod. "You two gonna be at each other like this the whole time? 'Cause that's gonna make for a long couple'a weeks, if so."

"Whadday want from me?" Chase says, gulping down a cheesy bite of the mash. "The guy's a dick."

"Yeah, he is. But you don't gotta egg him on all the time."

"Oh, so now this is my fault somehow?" Chase looks around, pressing his fingertips into his firm chest.

Jack opens his mouth, as if to speak, but stumbles on his words. "No, no one is saying this is your fault. He's just saying--"

"I KNOW what he's saying, dude, alright? I'm not an idiot. I graduated Phi Theta Cappa, with honors. I'm not stupid. I just don't see why, in this day and age, I still gotta put up with this kind of bigoted bullshit. If it's not because I'm black, it's because I'm fuckin' queer. I feel like I can't go any-damn-where without some idiot like that telling me whats right and wrong. Bet he didn't even finish high school."

A somber hush falls over the group and they start to eat. Chase drops his fork down, leaning back in his chair, too. He speaks with humility, bobbing his head.

"I'm sorry, guys. I didn't mean to ruin your morning with this nonsense."

Jack reaches out a bandaged hand and pats Chase's shoulder, as if to say its all going to be alright. A soft smile emerges from beneath the cowl of his hoodie.

Chase drums on the table repeatedly to chase away the darkened cloud that feels like it is looming overhead. "Alright y'all, what kinda activities are we gonna get into today?"

29

Jack smiles, bashful beneath the hood of his jacket. As Iris looks at him, he suddenly forgets how sweltering it is beneath all of the fabric in the late afternoon sun. He's no longer focused on roasting like poultry in an oven, as salty streams of sweat bead around the bandaged-half of his face and beneath his cotton t-shirt and hoodie sleeves.

No. When she smiles, he feels pleasantly dizzy, focusing on the wrenching fist grabbing his guts and twisting.

He can't, for the life of him, understand why she is giving him the time of day but, every day, she seems more genuinely charmed by him. She machine-guns questions at him, trying to get to know him, and he doesn't mind it in the slightest. Every one seems to make him feel a touch giddier than the last. There are moments that he almost can't even meet her eyes with his own because he knows he won't be able to pull away. Instead, lingering there for a too-long amount of time.

But he has a mirror.

He knows that the first time he makes a move, it will be met with the awkward silence and the, "I like you, but, more as a friend." Things aren't like they used to be for Jack. He can't just flash that charming grin to get someone's attention or spout a cheesy, effortless line and snag a woman's number. Those days are gone and Jack has, for the last few years, been able to wrap his head around that. No matter how much he wants to kiss someone, no matter how much he wants to feel what it's like to be inside her, to make her moan, to watch her body react to his, to feel her skin grow hot beneath his touch… he knows that those days are gone for good, living only in his wildest fantasies now.

As she takes the paddles from the hooks on the wall and grabs the front handle of the canoe, she giggles something about an old man she met in a nude drawing class. He tries his best to follow along, doing what he can to focus on her story and not the sweet smile on her face or the way her stunning skin glows, framed by faraway jellyfish-tendrils of hanging Spanish moss in the treeline near the road out.

He tries his best to enjoy the attention and the time with her before she wises up and realizes she could be in the company of anyone in the house more attractive than him.

As he replies with a story about someone he met in a college psych class and lifts the back end of the canoe, he catches a glimpse of Walsh's prying eyes, glowering at them both from around the nearby corner of his modest clinic. He's holding a metal bowl full of water, jaw tense as if his teeth are clenched at the mere sight of Jack.

Jack's story stops mid-sentence and he stands, frozen, locking into the stare with the old man. He's seen that look of burning hate from across the way before and, even years later, it still turns his blood to ice water.

"We were just…" Jack started but couldn't finish, standing impotently in the tall grass holding a heavy canoe.

Walsh sets the bowl down on the ground, never taking his eyes off of Jack until he stands fully again. He forces a placid smile at Iris and manages a half-wave. "You two have fun now. Watch out for the snakes while you're out on the water. They'll come right up to the boat."

Iris smiles, hopeful and bright, smoothing the obvious tension with her positive demeanor. "Thank you, sir."

"Gonna be a nice sunset soon." He says as he shuffles back around the corner. He whistles, ultra-loud and clear. From across the front of the property, the catahoula comes running full-speed, like a playful pup, even though he's aging. He skids to a stop at the water bowl, lapping up the cold fluid with unflappable greed, gobbling it sloppily as the two make their way toward the bayou's edge with the dinky boat for two.

The sight of the spotted fur and judging eyes of the canine make Jack feel light-headed.

"What did she do then?" Iris chuckles, already reverting back to their prior conversation. "Did she concede on the Freud thing?"

"Huh?" Jack asks, far away now. The sight of the dog is too jarring. He can feel his heart racing at the sight of it.

Iris looks back over her bandaged shoulder blade, flashing a gleaming smile that wrenches his insides like an alligator in a death-roll. He feels like he wants to drop the canoe and collapse into the damp thatch of wild grass beneath his feet.

Instead, he utters, "Yeah," and laughs nervously.

But the word is just meaningless noise to him, trailing into some empty abyss. Between the sudden appearance of Walsh and that goddamned dog… he's completely forgotten what he's even agreeing to.

30

Walsh leans back in his office chair, bobbing mindlessly as he studies Fisher's patient journal, flitting his eyes back and forth between the handwritten pages and the twenty-eight-year-old's oceanic eyes, brimming with excitement. Fisher hangs in the silence, waiting for the doctor to smile.

Walsh places the journal on his desk and rubs the gray stubble on his stern face. "Is this true?"

He nods so hard he resembles a flicked bobble-head doll. "If I'm lyin', I'm dyin', doc."

Walsh motions with his head for Fisher to head out to the exam room. "Hop up there in the chair so I can take a look."

In a flash, Fisher is crunching the butt of his designer jeans down onto the paper liner on the exam room chair. Walsh shuffles over, pulls the glasses hanging by the cord around his neck onto his face and peels back the bandages on the back of Fisher's right bicep. Where there were once gnarly lumps of scar tissue from skinning himself on jagged asphalt, Walsh now studies the perfectly-healing skin of Fisher's forearm and elbow.

Instead of celebration, a stony look spreads across his withering face. Fisher can swear he sees a glimmer of panic in the old man's eyes and his smile fades.

"What's wrong, doc?" Fisher braces himself for the bad news.

Walsh realizes he's battling a panicked scowl and his expression flits to joyous as if he was walking onstage to give a theatrical performance. "Nothing's wrong. This is exemplary. You're healing just as promised."

He open-palm slaps Fisher in the arm. "Well, then. Congratulations. Looks like you don't need these any more." Walsh's trembling hand peels off the taped-on gauze pads and tosses them in the trash.

Fisher smiles a little, still unnerved by Walsh's initial reaction.

"Nurse Tate will be by later to return your journal, as usual," Walsh says, tapping the young man on the shoulder, shooing him up off the seat and out toward the front door. As Fisher collects his water bottle from the interview desk, Walsh grabs Fisher's packed, manilla patient folder and places his newly-printed hematology results in it from the printer. "I'll see you tomorrow. Same time."

Fisher nods with a reverent bow and presses out the glass front door of the building.

The minute the door seals, Walsh screams and tosses the patient folder at the wall, exploding it into a flurry of flying paper like a white firework. He turns back to the blood-work desk and backhands a tray of glass test tubes at the opposite wall. It bursts into a bomb of shattered glass fragments and crimson fluid, leaving Jackson Pollock-esque splatter dripping down the fresh coat of gray-blue latex paint.

He grabs the rolling desk chair at the hematology station and whips it across the room, with a throat-shedding roar, as hard as his aging body will allow.

His chest heaves as he struggles to catch his breath, grinding his brittle molars until they feel like they will crack. He slams his finger down so hard on the intercom button that he nearly breaks the machine.

"Tate! Lab! NOW!" He releases the button and slaps the machine onto the floor.

He's growling now. He doesn't know when it started, but he is. He clutches his tightening chest, walks over to the desk safe where the pills are kept and sits in the chair in front of it. He eyes the lock, and rubs his papery fingertips over a tiny gouge where the metal is marred. He leans in, examining the damage closer, and his heart races.

Evidence of tampering…

He can't seem to get air.

He gasps big breaths in, feeling as though nothing is entering his squashed lungs. He feels like an overweight person is sitting on his chest, just how his fat older brother Louis did when they were kids, threatening to spit on him, crushing the oxygen from his ribcage with thick thighs…

Tate bursts in through the door, already panicked from his tone. She hesitates for a minute, taking in the shattered glass underfoot, the strewn paperwork and an overturned rolling-chair. She sees Walsh struggling for every breath.

"What's going on?!"

"The… the…" He tries to speak but he can't, gasping like a drowning man coming up for air.

"Are you having a heart attack," she shouts, rushing to his side.

He shakes his head. "Panic." He gulps again, wheezing between breaths, looking like he's going to pass out. "Attack."

"Okay. It's going to be okay. You're alright, James. Just take slow breaths. Lean over. Head between your knees." She presses his back and folds him a bit, until his head is below the height of the desk. Her tone is soothing.

"Okay, jeez, I'm rusty at this. We haven't had to do this in years." She takes a deep breath herself, thinking. "Okay, lets do the 5-4-3-2-1 thing."

He nods, sucking in air so fast he's lightheaded.

"Name five things you can see."

He looks around, through the black fog, through the stars clouding his dimming vision. "Boat shoes." He looks down at the brown, canvas shoes on his feet.

"Okay, that's one."

"Gold… wa… watch." He struggles.

"That's two."

Walsh looks around, trying to use the intended distraction to find a third item.

He does.

It's a stray, black pill sitting in the groove of the grout between the floor tiles beneath the desk. His eye grow large, filled with terror.

He's meticulous about cleanliness. It wasn't put there by him.

No, no, no, no, no, dear God no, he screams in his own mind, mentally begging deities he doesn't believe in to make this all some strange misunderstanding.

"Come on, we need three more things you can see," Tate coos.

As he opens his mouth to speak, he vomits heavily beneath the desk, splattering bile across the clean tile, washing over the loose pill like a violent, ebbing ocean wave.

31

An evening storm rages outside, filling the southern night air with thick, oppressive humidity. Lightning sends bursts of shimmering light through the tufts of clouds looming in the heavens above, momentarily illuminating them like diffused, gray lanterns. The bayou beyond the compound glitters, waters churning and disrupted by the pattering rain falling from the concord-grape-colored sky. The wildlife is quiet, tucked away for the evening in the safest hiding places they can find, and all that sounds out across the vast landscape is the inconsistent roar of bass-filled thunder as it vibrates everything in sight.

Inside, the gaggle of patients are playing charades in the den. It has a breathtaking view of the storm with its wall of windows and large sliding doors. Every time the lightning cracks it illuminates the jovial expressions on their faces.

Iris is up next. She faces her teammates, Jack and Mick.

"Aaaaaand go!" Fisher yells out, staring at his watch.

Angie giggles, popping a square of cheese from the deli platter into her mouth as she watches her competition. Chase hops off the couch to go refill his empty glass of water.

Iris' arms shoot out to the side and she stands proudly, flicking her hair as if the wind has taken it before jutting her arms back out.

"*Passion of the Christ*!" Jack screams, laughing.

She shakes her head. She repeats the move, proudly splaying her arms on either side of her, legs together.

"Uh… uh, *Ten Commandments*." Mick shouts.

Not right either.

"Why do you guys keep guessing religious ones?" Chase laughs.

"I thought Alan might have put it in, you know, after his stupid little Leviticus outburst. She's clearly, like, crucified."

Iris sighs, relaxes her body in defeat.

"Thirty seconds left!"

She rolls her neck and tries a different approach. She drops to the floor, draped over on her side, posing. Then she hops up, races to the bare floor across from where she'd posed and pretends to draw something.

"*Lolita*?" Mick calls out.

She looks up at him, confused and almost offended.

"What? I think 'da pedo draws baby Clarice Starling in 'at one, right?"

She waves her hands and goes back to pretend drawing. She races back to the spot on the floor, poses herself again and touches an imaginary necklace.

"Oh shit, I know this one."

"I don't, man."

"Aaaaand that's time." Fisher calls out proudly. The other team moans as a group.

"*Titanic*!" She yells, pretending to be furious, looking adorable as she does so.

Jack throws his arms up in the air.

"You know… *I'm flying, Jack*!" She motions the first pose. "And the heart of the ocean?! *Draw me like one of your French girls*?! C'mon! Y'all are killin' me here!"

"Why dinn't you lay down on 'da door 'dats big 'nuf fa' bof an' let Jack die? I'dda got it '*den*!"

Weeeeoooooo.

The electronics make a subtle noise as they power down, leaving the whole house in pitch black.

CRACK!

Lightning smacked through the landscape, shooting a burst of white light through all of the windows.

"Oh, I know 'is one." Mick snickered. "*Poltergeist*."

The others chuckle.

"Well, fuck. What a buzzkill." Fisher laughs.

"We could play…" Angie thinks for a moment, "light as a feather, stiff as a board."

"Shit. Le's have a seance while we're at it." Mick scoffs. "Plus, I'm stiff as a board all the time."

Angie can't see him bobbing his eyebrows at her flirtatiously so he rolls his eyes.

"I think I'm gonna go get ready for bed anyway. Gotta get my beauty sleep." Chase says, trying to sound more effeminate than he already does.

"You guys aren't going to bed, right?" Fisher points around the room.

"Hell naw, not yet!" Mick howls.

Chase ambles his way up the cold stairway to the level above, darkened completely by the closed doors throughout the hallway, blanketing the narrow strip in pitch blackness.

He doesn't see Alan coming out of his room at the same time, heading for the same hallway bathroom until he bumps right into him, spilling his glass of water on the specter lurking in the hall.

"Oh fuck, who is that?"

"Alan."

"Jesus, you scared the fucking HELL out of me!" Chase laughs nervously, patting Alan's chest to see where he is. He gasps. "Oh shit, I spilled all over you."

"Yeah." His voice is annoyed.

"I am so sorry!" Chase pats him down to feel the extent of the mess.

Alan goes silent.

Lightning strikes again and his face is lit up by the flash of white that streams in through his open bedroom door. In that moment, Alan is grinding his teeth, wincing, eyes shut tight, towel and toiletries bag in the crooks of his arms.

Chase pulls his hand away like Alan is a burning stove top. "I'm really sorry," he says through the blackness. "Its just water, but still."

"It's fine. Just don't fucking touch me."

Chase doesn't need to see his face to know he's grinding his molars even harder.

"Okay, I'm gonna go right. You go to *your* right."

With that, they shuffle in different directions.

Alan feels his way to the bathroom, feeling for the sink, tossing his things into the concave basin. He slams the door behind him and locks it. He jams his knuckles and forehead against the wood, breathing wild. His heart thumps like a cranked subwoofer, thudding violently against the inside of his rib cage.

The blood rushes south, surging between his legs. His erection throbs between his thighs and his breathing becomes so erratic he fears he might hyperventilate. Gusts of expelled air refract off the bathroom door back into his face.

He spins with ferocity, rearing a clenched fist back to punch the door but refraining so as not to draw attention.

The lights buzz back to life, blinding him like heaven's welcoming glow from the too-bright, 100-watt bulbs installed above the mirror. He narrows his eyes, grinding his molars hard.

In his sweatpants, his rigid, engorged cock has fully sprung to attention, tenting the gray fabric in an obvious way. He runs his hands up the sides of his black hair and pulls so hard that his vision lightens. The bandages on his forearms crinkle in the silence. He revels in the pain and self- punishment, wishing he could scream or hit something.

In the toothpaste-mottled mirror, all he sees is the *pure fucking hatred* for himself that he feels.

He remembers the way Chase's hands felt, racing over his body and his dick swells, throbbing with an almost pleasant pain and desire for release.

But he wouldn't dare wrap his hands around it to finish the job. He wouldn't dare give in to that kind of filth. *You're not some fucking degenerate faggot,* he thinks, berating himself internally.

He tries his best to think about pussy. To divert his mind to his high-school sweetheart after she spread her legs on prom night. But his thoughts re-routed to the image of Chase by the bayou, sunning his skin, the color of brown sugar, in the afternoon light. The beads of sweat tracing his toned musculature…

He can't jerk off with the barrage of thoughts racing through his mind. Too risky.

He scrambles over to his toiletries bag, shuffling through the hygiene items with haste. His lips curl into a smile as his fingers finally find the thin, cardboard-wrapped item he was searching for:

A pack of straight razor blades.

He pulls out the pack and unwraps one, feeling a rush of dopamine. Like he's opening a long-coveted Christmas present. It glimmers in the painful light of the bulbs lining the mirror.

It's the first time he's smiled in weeks.

He breathes out a long, slow exhale, centering himself for what is about to come. He sets the sliver of steel down on the marble countertop and pulls off his t-shirt, tossing it to the floor with abandon. He runs his trembling fingertips over his sinewy midsection eyeing the perfect spot for his newest art installment selecting a fleshy, unmarred spot beneath his lowest right rib. He plucks the blade off the counter and steadies his hand, poised over the skin as it rises and falls with his slowing breaths. His eyes dart to his erection and then back to the reflection of his abdomen.

He presses the blade into the flesh, feeling a rush of power from the edge burying itself beneath his epidermis. He slices into the meat with slow, calculated movement, diagonally, toward his navel.

A rivulet of hot, claret liquid curls downward toward his aching groin, following the curves of his body and resting at the tight waistband of his sweats.

His head falls backward like a heroin junkie, enraptured in the painful ecstasy of the moment.

His lids close tightly, seeing the bulbs through the thin veil of his eyelids as they flutter with excitement.

His chin presses downward, grinding hard against the top of his chest, and his empty fist balls up so hard that his black-painted fingernails could almost draw blood. The shameful pain between his legs begins to ebb, washed away like litter out to sea in lowering tides.

But when his eyes open, he is not prepared for what he sees. There, between the torn flaps of skin, he could swear he sees a bubble of something peeking through the wound. Darkened circles of off-white and blood-stained green…

With a pupil in the middle. Like some sort of malformed human eye, bulging from upper and lower lids.

He feels the skin, two halves, once connected by perfect layers of skin and meat and nerve endings close together and spread again…

In a blink.

He drops the crimson-streaked blade into the basin, jarred by the involuntary bodily function.

Alan steps closer to the mirror to examine it more closely and the lumpy, tumorous object retracts, retreating into his musculature. The open, gaping flesh sits flush again as if nothing was ever there. He shakes his head and stares at his pallid, sweating reflection in the toothpaste-spattered mirror.

"What the *fuck*?!" He whispers to himself.

His hands shake. Not from the pleasurable adrenaline he received from the self-punishment… No, this time, from *fear*.

32

As Chase nestles into his bed for the night, Alan is the furthest thing from his mind. Heart still racing from his nightly crunches (*a hundred in the morning and a hundred at night to keep the abs tight*).

He rubs a hand across the bandage over his appendectomy scar beneath the covers, letting his fingertips linger on his dewy torso. With great sorrow, he recalls the night he had to be taken from the table-read of a new series he'd been cast in. He recalled the shame of being hoisted into an ambulance in front of producers and crew. He remembers the feel of the embarrassment, hot on his face, as paramedics closed the door, rushing him off for emergency surgery.

A week later he got the call that his role had to be recast, due to the amended shooting schedule, and they told him to rest up, saying it like they cared even though he knew they didn't. It was show *business*, after all.

He closed his eyes and let his mind wander back to the last photo shoot he was cast for, the one that made him decide to sign up for Walsh's trial in the first place.

***

"Alright, I'm ready. Send him out." Stuart *hollered, mentally preoccupied with the buttons on one of his remote flashes. It was on the fritz again and he could feel his pulse throbbing in his throat. So much for getting his numbers down like the doctor ordered.*

The PA touched Chase's glistening arm as the makeup artist finished misting him. She said the spray made black skin stand out even more in the high-contrast black and white photos. But he didn't need an explanation. He'd modeled for Stuart before, on a smaller scale. The guy was a cocksucker, both literally and figuratively. He was as good at his craft as he was at giving oral, but he was a cold bastard, treating people like expendable props from his shoots.

Both men had risen in the ranks of their profession slightly and Chase smiled as he saw Stuart's face troubleshooting behind the flash umbrella.

"Good to see you again, Stu." Chase smiled and offered a polite wave, bare, black feet stepping gingerly onto the white infnity wall material. He was wearing a pair of simple, stylish, new boxer briefs with a rainbow striped waistband and nothing else.

"Yeah." Stuart bit his tongue, pulling the batteries out of the flash unit and blowing off the contacts. "Carol!" He screamed.

Carol rushed over dutifully, standing meekly by his side. She was middle-aged, soft in the middle, and reminded Chase of a human version of Miss Piggy from the Muppets. "Yes, sir?"

"Get me two FRESH double A's." He palmed the batteries into her hand and she scurried off. He finally looked up. Chase thought he would smile when he recognized him but he didn't. Instead, he frowned more.

"What the fuck is this?" Stuart hollered over his shoulder. Carol rushed back with two fresh *batteries and took the initiative to replace them in the flash unit. "Where's the fucking producer? Someone get me Greg. We got a problem."*

Carol nodded and rushed off. Chase felt nervous at the sudden displeasure as Stuart's eyes studied him up and down.

Greg shuffled over, overweight and clad in khakis and a bulging polo. His breathing was loud. "What, Stu?"

"What the fuck is this?" He splayed his hands at Chase and then picked up his Canon DSLR, tethered to a thin, open laptop on a trolley by a long red USB cable. The lens on the camera was huge and looked like a white thermos. Chase was surprised the rail-thin man picked it up with such ease.

"Goddammit, Stu, just tell me the problem this time. I hate these fucking guessing games." Greg took another taxing breath of air and rubbed his eyes in frustration.

"This!" Stuart smacked the Canon down on the trolley and marched up to Chase, waving both parallelled hands above and below his appendectomy scar like he was sawing the model like a slice of pizza. "Thiiiiiis! Dammit, Greg, this is a fucking underwear ad. And you guys send me this guy? All people are gonna see is this big fucking dimple right here. Look! Look how the light is already hitting it!" Stuart motioned to the massive blue and silver Skypanel beaming its light onto Chase. "Its so deep, the key isn't doing a damned thing to fill it."

"Then move the key. The damned thing's on wheels."

"You are missing the fucking point, Greg--"

"Then Photoshop it! It's not a big fucking deal, Stu. It's a scar. People have 'em."

"You fucking guys and your Photoshop. Why don't I just digitally alter the whole thing? Or hell, lets just have an AI render us an image and send this asshole home? Dammit, Greg," he said as he shuffled away. Chase clamped a hand around his other wrist and held it straight down, to block the offending scar. *"With the money you pay these vapid fucks, you shouldn't have to fucking Photoshop the Grand Canyon out of the picture. This is an* underwear *ad. Someone should have caught this."*

"We looked at his portfolio. We didn't see anything."

Chase cleared his throat. *"I'm sorry, this is my bad. This was recent. I haven't had a shoot since then. I should have said something. I didn't think it would be an issue."*

Greg held a hand up. *"It's not!"* The gesture was meant to assure him but it did little to assuage Chase's anxiety about the imperfection.

Greg turned to Stuart and poked him in his bony chest. *"Take the damned pictures and stop bitching. We will have Belinda retouch it. Its not the end of the world."*

"This is going on a fucking billboard, Greg--"

"Not another damned word. Are we clear? Take the photos. I have raquetball at four and I'll be damned if I'm missing it over a damn appendectomy scar."

Stuart picked up the camera, gritting his teeth, and took a test shot. The remote flash went off as it was supposed to. Stuart looked conflicted about what he wanted to say. "Turn to your right."

Chase did as instructed.

"Put your hand on your hip. Maybe we can hide it with the goddamned shadow."

Chase was so embarrassed in that moment, posing in different ways to try to hide the scar that kept him alive, yet had already cost him so much in his career. He tried to zone out, tried to think about the lackluster hookup he had the night before with the good-looking Peruvian on Grindr who was in Nola for a friend's bachelor party.

But his mind kept wandering back to the tiny two-inch scar on the side of his abdomen. He wondered if it would continue to befuddle his career and maybe even creep into his love life. Maybe he would end up as one of those guys who only has sex with a shirt on.

He thought to himself, I have to do something.

33

Outside, an ominous sky trickles through the darkened trees, foliage waving in the wind. Spanish moss flutters like clothes on a line. The expanse above looks like crushed, violet velvet, sucking up every bit of errant light that rural Louisiana has to offer. Steamy gusts whistle through the ill-fitted windows, pouring in like subway steam, mixing with the icy blast of the window units as if a sinister force is slinking through the night.

An opossum scuttles across the rooftop overhead and Mick looks up, as if he has some sort of x-ray vision that can see through boards and shingles.

He looks back down, placing his four of hearts onto a lengthening stack of vintage playing cards with nude women draped across each in a torrid pose. His makeshift flask and card deck are lit up only by the 40-watt bulb seeping out from under a thick, linen lampshade on his nightstand.

He's growing tired of playing with himself once again, head bobbing as he fights sleep.

He snaps back up, blinking with a sudden alertness, and looks at the clock: 3:30 am.

He hears a rustle in the hallway. Heels clicking on hard wood. He cranes his neck, anxious for a fellow night-owl to keep him company.

Only catching a glimpse of her in his periphery, he grumbles, "'bout damn time. Got you a present." He produces a plastic bottle of tequila from beneath his cot. "Come, have a shot wit' me."

Angie saunters in, high heels leading the way. His face brightens. Not just at her presence, but her attire.

As he spins his wheels around, he gets a full view of her. Soaks in her wardrobe: A pink negligee with a netted lingerie robe loosely tied over the top of it. The negligee beneath is so short, the curvature of her toned ass nuzzles its way out into the humid night air beneath its lacy hem.

His eyebrow cocks, his grin impossible to stifle. "Well, well, well. Look what 'da cat dragged in."

"All week, you've been staring at me." Her voice buzzes with sexuality, her glittering eyes narrowed into a sultry squint. She softly runs her hand up her top, dragging the material up, exposing her stomach and the lack of panties beneath, flashing him a glimpse of the landing strip of ginger, tightly-manicured hair beneath.

Mick stares hard, steely-eyed. His elevated pulse thrums hard against the taut flesh of his throat.

She leans in, showing off a bountiful amount of cleavage from her pale, heaving tits. He wants to hold them. Feel their heft in his sweating palms. Her heart beats wild and fast beneath the jiggling flesh.

"You've been undressing me with your eyes." Angie peels back the belt on the robe, slinking the whole thing off her shoulders, discarding it on the floor.

She lifts the hem of her nightie again over her head, exposing everything now. Standing stark naked save for high heels, before him now. A looming goddess with blessed proportions. She pouts as she coyly approaches. "You want me, don't you?"

Mick lobs the cheap bottle of tequila onto a rumpled pile of dirty clothes in the corner and nods. He grabs her wrist. *Hard.* Pulls her close in a dominant display. Just because he's in the chair doesn't mean he doesn't demand to call the shots.

She braces against the bedside table. It wobbles, spraying playing cards to the floor like flat, white rain. Angie leans in with a wicked half-grin.

Mick reaches up, grabs her by the hair, and pulls her down to his face with force. She grins, bent at the waist, her bare buttocks jutting out from the height of the heels. He kisses her deeply, leaning into her as far as the chair will allow. Drawing her in further by her rust-colored locks. The other gloved hand caresses her, meandering his bare fingertips up the gooseflesh on her curvaceous body until his digits are squirming through the damp flesh between her thighs.

She moans with pleasure, the sounds of which seep out into the pitch-black hall.

34

The wretched smell of the smoking car...

Even in his nightmares, he can smell the pungent stench of gasoline as it leaked into the wild grasses below the CR-V tank. He watched it pool out the window, creeping toward the flaming engine like the boogeyman's hand under covers.

He heard the sound of the sirens, too, howling in the distance like wolves to a full moon. Too far away to help Kate.

To help any of them.

The humidity was like a wet blanket around his throat, choking back his guttural screams. His voice was the only noise echoing across the bayou. Even though he was not alone. He had to scream loud enough for them all.

His blood-soaked hands tremored as they tried to dislodge Kate's cranium from between his caved-in lap and the spent airbag.

The dog pants. It watched like a reaper come to claim his soul. Patient. Eyes locked.

That goddamned catahoula. *The thought rings out through the shock over and over. As if the mutt were somehow at fault. As if the canine were responsible for his crushed pelvis and what little remained of Kate's face.*

The wreckage of her skull.

Hot, oozing brain matter slipped across his hands as he yanked at the steering wheel, the contents of her once-intelligent mind aired out for all to see.

He cried hard, spit trailing down like alien slime onto her matted locks of black hair. Hair that came away from the scalp in hunks as he pulled at the machine.

But there's more to the story. More to mourn. More guilt to swallow.

Outside of the shattered windshield, beyond the engine that's caught fire...

It was a little girl.

Head slumped. Forced to stand by the pressure of the mangled grill. Pinned against the tree.

She was so young. He could barely see her through the rising smoke, black billows of it crawling up her body like a magician who wants to disappear in a blackened puff.

A stream of crimson dribbled from her mouth onto the silver hood, coated with exploded fractals of glittering glass. Her arms dangled limply.

On one, lettered beads read "JESSICA."

He could see the gas, reaching the flame like God's index finger in Michaelangelo's Creation of Adam.

Jack clawed at the window. His handsome, chiseled features twisted into a full earth-shattering scream as he struggled with all his might to escape.

But he didn't get out.

Even in his dreams, he never gets out.

***

As Jack awakens, sweat dousing the outer rim of his gray hoodie. He hears something akin to a moan from the room next to his, but not one of pleasure.

He listens closer, sitting up, wiping his dripping, gnarled brow with a damp sleeve.

Mmmmmpf!

He hears the noise again. As the sound rings out again in the oppressive darkness, he realizes it's not a moan at all.

It's a female's pained *whimper*.

It's *Iris*.

35

Jack's eyes struggle to adjust to the moonlight beaming through the shade slats. His eyes pass a row of construction-paper origami gifts on the lit windowsill and finally settle on Iris. She is sitting bolt upright on her bed. The torn bandage is flopped backward, dangling with a crust of dry blood down her bare back, slapping against the back of her bra with every violent movement. She stares blankly out the window ahead, her eyebrows furrowed in pain, mouth twisted in a grimace. Her left hand is over her right shoulder, digging a fresh hole into the skin on her shoulder-blade where there was once a twisted scar that clearly read the word SLUT.

Her skin bleeds down her back from the gaping crevice she's opened in her own flesh. She doesn't react to Jack's presence, grunting furiously as she digs harder, staring off into nothingness.

Jack approaches with a mix of caution and panicked speed. He speaks, unsure if she's alert or somehow asleep. "Iris, what are you doing?!"

Iris stares ahead, blank, digging deeper into her shoulder as a stream of blood trickles down her arm.

"I have to get it out," she mumbles, tone terrified. Suddenly, with more fear, she yells it again, louder this time, "I have to get it out. I have to get it out!"

"Get what out?!" Jack's voice is low and commanding, like a paternal figure.

"Something's in me!" She's crying now, still focused on the blinds ahead as if she's far away, trapped in a dream. "Get it out of me! Please!"

Jack snatches her up with both arms, swiping her offending hand away, clutching her inside a tight hug for her own safety and dragging her upward to her feet.

She struggles in his grasp, screaming as if she's being attacked and starts to try to wrestle free, hitting him.

"Get off of me you bastards!" Her scream rips through the house and light spills into the hall from neighboring rooms. Jack lets her go, afraid of how it will look if someone comes barging in, hearing her words, and seeing the stream of blood trailing down her spine.

But as he steps away, he can see her eyes snap to life, as if she's awake and fully-conscious. She seems confused by her surroundings. The look on her face melts from rage into worry and she runs to Jack, wrapping her arms around him like a scared child. He embraces her, feels her wordlessly trembling in his grip.

36

After trying the locked doors to the infirmary, the duo find themselves next door in the shed.

Iris sits on a card table, surrounded by shelves stocked sparsely with cleaning solvents, canned goods, kayak equipment, garden tools, bulk medical stock and toiletries. She is in pajama shorts and a bra, the back of which is streaked with rivulets of crimson. She seems calm, trying to modestly cover herself with her folded arms. A cascade of blonde hair drapes over her uninjured shoulder. She watches Jack scuttle through the shed, upturning bins and haphazardly searching for supplies.

Adrenaline surging through his veins, Jack finally finds a large first aid kit and rifles through it for some cotton balls. He opens a brand new bottle of peroxide frantically, tearing off the safety tab with his teeth. Sweat drips down his face from the heat, the hoodie and the urgency.

Her voice is soothing with a tinge of happiness. The fear has died down. Watching the amount of care he's putting into treating her is endearing. "It's okay. It doesn't even hurt." She insists. "*Really.*"

"You're going to get an infection if I don't clean this out."

They lock eyes for a single, tender moment and it's then that she can see how much he likes her. It's the worry and terror in his eyes that gives him away.

The air is thick, buzzing with electric anticipation. The muggy night fraught with romantic words unspoken.

He pours peroxide on a cotton ball and walks behind her, dropping the brown, plastic bottle on it's square side. Peroxide glugs out onto the floor in arterial-looking spurts, bubbling on the dusty floor. He makes no attempt to retrieve it, entranced by the sight in front of him, unable to trust what his eyes are seeing.

"What?" She whips her head around to see, but can't because of the location.

Jack stares at her back. *Speechless.*

Her wound is completely healed.

"It... it... Iris... it was a *crater* in your skin a few minutes ago!" He's both terrified and astonished. "Now there's... there's nothing." He stumbles over the syllables, stuttering in astonishment.

"Oh my God! Jack, do you know what this means?! *This means... the medicine's working!"*

Jack's face grows hard like a rock. And he responds weakly. "I'm so..." he looks down at the unchanged scars peeking beneath the bandages on his left hand, "happy for you."

His forced congratulations are clearly rooted in his own pain.

But Iris is so elated, the obvious melancholy isn't registering over her own excitement.

"I can't believe this!" she gasps. "It worked!"

Tears of joy flood her bright, blue eyes. She wraps her arms around Jack in celebration and abandons caution. She leans in to kiss him, overcome with joyous emotions and a sudden burst of freedom and lust she hadn't felt since the attack years prior.

But Jack pulls away, changing the mood in the dusty shed like the flip of a light switch.

He desires her. Intensely. But the thought of things escalating…

The thought of her seeing the horrific extent of his burns, his scars…

The thought makes him want to throw up.

He sees the dejected look on her face and he's furious with himself for causing it.

Silence hangs like a sheet of ice between them. He grits his molars, pinching his eyes shut tight.

He wants to make her feel better.

Wants to make *himself* feel better.

More than anything, he wants to feel that raging inferno of desire again, something he was positive had died in the accident, too.

Jack finally musters the courage and thrusts himself forward before he can talk himself out of it again. He stops for a moment near her face, giving her a chance to pull away. Giving her a chance to abort the whole thing. But she doesn't waver. Instead, she slides her slender hands on the sides of his damp sweatshirt. He swears he can feel her pulling him closer.

He kisses her.

Deeply.

A rush of chemicals and emotions flood Jack's swimming mind. Iris draws him closer with her legs, coiling around his like a slow boa constrictor, pressing her bare skin to his chest. The sweet taste of her mouth makes his heartbeat thump in his skull, fighting the blood rushing between his legs in a woozy rush of light-headedness that feels like Heaven.

She slides her slender hands up and gently lowers his hood. He withdraws in a flash, prying himself away from her, raising the hood back up to cover his burns.

This is all wrong. He doesn't want her to see him like this. To see the ugly, warped shell he's trapped in. Like a caged animal. His heart is racing, crotch engorged. He wants to scream.

But he calmly whispers instead, barely finding his voice, "I'm gonna, uh, call it a night."

She is unsure what to say. He's a skittish deer, ready to bolt, and she can see it in his body language as he leans toward the door. She covers her chest modestly, suddenly feeling totally naked even though she isn't. "It's fine. Really." Her tone sounds like she's begging. Maybe she is. She has been longing for someone to show her affection for so long. Longing to feel good enough about her body to expose it to someone. Her face still burns from the excitement of the kiss they just shared.

The dangling, caged drop-light dances in her azure eyes, full of sincerity and stifled tears. "Whatever is under there, no matter how *bad* it is, I promise you, Jack, I'm not scared."

The fact that she even has to mutter those words makes him physically sick

"When I look at you, I see… you." She manages a smile.

But the idyllic platitude and optimistic tone are completely lost on him. He turns away, unable to face her, and shuffles out quietly, humiliated. Unwilling to let her see the water welling in his own eyes now.

As the door shuts, she sits in silence, feeling the painful sting of rejection and the quelling rush of adrenaline.

37

DAY EIGHT OF TRIAL

Patient Journal Entry provided by the St. James Parish Police Department.
Evidence Item #SJPD-112733C
Criminal Case #: 7-23-mu-187462-OB
Translated to digital transcript by Mary J. Stearns
Subject Name: Jack ████
Date: 7/05/████

Written Journal Entry: Last night I had a startlingly-vivid nightmare of the accident. I know I don't want to talk about the details of it for obvious reasons but it's worth mentioning that this was the most vivid nightmare I've ever had. I had horrible night sweats, just like the night before. It was bad. I swear, I was reliving every horrible detail.

Then, when I woke up, I hear Iris making noise. I went into her room to see that in her dreamy fugue-state, she had carved a deep gouge into her back with her fingernail. Blood was running down it. She had dug all the way into the meat. I feel like she was deep enough to graze bone. When she finally came-to, she had no idea what was happening. We rushed to the infirmary and banged on the door and no one answered. The door was locked (It seems dangerous to not be able to reach you in a time of crisis. Is there a number or something we are supposed to call in case of emergency to have you come?)

By the time I found the first aid kit in the supply shed, her wound HEALED! It was as if there had never been a bleeding hole in her skin. The meat, the skin, everything had healed and sealed up.

I'm really happy for her. She deserves it. I'm glad the medication works... I guess, just not for me.

I know you promised that I wouldn't be on the placebo so I'm not sure if the medication is just not working or if... maybe it's just something you told me to get my hopes up.

I wouldn't blame you for wanting to hurt me like that.

I wouldn't blame you if you wanted a lot WORSE for me too.

Time Symptom Started: After midnight
Time Symptom Cleared: N/A
Location on Body: All over (night sweats)
Describe the Symptom: (see above)
Severity: Feels like the nightmares are worsening.

38

The sizzle of eggs is in the air as Mick rolls in, hair cow-licked in the back from being recently mashed against his pillow. Angie leans against the oven, scraping sticky egg whites from the bottom of the pan. Her blessed curves jiggle with every tough movement.

Mick rolls in as silent as a cobra and pinches the bottom of her perky ass escaping through the gap under her sleep shorts.

"*Hey, girl.*"

She jumps, reflexively grabs the frying pan as if she's going to hit someone with it. Burst yolks dribble down the lemon-pepper seasoned whites and she frowns, growling, "Jesus! What the *fuck*?!"

"Take 'er down a notch, jumpy. I just wan' to say... last night was," he rolls back and forth playfully biting his lower lip in an attempt to be crass and funny, "jus' *wow.*"

"What the hell are you yammering about?" She concentrates on trying to salvage the eggs. Maybe there's still time to commit to scrambling them. "And what gives you the right to fucking touch my *ass*, creep?!"

"Creep, huh? Da's a pet name I ain't got yet." Mick tries to hide his shit-eating grin, glancing around to make sure they're still alone. "You don' have to put on a show. No one' here but us."

"Put on a show?" She whips toward him, stooping down to an offensive height, pointing with the pancake flipper. "The fuck are you talking about?" She hollers, aggressive and confrontational. "I don't know how many languages I need to tell you this in, but you're *delusional*. You and me, that's *never* gonna happen. "

She slams the utensil down in the pan of eggs and presses both hands into the sides of the stove. She turns finally, facing him, venom in her words. "You're seriously fuckin' *loco* if you think I am ever gonna sleep with someone like you."

He purses his lips, growing a little annoyed, though it takes a fair amount to rattle him. "Listen, I won' blow up your spot with the hubby if *dat's* what you' worried about." He holds his gloved hands up in surrender.

"Tell my husband *what,* exactly? That some lunatic paraplegic thinks we fucked?"

"Oh, you're just gon' pretend it didn't happen?"

"*Nothing happened!* You," she growls, furious, "fucking *psycho!*"

Mick wheels closer, speaks quieter. "Oh, really?" He rolls closer, angry now. "So none'a 'dose three orgasms I gave you ringin' a *bell*?

Angie giggles and pats him on the top of the head, "Aww, that's cute."

Mick whips his face away and his mood snaps from lighthearted to dark as if his emotions are on a swivel. "Get 'at 'good dog' *bullshit* outta here! If I was *standing* in front of you, face-to-face flirtin', you wouldn't fuckin' *pat my head* like I'm some kinda *pet*! I'm a *man*, goddammit! You' over hea' treatin' me like I'm some *chihuahua.*

Y'all motherfuckers don't take me *seriously* 'cause I'm in this goddamn chair."

"What the hell is wrong with you?" She is being genuine, truly confused and unnerved.

He wheels back a little, chewing his lip roughly. "Yeah, 'ats right. Best claim you was sleepwalkin' or some shit so you don't have to admit you banged ya'self a lowly *cripple.*" He rolls toward the common area, furiously muttering just loud enough for all to hear, "you's a lousy piece'a ass anyway, selfish bitch."

Angie hollers behind him, pointing an yolk-coated pancake flipper in his direction. "Ya know, hallucinations are supposedly one of the side effects of the medication, you psycho. Better get Walsh to check your *head*!"

39

Later in the afternoon, Jack sits on the couch folding a piece of hot pink paper into an origami dinosaur, taking breaks to gaze out the window at the threatening sky hovering above the placid bayou. From a long ways away, he sees a young alligator slither into the murky depths with a splash that breaks up the still waters. He looks back down at his folded paper.

"You' awful quiet today." Mick finally says, picking softly at the healing scabs on his knees. "Got somethin' on your mind?" His voice is gravelly, but he cares about his friend and it's apparent in the sincere look he flashes.

"Yeah, but I don't really wanna talk about it."

"Girl trouble?" Mick snickers.

Jack breaks his gaze from the paper and stares at Mick. His silence paired with the downtrodden look in his pained eyes, says enough.

"Yeah," Mick sighs loudly, "me too. Got 99 problems and a bitch is all'of'm."

Jack snickers too, fidgeting with the folds, mind a million miles away. "What's the *first* thing you'd do if you could walk again?"

"This morning I'da said *bend* Angie over that kitchen island and get in them *guts* again, but afta' 'dis mornin', that lying ho' can rot in hell. I wouldn't piss on her if she were on fire after the way she talked to me."

Jack is silent, eyes large and wide beneath the hood of his jacket. "What happened?"

"Dude, she came into my room last night. I went down on her for like two *hours*. She rode me like a carousel."

"*Get the fuck outta here*." Jack giggles. Total disbelief.

"Sure-as-shit, I made her cum like three separate times, an' then this mornin' she suddenly got *amnesia*."

"No fucking way." Jack doesn't believe a word of it. He knows how standoffish Angie has been toward Mick's advances.

"Jack, I swear on my mama's grave."

"Your mother's *alive*! She lives in *Chalmette*. I've *met* her, remember? Couple of times, actually."

Mick pushes his limp foot off his knee and it drops to the floor with a *thunk*. He yanks it up and wrestles the dangling extremity into the chair's foot cradle.

"I forgot you fuckin' met her, alright? I'm telling the truth, though." He shakes his head and laughs, forgetting how good Jack's memory is. "To answer your original question—"

"Yes, *thank you*."

"I dunno, guess I'd go play golf. I used to love playin' through a nice course."

"You don't strike me as the golfing type."

"Oh 'cause you know so much about me before the chair." He jests. "I loved playing a round at the club, man. Used to be real good at it, too." He rolls over to the door to gaze out at the sprinkling rain. "Either that, or I'd go find some shit to sell to rustle up some fast cash so my shit-stain landlord wouldn't throw me out on my ass."

"You told him you're getting paid for the trial soon, right?"

"Oh, my place is about to be gone, bruh. Asshole said he can't wait that long."

"You can crash at my place when we're out."

"Thanks, man." Mick sounds dejected.

"Hey, at least the move'll be easy." Jack chuckles a little. "Just gotta drag your shit three doors down."

"Yeah," Mick sniffs. "True, I guess. 'Preciate that, Jack."

Jack nods as if to say *No problem*.

Mick changes the subject and scratches his knee-caps again. "Itchin' means it's healin', right?"

Jack stares at Mick's knees for a moment and then forces another fake smile. "Yeah, I think so. That's awesome."

"It don't do me no good, really. I guess at least now I look better in swim trunks." He giggles, cheering Jack up, too. "Maybe get my modeling career off the ground, finally."

Jack grins. "You'll be on the cover of Vanity Chair in no time. Makin' that *fuck-you money*."

Mick's tone turns more serious. Its obvious from the deflection that Jack is hurting. "Don't worry, man. Yours'll heal too."

Jack's face grows sour and he throws the tiny paper T-Rex on the coffee table, pulling a couch pillow into his ribs in a subconscious attempt to hide himself. "Nah. I'm probably on a damned placebo."

"No." Mick snickers. "You're *not*." His words sound confident, factual.

"You don't *know* that."

"Yes, actually, I do." He can't contain his broad smile. "For a *fact,* actually."

Jack straightens up. "Wait... *how?*"

Mick smirks giddily, dimples puckering his bearded cheeks.

"Mick?" Jack's look is dead-serious. "What'd you do?"

40

Alan checks his smartwatch beneath the constant overhead spray and instinctively fights the urge to roll his eyes at the time. Despite the lack of things to do around the compound, he is still shocked that he has managed to spend forty minutes in the shower.

No scrubbing. Just feeling the deluge of cool water rush across his flesh. He cranks the handle with pruning fingers to shut off the spray, wraps a towel around his waist, and pads his sopping body out the door and down the hall. He leaves a watery trail on the hardwood leading into his room, where he eyes his shirtless body in the mirror.

His self-inflicted wounds, new and old, are nearly healed now.

Chase's toned body fills the door frame, jolting Alan out of the private world he's once again found himself in.

"Can I *help* you?" Alan snarks in a nasty tone, awkwardly attempting to cover his chest with his arms. Feeling exposed.

Chase's smile never wavers. He enters the room and walks behind Alan.

"Yeah, get an eyeful, queer." He angrily swings his arms open wide in a crucifixion pose, exposing his damp, sinewy chest for Chase.

Chase's eyes follow the beads of water down the pale man's sternum, tracing their way down the tuft of black hair below his navel, like an arrow to the treasures below the towel. He bites his thick lip, stifling a grin and strips off his own shirt. He tosses it on the ground behind his muscular frame, cocoa abs catching the daylight when he twists.

As much as he wants to, Alan can't pry his eyes away.

Chase steps forward, murmuring something into Alan's ear. "You were great out there, Ace. Threw that curve ball JUST like I showed you."

Where's he heard that before?

This doesn't seem right.

None of this feels right.

Alan has the sudden urge to relax into those familiar-sounding words. To press back against the man's warm body. To drink up the sound of Chase's voice like a drink laden with honey. He feels drunk on the exchange. Woozy, like he wants to fall over. No, fall back into the man's arms.

"C'mon, time to hit the showers."

Alan's eyes are barely open now, head lolling backward as if he's riding a potent high. "I just got out of the shower."

Chase is whispering the words into his ear now. "Well, why are you still so dirty then? Huh?"

He grabs Alan's shoulders lightly. Playfully. But his touch lingers too long. Alan's eyelids part and their gaze locks in the mirror.

"There's enough hot water for two." Chase runs his brown fingers down Alan's water-beaded skin.

Alan is turned on. He feels a rush of blood vacate his brain to head south.

"Mmm. God, you're really somethin' special." Chase turns the malleable man in front of him, craning his head down to kiss the neck of the dizzy man in his grasp. Then his ear, nibbling his lobe. Alan can feel the man's hot breath on his jaw, though he makes no effort to engage. Chase makes his way up to Alan's lips and he kisses them softly.

As their lips touch, his fist balls by his side. His mind flips like a switch and Alan's demeanor changes like a wild animal, attacking in anger.

He snaps. Alan punches Chase's face as hard as he can with a closed fist, attacking with pure rage.

As Chase clatters to the floor, things change, ever-so-subtly. Alan blinks out of his foggy hallucination and peers down at the injured man before him.

But Chase looks different...

He's on the floor, fully clothed. Blood splashes down his shirt like the start of a red rainstorm, gushing from his nose.

He stares up at Alan, terrified, scrambling backward through the pile of freshly-washed towels now strewn around him like a lavender terry-cloth moat.

"What the *fuck*?!" he screams through his bloody hand.

Alan can't believe what he's just done. Flooded with fearful confusion, he panics. "I... I'm sorry! I thought–"

"I was bringing you clean *towels*!" Chase screams, sliding away from the extended hand of his abuser. "*Asshole*!"

Trembling, Alan fetches a clean towel from the floor and kneels, bare kneecaps grinding on the hardwood slats.

He tries to hold it to Chase's face, but the bloodied man isn't having it. "Get away from me!"

"*I don't know what I –* something's very, very wrong with me!"

"*No duh!*" Chase flashes a steely glare and clutches the wide, bleeding gash across his swollen nose. "This is a fucking *hate crime,* you homophobic prick!"

"I'm sorry!" Alan is sincere, distraught, crawling toward Chase on his knees, hoping the towel around his waist doesn't fall. "Let me see."

"Get the hell *away from me!*"

"*Please,*" Alan screams, flinging his hands wildly in the air, in an act of frustrated aggression. Chase flinches. Alan instantly feels worse seeing his reaction. "Let me make this up to you. What can I do?"

He's humiliated. Frantic.

"Punch me," he exclaims, as if having a sudden revelation of how to even the playing field. "Please! Right in the face! Hard as you can."

Alan notices his hand is resting on Chase's shoulder. He removes it like Chase is a hot stove and curses himself silently. Chase can see it all in his eyes. He recognizes the self-hatred. The frustration.

"God... you're a mess." Chase stands, collecting himself. He holds the bloody towel to his face. "Listen, you selfish little prick, I don't know why you hate me so damned bad. Or... who *knows*, maybe its *all* gays. But I am a *goddamn human being!*"

"I'm sorry." The apology is so soft it's almost inaudible. Alan wraps his arms around his chest and bites his lip to keep the tears from welling. He watches another drizzle of blood ooze down the man's angular face.

Chase lets the words hang in the air for a moment, fury brimming in his brown eyes. "You wanna make it up to me?" He jams his index finger into Alan's chest several times. "*Keep... the hell... away.*"

41

Iris, Angie and Eddie are perched at the edge of their couch seats, hovering over a dusty, old board game with missing pieces. Jack sits on the floor, counting his stack of fake money.

With the roll of the dice, Iris springs onto her feet, arms in the air. "Yeah! Twelve! You know what that means!" She starts to gloat, doing a ridiculous dance in place that makes them all laugh. Most of all, *Jack*. "Freeeeeeeee parking!"

"How does she keep landing on free parking? Every… single… time?!" Eddie flops back in his seat and slams his head into the cushy backrest of the couch in momentary defeat. "She's got crooked dice! I'm calling a crooked set!"

Iris bursts into chipmunk-esque laughter. "Look at 'em! You can see they aren't rigged! They're almost the only original thing in the box, man!"

"You land on it every time!" Eddie says, flustered but still smiling.

She drags her dime to the FREE PARKING spot on the board and scoops up the pile of cash in the center of the board. She pretends she's going to make it rain on Jack, strip-club style. He leans back, playing into the joke, offering himself up below the wildly-colored bills.

"Doubles, girl, that means you roll again. One more double and you go to jail." Angie says, mind focused on the pathetic assortment of properties she owns but can't build any houses on.

Iris rolls the pair of dice again. *It isn't doubles.*

Eddie sighs, throws his hands up, rolls his eyes. "Godddddd! She's got a damned *horseshoe* up her ass or something! What the fuck?!"

She hands off the set of white cubes to Jack. He runs his scarred fingertips over the divots in them, subconsciously enjoying the tactile sensation.

"You're up, buddy," Eddie announces, leaning forward. "You got all that cash. Marvin's Gardens is open. You get that, you can throw hotels up on 'em bitches and stop this psychopath in her tracks."

"Even if he does, I've got plenty of money to pay for rent now that I just got that haul," Iris gloats.

"*Yeah, yeah.*" Eddie flashes a fake-angry glance at her and leans down near Jack's ear. "Stop… her."

Jack snickers and rolls. The second the dice settle, he crosses his arms on the table and thumps his head between them, making all the green houses and red motels on the board jump in place.

"You're goin' to *jail*, son," Angie's voice is low. She's over the whole game already, barely in it now.

Jack exhales and without thinking, he says, "Dammit, not *again.*"

Iris laughs, unsure if she heard him right. He hadn't been to jail in the game yet. "Again?"

"I wish I could say this was my first time in the clink but, alas," Jack shrugs, sucking in a deep breath.

"Oh fuck, I forgot about that," Eddie chuckles, chugging the last of a can of sugar-laden soda and smacking it back onto the table with a loud, aluminum *clunk*.

Jack slides his coat button over to the orange jail square on the board. He doesn't even notice that Iris looks shocked. A little *betrayed*, even. Her tense eyes lock onto him for any sign of an explanation, but none comes.

He doesn't feel it when she inches away subtly. Allowing her smile to fall into a flat expression.

"Angie, *sha*, you're up," Eddie says standing to get another drink.

"I'm the penny, right?" Angie finally snaps her gaze from the view outside onto the board again.

"I'm the penny. You're the button off the couch, or whatever. Iris is the beer cap."

"No, I'm the penny." Eddie hollers.

"You grabbing a soda, man?" Jack perks up, sliding the dice over to the bored redhead beside him with a bandaged hand.

"Yeah, you want one?"

"Yes, please."

Angie rolls. "Aww, yeah! Electric Company. Lemme buy it. Gimmie-gimmie!" She holds her claws out like a raptor, grabbing at the card with a sudden, reinvigorated interest in the game.

Iris sits back, pressing herself into the couch behind her, wishing she could be swallowed by its comforting folds of fluff in an upholstered bear-hug. Jack glances back at her, his rich, brown eyes peeking out from the cotton hood followed by a genuine, caring smile. He is oblivious to her sudden change of demeanor, seeing only the good in her. He turns back to the board and runs his palm over her shin in an effort to comfort her. To feel close to her in even the smallest of ways.

But she can't seem to find it within herself to smile back. She can't fake it. She can't shake the comment.

She realizes that despite the days they've spent together in close proximity, killing time and getting to know each other, they don't mean anything because at the end of the day, she realizes she still doesn't know Jack at all. The burned man remains shrouded in mystery.

***

Dr. Walsh watches the live security feed streaming over wi-fi to the screen in his office. He watches Iris lean forward to roll the dice again, eyes locked on the healed patch of flesh over her scapula where her carving used to be.

Where it *should* be.

His withered eyes, tucked beneath jutting tufts of white eyebrow hair, narrow with suspicion. He feels the nausea swirl in his gut again, wishing he had a pill in his desk safe that would quell the panic rising in his belly.

Terror roils within him like a pot of slow-boiling water. In a sudden burst of energy, he launches himself from his chair, clattering awkwardly to the floor next to the tiny trash bin. He picks it up with both hands, pressing his face inside just enough to hurl the contents of his stomach into the liner. His groaning voice echoes back to him and he collapses against the wall when he finishes, cradling the bin like something precious. He doesn't want to look, but he can't help it. His eyes drift back to the screen.

Back to Iris's shoulder. Back to the spot on Angie's exposed thigh where her dog bite used to be. Back to laughter and friendly chatter…

Back to the *healing*.

It's all so wrong, he thinks. *These poor people. What the hell have I done?*

42

Iris slinks timidly in through Mick's open door. Eddie's lying on his back in Mick's bed, murmuring something about Kim Kardashian's newest surgery, catching Mick up on all of the truly essential bits of world news happening on the outside.

Mick hasn't been listening. Instead, he sits in his chair, practicing a coin flip on repeat while his best friend drones on.

As soon as he notices Iris, Mick's face softens. He pockets the coin and wheels himself in a three-point turn so that he can face the delicate woman leaning against the jamb.

"Am I interrupting? I can come back." Iris's voice is meek, apologetic.

Mick scoffs. He doesn't have a damned thing going on. *None of them do.* "We was just reviewin' Eddie's will and trust, but I 'spose we can suspend any-and-all fiduciary responsibilities. Right, Eddie?"

Eddie groans. "You know damn well I don't know what *fiduciary* means." He wriggles stubbornly on the twin bed like a child throwing a tantrum. "Shit, man, this place is so *boring*. I feel like I'm watchin' grass grow. I don't know how y'all do it. I'd go crazy in here."

"Why 'da hell you think I keep inviting you ova'? *Entertain me, clown.*" Mick hurls the quarter at his friend, hitting him hard right in the side of his exposed pectoralis.

"Ow! Jesus!" Eddie bolts up, temper flaring. Zero-to-sixty in a second. "Keep callin' me clown, jerk-off. I'll put a parking boot on your chair, lock up 'em wheels like a towing company!"

Even though Eddie is genuinely infuriated, Iris can't help but laugh. The simple guy has been nothing but a sweetheart to her every time he's visited and she has a hard time taking him seriously. She's seen them play rough on multiple occasions, enjoying a form of strange, twisted tough-love like two brothers might share in a tight-knit family.

"You know what," Eddie continues, staring hard into Mick's eyes, "how 'bout you clown for *me* for once? Do some tricks in that thing. Pop-a-fuckin'-wheelie! Do *somethin'* with your life, man!" His southern accent has never been more prominent. The country bumpkin is fired up.

Mick takes it with a grain of salt, comments rolling right off him. He giggles and crow's feet form in the tan skin around his eyes. "I ain't ya' damn circus monkey."

Mick finally breaks eye contact, rolling his head to the snickering woman in the doorway. "What brings you to my lair, doll?"

Iris sits next to Eddie. *Perches*, really. Like a bird ready to flit to safety at a moment's notice. Her hands drum anxiously against her tight jeans. "You and Jack are close, right?"

"Last I checked." Mick nods, pursing his lips, granting her his full attention.

"Today he made a joke about being in–"

She struggles to say the word. She just doesn't want to believe he's capable. As if saying it, putting it out there in the universe, would somehow make it *real*.

"Jail." The weight of the word is heavy on her mind.

There it is. In the universe now.

"No," Mick says, with total seriousness. "Not jail."

Just as she breathes a sigh of relief, he speaks again.

"Prison." After a pause, he speaks again, shaking his head. "He had a helluva time jus' getting' his probation officer to even let 'im come do 'dis trial."

A silence lingers, thick in the air. Air that suddenly feels like it's been sucked right out of her throat with a high-powered vacuum.

"I see." She feels dizzy, wanting to stand but afraid she will hurl instead.

She's been spending so much time with him. She feels like a fool. She's been alone with him on mutiple occasions. In the woods, in the bayou, places where a former wing-slinger wouldn't just have to be found and taken to the hospital. No, she's been kayaking with him in places her body wouldn't even be found. Thoughts of those outings ending in violence make her head swim.

"Why you ask? I mean, what's it matta'? 'Dat ain't, like, who he *is*."

"With what I've… I've been through a lot and," she struggles, "I guess I just needed to know if he was, *you* know…"

She chokes on another word. It's a brick in her mouth, wedged tight.

Mick stares at her, baffled by what she's trying to say.

"Dangerous." She winces.

Mick laughs aloud at the ridiculous notion.

Eddie expels air in a comical *pffffft*. "Jack? No, girl, Jack is *harmless*."

Mick's face is gravely serious now. "Listen, you didn't hear any of this from me. I'll deny every mu'fuckin' word of it if you blab." He hesitates, looking at his fidgeting hands, picking at his short, chewed nails, then lifting his mocha-brown eyes back to her. "He and his wife got in an *accident*–"

The words smack her like a bag of sand now. *His wife???*

"He's *married?*" Her words are quiet but her expression screams: appalled.

"He *was.*"

There is a moment of quiet reverence between them all. Iris feels a twinge of shame for her reaction.

"One day, he and his wife were suppose'a have dinner at her mom's house. Her mom was a… real intimidatin' woman. She scared the shit outta Jack. Kate offered to, uh, help *relieve some stress* on the drive home, if you catch my drift." Mick starts to mimic oral sex and then thinks better of it, offering some rare tact. "Next thing you know, *BOOM*. The engine, it…" he smiled.

He didn't know exactly why he was smiling, though. It was some strange coping mechanism he'd developed at a young age, grinning through the painful times. He swallowed hard, looking down at his finger-less gloves.

"Crushed her skull in his lap. Shattered his whole pelvis, broke some'a his ribs. Her head bein' wedged against the steerin' wheel pinned him inside the car. SUV caught fire." He made a *poof* noise and flicked all his fingers out like a quiet bomb. "Burned him up all over."

She's speechless.

Eddie lifts his head a little. "Guy likes to act like he's fine, but inside, he's still all fucked up."

Mick glanced up, his intense eyes finally locking onto hers. "Doctors put him in a coma 'til the burns healed and 'den he and I met a few weeks later in physical therapy for my knees. He was out on bond. After he was well enough to stand trial, they sentenced him. *Manslaughter*, I think. He did a couple years and when they let him out, he-done moved in next to me."

"Wow." Her eyes bulge, staring at the hardwood floor. "Poor guy."

Mick points at her. "No!" The motion seems aggressive, but his voice is informative. "See, *that's* why he doesn't tell people. He don't like the pity. Still feels guilty about it. I'm sure he will 'til the day he dies. Thinks it's all his fault, that he's some horrible person."

"He's a good guy," Eddie nods, "just a little fucked up in the head's all."

"But, hey," Mick laughs. "*Ain't we all?*"

43

Alan stands against a tree on the sprawling back lawn near the water's edge, comforted by the shadows of the southern night. Lightning crackles through the clouds overhead, but no rain falls through the steamy fog of oppressive heat lingering across the bayou. The booze is hitting his empty stomach and he feels his body growing to match the stove-like temperatures of the summer night. He relaxes into the shadows, chugging greedily from the bottle of tequila in his hand. He enjoys how the inebriation seems to silence the thoughts in his head, rushing and swirling anxiously, all the time. Despite not doing anything strenuous all day, he feels exhausted. The mental toll the last few days have taken on him weigh heavily on his conscience. He's replayed the hallucination and the attack in his mind a thousand times.

It all seemed so real… *until it didn't.*

He was amazed with his own strength, remembering the way Chase's face bled. Rivulets of crimson streaming down the curves and features of his frightened face. Features that were flawless until his balled fist met flesh. He found something strangely erotic about the marring, finding a sick pleasure in transforming something so perfect into flayed flesh and twisted bone. It was similar to the feeling he got when he carved his own…

Footsteps approach in the grass, preceded by the weak glow of a hanging lantern.

He hopes to himself that it's Chase. He's eager for a chance to explain. Eager to apologize again.

Eager just to be around him for any reason.

To his delight, though he'd never show it, Chase appears, waltzing up to a lawn chair.

As he goes to sit in it, he spins, notices Alan, and groans a terrified, "woah," while clutching his heart. He stands fully, still clutching at his shirt. "Jesus, I didn't see you there."

"Sorry." Alan breathes after a painful swig of cheap liquor.

"You're just standing out here in the dark? No flashlight or anything?" Chase's tone is almost accusatory, angry.

"Easier to see the lightning when its full dark." Alan points up at the roiling sky with the half-filled bottle, and instead of looking where he's motioning, Chase notices the bottle instead.

"Holdin' out on us?" He points to the bottle and Alan laughs a little with an inebriated sneer.

"Mick gave it to me. Said he didn't need it *for that ho' any more*, whatever that means."

Silence.

"Want some?" Alan offers the container up and Chase approaches with hesitation. "You don't mind?"

"What? Like I'm gonna drink the whole bottle by myself?" Alan scoffs.

Chase doesn't think it's that far-fetched. He wouldn't put anything past the guy. *He's a wild card, and not the fun kind,* he thinks.

"It's a liquid olive branch." Alan approaches, leading with the bottle. Chase takes it, suspicious.

"You mind if I…?" He points to the lounge chair right beside the one Chase was about to sit in.

"Free country. At least, last I checked," Chase says, his anger biting.

Alan takes a seat, the back of his bare thighs already sticking to the plastic with a dew of July sweat. He smacks a mosquito on his irritated neck and looks to his lap, but it's fallen into the darkened abyss of night. He sweeps off his black surf shorts just in case. "These fuckers LOVE me!"

Chase swallows a mouthful of the stinging amber liquid and grimaces, pulling the bottle away to look at the label. He cocks his head to the side and laughs, "At least *someone* thinks you're sweet."

Alan smiles at Chase, grinning at the burn, taking it as a positive sign that Chase is even a tiny step closer to forgiving him for the attack.

Alan leans in, their elbows nearly touching. He examines Chase's face, a look of surprise plastered on his own. When he'd last seen Chase, sitting on his floor, towels scattered around him in disarray, he feared that the man would need stitches for sure. But now, only a small butterfly bandage held everything in place, the busted skin nearly healed. *It really was a miracle.* "Damn. Nose is almost completely healed."

"Yeah," Chase stares forward, trying to stifle the urge to say something sarcastic. He knows it won't help anything. "Can't believe these pills really work. Shoulda seen Walsh when he had to set the bone straight earlier. Looked like he was about to shit himself. Not because of the damage but just… how fast it was healing."

Alan smiles weakly, glancing down at the tall grass, bugs frolicking through waves of it, blackened by night, whipped by the wind of an incoming storm. Illuminated only by the lamp. "I'm really sorry." He can't even look Chase in the eye as he says it. His tone seems genuine though, and Chase softens a little, taking another sip from the bottle and handing it back.

Alan takes it timidly and carefully wipes the rim of it before taking another sip.

It's a gesture Chase notices. Even through the darkness.

His smile fades. "Hey," he's nervous to even ask, "I'm curious. What did you see before you decked me? You were… *clearly* hallucinating. In retrospect, I can see that now. Talkin' to yourself and everything."

Alan swigs, clearly tortured by the answer to the question, but doesn't speak. He can't.

How can he talk about something so personal with a stranger who probably hates his guts? How can he put into words what the hallucination was of… and why it infuriated him?

Sensing he won't respond, Chase speaks up in in attempt to make things easier on him.

"You know, growing up, I carried this crushing weight around. Scared of what people would say when they found out I was, you know… *Fabulous.*"

That makes Alan snicker. His eyes soften and drift up to the ghostly imprint of Chase's black face against the dark night. A shimmering bolt of lightning flickers through the cumulonimbus clouds above, rising into the violet-tinged sky like the smoke from a detonated atom bomb, never striking down into the swampy land below it. It flashes again, making Chase's eyes twinkle. Alan can't tear his gaze from them.

"I'd try to overcompensate by acting super butch to throw people off when they'd say things about me being flamboyant. I didn't know it at the time, but I had a beard. I dated her from seventh grade til my junior year of high school. I played football, basketball, baseball, you name it. I drank beer out of a can. I did all the things I thought men were supposed to do. But I wasn't being… me. And, you know, folks sometimes don't take kindly to that stuff. Case in point." He points to his nose, getting a dig in.

Alan feels remorse when he says it.

"When I finally knew I had to say something, to… be the real *me*… I was so scared of how my parents'd react. I'll never forget the day I told my mom and dad. I'm 17, sitting at the dinner table, sweatin' like a whore in church. My mama said grace and then I just blurted it out: 'I'm gay and I'm in love with a man named Tim.'"

Alan nearly spits up the swig of tequila he's downing. "I'm sorry."

"No, it's fine."

The way Chase is enunciating and motioning with his hands makes Alan wonder if he had always expressed himself like that. *Or was it a more recent development? Like sonar to non-verbally attract other gays or clue them in without outright saying it.*

Chase smiles a little, suddenly forgetting that Alan is a foe. His southern ways seep in and he forgets for a moment that not everyone in the world is a friend.

"I was young, dumb, full a' cum, and head-over-heels for my baseball coach. He was gorgeous! Oh my God," he waves his splayed hands in front of his face. The sheen on his nails almost looks like fireflies in the glow of the lamp. "I digress. So, I tell them I'm gay and then my dad turns to me and says: *I know*."

Growing more animated, he clutches Alan's shoulder and laughs. "Turns out, they'd known for *years*. Like, since I was little. And yet, I had only just figured it out for myself. It's like… I was the last to know."

Chase leans all the way over to him. Alan can feel the gentle whoosh of air that pushes into him like an errant breeze from the approaching storm. His whole body stiffens.

"I'm not blind, babe." Chase touches the almost-completely faded scars running the length of the man's pale forearms. "You went up the highway, not 'cross the street. Seein' that road map of self-hatred carved in your arms," he slides it up, wraps his hand around Alan's bicep, and gives him a comforting squeeze, "that *there*… that tells me you might just be the last one to know."

Alan feels like Chase is looking straight into his soul. The feel of Chase's hand on his skin makes his shorts feel tight and the blood in his head rush elsewhere. He swallows hard and tugs his arm from Chase's grasp.

Chase looks down at Alan's writhing legs, squirming uncomfortably and his gaze rises to the bulge in the man's shorts. He is not sure how to react and remembers squeezing his arm, a gesture he thought nothing about in the moment.

Alan's glare is steely and Chase can't make heads or tails of it. He wants to believe that it's all just a trick of the light as Alan slides his hand down to disguise the bulge. He wants to believe that the misguided guy truly heard what he was trying to say. But the expression on Alan's ghost-white face is one of bitterness, evolving into fury, all-too-familiar with the look of self-hatred.

Alan finally looks away, gritting his teeth so hard that his jaw flexes. He knows Chase noticed his erection. He knows he didn't hide it fast enough.

He prays to God in his mind that this is just another hallucination. Another all-too-vivid haze that he will snap himself out of.

The soft tinkle of rain sounds over the water in front of them, sending a million tiny shock-waves through the surface of the water. Alan feels the cool patter of it thrumming against his pulsing skin and breathes deeply, hoping his hard-on will die down enough for him to pull the rip-cord and eject himself from this uncomfortable situation.

"Well," Chase sighs hard, takes one more swig, and hands the bottle of booze back, "I'mma head in." He stands, avoiding looking anywhere near Alan's direction as he ambles up the slight hill toward the main house, leaving Alan to sit in the rain.

44

Iris is on her belly, sprawled across her bed, feet bobbing playfully in the air behind her. She struggles to find the right wording to fill out her patient journal.

How do you say *thanks Doc, you gave me my life back?* Or *thank you for ridding me of the constant reminder of the worst day of my life?* She wonders, instead, if she should give Eddie the cash to buy a thank you card…

Just then, an orange paper airplane soars through the air silently, landing on the floor just in front of her. She smiles, recognizing the construction paper as Jack's, brought from home for his origami creations. She shoves her journal and pen to the side, creeps to the edge of the mattress, and strains to pick it up from just within reach on the floor. She sits up, legs crossing, and unfurls it, fighting the grin that is manifesting on her face.

R U STILL AWAKE, it asks in blocky permanent marker.

She writes YES below it in pen, refolds it, and sends it careening back through the open door, across the hall into his room. She hops down and pads across the hardwood floor after it, leaning against his door frame.

There he sits in a confetti pile of construction paper squares, like boredom incarnate. She can see the glimmer of his grin reflecting in the blue-tinged security light seeping through the slats in his window blinds, basking him in slivers of pale teal light. His hood is down and his mop of brown curls glints as he looks down, bashfully, picking at the fingernails on one hand with the ones on the other.

"Hey," she whispers. She instinctively starts to reach for the light switch but thinks better of it, knowing that will spook him back into hiding, like a nocturnal animal, shooting down into its darkened burrow for safety.

The amount of trust he's putting in her, even aided by the veil of the darkened night, makes her feel somewhat special. She wonders how long it's been since he didn't have it pulled up around other people.

He fights a sudden grin when he looks at her, pulling his face away toward the window. She can see that his bandages are off. The the texture of his skin on the burned half of his face is shiny and warped, taut in places and lax in others. She sees the hint of mismatched cheekbone and grafted chin and the garish seams where the scarred skin meets the rest. Despite being malformed in the burned corner, his smile is sweet, and if she's being honest, surprisingly attractive.

His eyes dart back to her, glittering in their movement as they lock back on hers. "Hey," he says in a whisper as timid as he is, "so, I've been thinking…"

"Sounds *dangerous*." She grins, knowing he wasn't finished speaking.

Jack smirks at the smart-ass retort. "I was wondering if tomorrow for lunch you'd like to check out this cool little spot I found on the trail up in the bayou a little ways. It's a perfect spot for bass and catfish. We could bring some snacks and some fishing rods–

"I don't really… fish."

"Oh, we don't have to–"

"No, I mean I don't know *how*."

"Oh, I can teach you if you want. If you suck, I promise I'll only make fun of you a little bit."

She snickers and then says, "I dunno, man. Sounds like a date."

Jack's mood shifts. "Yeah. I'm sorry. I guess it did sound… I just… made it weird. Nevermind."

"No, I mean… *sounds like a date*." She winks, knowing he can see it. She can feel the slices of illumination horizontally-striping her face.

He feels elated suddenly. As if he's ten feet tall. He looks down, fighting a bigger smile. His blushing, un-damaged cheek radiates heat.

"Really?"

"Yeah." She answers without hesitation. Her dimples are out and she mindlessly nudges something on the floor with her bare toes.

"Alright. It's, um," he chuckles a little, in disbelief, "it's a date."

45

Mick's eyes dart beneath a thick row of lashes. His mouth murmurs something unintelligible into the acrid, night air. His spasming fingers thrum the bed sheets beneath them and his legs lay still, splayed before him, unmoving. His worn-out socks are ripped and a scrawny toe peeks through the hole. New ones haven't been a priority in years since they merely exist, like his useless lower extremities.

His head thrashes a little, bobbling from side to side with the vivid dream. But the dream is not a dream like most, consisting of nonsensical surrealist concepts and events that suddenly, somehow, seem commonplace and normal. No, this is a vivid memory instead. A horrid recollection of the afternoon his life changed forever.

***

Tall grasses whacked his tattered, black Danzig t-shirt as he was yanked through a tall field by the gruff hands of a pudgy brute. The blindfold was cinched tight, pinching his scraggly, unkempt hair and sideburns in the knot. Another clump of wavering foliage swished loudly and beat against his chest with a percussive whap-whap-whap. Bristly blades caressed his jutting ribs and tickled his bearded chin as he passed through marshy, treacherous swampland. He spit out pieces of minnowed-chaff that stuck to his lips like huge, golden sesame seeds. His feet sloshed in muck, nearly sucking his designer tennis shoes off with every step. Thoughts of pissed-off water-snakes filled his mind as he slunk onward into the dark unknown. The sound of spooked birds halted his fearful thoughts as a cacophony of screeches echoed across the land.

He struggled against the burly figure that dragged him along, against elegantly-simple zipties that cut into the flesh of his sweat-covered wrists. Against the heavy clods of soaked dirt that clung to his new shoes. He breathed hard, gobbling up mouthfuls of stinking, muggy air, thick with the scent of detritus, stagnant water and organic decay.

He wondered how many others had gone missing in the same bayou, decomposing in the murk beneath his soles, the questions of their disappearances unanswered...

He felt the hefty man's pace slow and the water disappeared as he tripped his way up onto what felt like shorter grass.

"Up!" the voice ordered, low and booming.

Mick felt the swift upward jerk of his shirt as he was partly lifted into the air. The toes of his sodden sneakers smacked against wood and he knew to lift his foot higher or he'd trip. There was a step. A rickety one. And then another. He took one more but there was no step there. The asshole next to him snickered at how foolish he looked taking a huge step up into nothingness. His feet smacked down hard on floorboards that were squishy and rotten.

The large man hurled him through the doorway and his feet caught on a raised lip in the threshold, which sent Mick soaring through the air, cracking down on his knees, sliding on something crinkly and unknown like a slip-n-slide. He lost balance quickly and flopped onto his face, letting out a furious yowl.

"That fucking hurt, you prick!" He struggled to stand but couldn't get enough leverage.

The giggling brute grabbed him by a wrist and wrenched upward, sending a shock of pain running up through Mick's arm and shoulders.

"Ow! Goddammit! You' gon' break my arm, you fat fuck!"

He was shoved into a rickety chair. It groaned beneath his weight. He writhed as his captor looped ropes around his ankles, binding them to the legs of the chair so hard that he immediately felt blood pooling in his soaked, constricted feet.

Next were his wrists. Still zipped tight in the thin straps of plastic, he felt a looped length of rope wrap around both hands and then the jiggle of someone tying them off to the backrest.

The captor yanked off Mick's blindfold in a flourish, taking a painful hunk of the Cajun's hair with it. Mick growled in pain, face whirling in every direction to take in his surroundings.

They were in a shack. One that was dilapidated and ravaged by the cruel elements of the southern wilderness, beaten down by time and rain. It looked like a dusty box of tinder, one he was amazed hadn't been torched by lightning at some point. Faded remnants of once-shamrock-green wallpaper remained in weathered strips, peeling down the walls like curled, gangrenous claws. It sported images of mallards in flight, *hunters poised, guns readied, with loyal dogs at their side. The pattern repeated until it reached the vertical strips of wood panelling that would have made him nostalgic for his youth if not for the adrenaline and terror pumping through his veins.*

The only furniture was a wooden coat rack, a poorly-stained, homemade shelf full of dusty mason jars, and the remains of a fireplace that had long-since caved-in on itself. Unable to ever host a crackling source of heat again. It was filled instead with crumbled bricks and a dead-grass nest of some kind.

Mick's gaze plummeted to the floor where he saw the source of the crinkle he'd heard. It was painter's plastic, tacked to the walls behind him and laid out on the floor all around him, held in place by a few errant bricks in the corners. The sight of it made his stomach twist tighter than the ties around his feet, which were already starting to go numb.

He heard the steady gait of someone large, walking in the next room. The new set of footsteps told him he was outnumbered. As he came into view, the sheer size of the second man made him want to let go of the bladder full of piss that he'd been holding ever since he was attacked in his computer chair.

Mick watched the shadow of the massive man lumber forward, eclipsing the light trickling in from the back porch door. Something was in his hand. A toolbox, from the look of it. As he made his way through the threshold into the main living area where Mick was, the hostage felt the first man's hands slide over his shoulders and clamp down on his collarbone, pushing with force downward. He chuckled something into Mick's ear.

"Well, well, Dorothy. You wanted to meet the wizard? Well, today is your lucky day. Welcome to the Emerald City."

"Does that make you da' scarecrow? You know, 'cuz you missin' a brain?" Mick retorted quickly. "Or the way you tied me up and blindfolded me to get me out here, maybe you's the Cowardly Lion." Mick lunged at the husky goon as much as his ropes allowed, but the man just cackled.

"Hmm, maybe you're not Dorothy. Maybe you're Toto. All bark." He barked like a canine in Mick's face and Mick tried to headbutt him. The goon stepped back and kicked Mick straight in the chest, hurling the chair backward. A shockwave of pain shot up through Mick, buzzing from the compression of his wrists, the impact, and forceful kick.

Mick heard the man giggle loudly as he stared up at a popcorn ceiling, stained brown in several massive spots from water damage. Near the entrance, where the front door sat cockeyed against the wall, ripped from its hinges and mangled from decay, there was a hole where some of the roof had caved all the way in and Virginia Creepers had started to crawl inside, latching onto the rot with grabby little tendrils. He saw a pelican flying in the gray sky through the foliage-framed gap.

"Now Toto, are you ready to play nice? Or do you need to be put to sleep?" The man's face had forced its way into his view. He wanted to spit on the lard ass but knew it would only lead to more punishment. These men wouldn't have hesitated to kick him while he was down. That, he was certain of.

"Enough." The larger man's voice boomed, commanding attention. "Sit him up."

"Yes, sir." The goon nodded up at the massive man, shaking a bit of sweat dribbling from his puffy cheeks into Mick's brown eyes. It stung, but it was the least of his pains. He could still feel the imprint of the fat man's boot on his sternum. His smashed hands felt like hammered sausages, plump with blood and throbbing.

The lackey lifted Mick's chair back into a seated position, forcing him to stare directly at the larger man who just entered.

"Do you know who I am?" The large man smiled.

Mick nodded reverently.

He did know.

It was Finn O'Malley. Kingpin. Outlaw boss of the shady circles Mick ran in. The source of most narcotics peddled in Orleans and St. James parishes. A man no trafficking or RICO case had been able to touch. A violent fuck that Mick had been warned time and time again not to cross...

"I'll bet you're wonderin' why I requested this meeting, aren't you Mick? Or, if you're smart, which I know you are, then perhaps you already know why you're here."

"It won't happen again, Finn." Mick wished he could scramble out the door. Well, the hole where a door once stood. Legends and talk of the man's violent displays of jealousy, anger, and revenge spread like the legend of the Loup Garou around these parts.

The man stood, looming nearly seven feet tall, cotton-like hair as wild as the look in his eye. "Oh, I know it won't."

Finn set the toolbox on the crumbling fireplace mantle, caressed the sides, and pulled out a battery-powered impact drill. He depressed the trigger and the machine whirred to life.

Mick's mouth ran bone-dry and his balls retreated toward his pelvis.

"You know why it won't happen again?" After he waited a moment for a reply, met with only the sound of Mick struggling against his restraints, he took a step closer. His waterproof black Timberlands thumped against the rotten floor with an audible thunk. "Because I'm not a forgiving person, Mickey. You see, fool me once, shame on you."

Finn walked toward him, tapping his heaving chest with the drill bit in it. "Shame on you, Mick."

The touch of it against his shirt, as it tapped its unforgiving metal edge into his concert tee, made him realize that this was all-too-real. No one knew where he was at. No one knew he was even gone.

No one was coming to save him.

"Look, Finn." He tried to sound calm through the fear. "I know it looks like I was

skimmin', but I assure you 'dis is all just, just a misunderstanding. I was gonna bring you the rest 'a ya cut soon, I promise," he lied.

"Didn't take long to track you down. Either you're one dumb motherfucker or--"

"I wasn't hidin'." He was telling the truth. He wasn't hiding because he was confident he'd never get caught. "Lemme explain--"

"You know where my name comes from, Mick? Over in Ireland, Finn's a famous giant. A real beast of a man."

"I can get you all the money soon. Very soon," Mick hollered in protest at whatever Finn wass getting at.

"My uncle's Irish, too. Whole family is, really."

"Seriously, with interest!"

"He was in the IRA." Finn continued as if Mick hadn't spoken a word. "Fascinating, violent group of people, the IRA. Lemme tell you a little story about Belfast." The growl to his voice was as demonic as a human voice gets, low like an agitated grizzly.

"Double? Gimme a few days I could probably do double."

"Belfast is divided into four parts." He used the drill bit to draw it out on Mick's right kneecap, snagging the already-torn fabric with the sharp edge. "Each quadrant is protected by its very own paramilitary. If you wrong someone in one of those quadrants, they'll serve justice long before any of the local garda get off their asses."

"I swear--"

"They control the crime." Finn pressed *further, inches from Mick's face. He was sweating bullets. But the giant before him, blocking the gloomy light that seeped in from the busted single-pane window, was calm. "Mickey, if you're caught selling drugs in an area you're not supposed to, you know what they do?"*

Finn gave him a moment to think. Silence hung like a guillotine between them and the only noise was the swish of the overgrown wheatgrass in the swamp outside, whooshing in on the wind through the damaged pane.

"If they like you, say, if you're a first time offender, they take a drill," he held the battery-operated tool up. "Much like this one. They roll up your pant legs and they drill through the back of your knees."

Mick thought he might piss himself. Finn derived a massive amount of pleasure from the exchange.

"That way, the offender'll be able to walk again one day. But he won't ever forget his lesson." Finn smiled, flashing a row of tobacco-stained teeth. Mick could smell a faint, fishy waft of the seafood he'd had for lunch.

"Please, Finn, it won't ever happen again!" Mick cried, tears blending with beads of sweat, rolling down his face. His eyelids fluttered. He wanted to pass out, both from the fear and from the heat.

"Now, if they don't like you, they leave your pant legs down and they drill through the front of the kneecaps. The guy won't ever walk again and he'll end up with an infection from the jean fibers

in his wounds. It's real nasty on the cartilage too. Lots of pain, from what I'm told. Even years later."

Finn leaned back and Mick sucked in a deep, relieved gasp of air.

"Oh, I wouldn't go getting too excited now." Finn put a large paddle bit with a razor-sharp point in the end of the impact drill and smiled. "I gotta say, Mick..."

He squatted down, hovering his ass over the weather-worn wood, surprisingly flexible and spry for a man whose weathered face looked like old shoe leather. Mick felt the goon's hands slide down both shoulders again. His fat fingers pressed into Mick's thin, drug-ravaged body.

"I really don't like you." Finn's smile faded into a look of sincere hatred.

Mick struggled but his ankles were still tied to the front legs of the chair.

"Please, for the love of God! Somebody help me!" Mick screamed out a terrified plea for a savior -- anyone who might be able to hear his cries. But he knew that it is a waste of time and physical energy. He squirmed against his ties, despite knowing the men would give chase if he got out. He wouldn't go far on numbed feet. He screamed again and heard the echo of his own voice scare a murder of crows from the cypress trees across the grass marsh.

People go missing out in these swamps all the time. *That thought terrified him, sending an icy chill up his sweaty spine. Long-gone members of his own coonass family were probably* decomposing in their own watery graves in the same parish.

He knew he was about to join them.

"Scream all you want, Mickey." Finn yelled the words right into his face, punctuating them with a villainous eruption of genuine laughter. "This' why I loooooove the bayou!" His gruff voice grew quieter, colder. "So quiet out here. So peaceful. Miles away from everything."

Without another word, Finn pressed the sharp tip of the paddle bit against Mick's knees and fired up the drill. It bit into his jeans, making quick work of the skin, cartilage and tendons.

Mick screamed like he never had before, shredding the inside of his throat with his excruciating howl. He thrashed his body, flopping back and forth like a fish out of water, but it only made the pain in his knee more intense. The bit was blazing hot. It smoked as it drilled through his kneecap into the femur below. Bits of bone and debris flew out of the sopping wet hole, lubricated with spurts of blood.

Finn released the trigger and yanked out the bit with some difficulty. It had become tangled in the sinewy tendons. He ripped back with force, tearing the rubbery, off-white strips in one move.

Mick's head flopped back. He fell silent.

"Wake him up, we aren't done yet." Finn growled at his goon. The lackey raised his arm and smacked Mick so hard in the face that his neck cracked. He sprung back to life, gargling spit, tears and sweat.

Finn pressed the button again and goes back in. Mick felt the pressure of the man's push and *the devastation of the tool as it destroyed him inside, doing irreparable damage.*

The bit squished out the backside of his knee and ripped through the other side of Mick's pants. Finn pulled it back through the swelling canal of gore and smiled at the crimson-slathered bit as tiny fragments of bone slid down it like crushed eggshell.

He smiled up at Mick who was fading in and out of consciousness. "Don't pass out, Mickey. One down... one to go."

Finn whirred the impact drill once more and started in on the other knee, making no attempt to hide the smile upon his face. Blood and bone dribbled onto the plastic sheets below, pooling in a tiny lake of gore and pant fibers.

***

Back in bed, Mick twitches violently, trapped in the recollection of the worst day of his life.

In the darkness of the night, glimmering in the flicker of a burning bedside candle, his sweatpants undulate in the knee region, tenting upward unnaturally.

Something needle-like presses through the fabric, tearing the material with its upward push. It widens as it emerges, leaving a tar-like goo on the rim of the tear.

The spiked tentacle presses further, feeling in every direction, crawling the perimeter of Mick's kneecap with a mind of its own, never waking its host. It palpates the area with its finger-like extremity before sucking back inside the material, back inside Mick's knee, leaving only a hole in the man's pants and a bit of black slime behind.

46

DAY NINE OF TRIAL

Patient Journal Entry provided by the St. James Parish Police Department.
Evidence Item #SJPD-118133C
Criminal Case #: 7-23-mu-187462-OB
Translated to digital transcript by Mary J. Stearns
Subject Name: Alan █████████
Date: 7/06/████
Written Journal Entry: *Yesterday I experienced a vivid hallucination about a bastard I used to know. It was intense. It led to the altercation with Chase when he came in to bring clean towels. I also had night sweats last night and trouble sleeping.*
Time Symptom Started: yesterday afternoon
Location on Body: head
Severity: intense

Patient Journal Entry provided by the St. James Parish Police Department.
Evidence Item #SJPD-114739C
Criminal Case #: 7-23-mu-187462-OB
Translated to digital transcript by Mary J. Stearns
Subject Name: Mick ████████
Date: 7/06/████████
Written Journal Entry: *I slept really hard last night at first and then had a really bad nightmare. Woke up this morning and there are tears in the knees of my pants and black crusted shit all around it. Not sure if someone is pranking me or what. The holes in my knees do look better though so I guess the drug is working. Keep it up, doc. Also, I gotta say, I don't know if its all psychoso... psycha... all in my head, or not but I feel like the chronic pain I've dealt with in my legs the last few years is going away. Maybe I'm just having a couple of good pain days in a row but so far, I feel less of a need to pop ibuprophens like they're tic tacs. So that's a plus!*
Time Symptom Started: PM
Time Symptom Cleared: when I woke up
Location on Body: head, I guess.
Severity: Meh

47

Mick rolls in his room with a full glass of soda wedged between the long, stalks he once called legs, careful not to spill the contents in transit. He'd do just about anything to avoid having to change pants again, or sit with his crotch a sugary mess all day, both of which sounded like an annoying chore. Though, he'd give his left foot for a tumbler with a lid…sippy-cup… any sort of container. He thought about chugging it straight out of a tupperware recently but held off.

Once in, he sets the flared glass on the round top of the rinky-dink bedside table, next to his deck of nudie playing cards and miscellaneous shit dumped out of his pockets the last few days. He swivels around to go back for the snack he left on the kitchen counter, fearful Alan would suck it down like his mama's old Hoover if he left it unattended for too long. The man was like a human carp.

As he swivels, the curled handles at the top of his backrest smack against the wonky table, toppling the whole thing over with a SLAM!

Soda and cards go everywhere, splashing onto the floor and bed-skirt, soaking the cards and bouncing up onto the fabric on his withering calves. The lamp on the table and the glass of a spent scented candle shatter as they crash down into the mess.

He screams out with rage, reaching over to punch the wall and falling short with a whiff, held back just out of reach, by the chair.

"Ahhhhhhhh, GodDAMMIT!" He howls again, whacking his closed fist in the air, this time connecting with the bed, rolling him back through the crunchy glass mess, coating his wheels in sticky Dr. Pepper.

He sees his vintage cards, *the only source of entertainment in this place beyond Eddie and Jack,* rafting down a stream of carbonated beverage. He thinks there may be time to salvage them. He picks one up and wipes the brown liquid from its linen face onto his Tenacious D t-shirt and tosses it on the bed.

He wheels backward to get a better angle to reach them, wetting the palms of his gloves as he does. The shards of the busted lamp and shattered bulb gnaw hungrily at his rubber wheels as he strains for a clump of them, struggling to retrieve a cluster from beneath the bed risers he curses every night for making it hard to crawl onto the elevated mattress and box spring. Walsh gave him the large ADA bedroom on the main floor since the compound doesn't have a ramp or lift to the second story, and, while the room *was* the swankiest from what he'd heard, he'd have much preferred just a mattress and box spring on the floor and a table that didn't tip over if you looked at it wrong.

Bracing one hand on the cot, he tips sideways a bit to reach it, as he has a million times before. He teeters during the delicate shift of weight, but doesn't take into account the slickness of the wet wheels and he loses the war with gravity. The wheelchair topples over and Mick rains down hard, slamming his ribs against the cushioned metal armrest.

"FUCK!" He punches the box-spring and, flustered, pulls himself into a sitting position on the floor, struggling to right his chair with a growl. It is going to be a pain in the ass to get back in it from the floor. He can do it, but he's too angry. He locks the brake and pulls himself up so that he's sitting in the wet mess with his back propped against the lifted bed. He huffs furiously and shreds one of his soaked vintage playing cards in a burst of anger, severing the playmate's body just below her rack of heaving tits. He flings it across the floor like a frisbee and slaps his head back against the mattress.

Why do even the simplest fucking things always come with such an advanced level of difficulty, he wonders. He ponders if his handicap is part of some karmic retribution for his twenties club-days. He was a tall, flirtatious womanizer all the LSU girls used to throw themselves at when he prowled around Baton Rouge like some filthy alley cat. More likely, it was, indeed, payback for the drug-fueled days he spent shooting up more heroin than he sold, skimming money from Cajun-Irish giants with a toolbox full of nightmares and an ability to laugh while his face was caked in gore.

Maybe Finn was right.

Maybe he did deserve this.

The thought made him shiver. He watched a melting ice cube slide slowly across the slightly off-kilter floor. Sitting there, waiting for his heart rate to die down, feeling his knuckles throb and swell beneath his damp gloves, he sees something utterly fascinating.

It can't be.

He feels like it's a dream. Something cruel that he is going to wake up from at any time.

It just can't.

But it *was* true. As impossible as it seemed…

Mick sits alone in a spacious room in chaotic disarray, ass steeping in tepid soda like a bag of tea, watching his foot waggle back and forth. Watching the toe of his white canvas shoes, covered in amateur permanent marker graffiti like a high-school student's desk, as it taps forward and pulls back, stretching calf muscles and tendons that had atrophied over half a decade.

He stares at the other foot, willing it to move with his mind as it once did. Wanting the miracle to be real, not just some horribly cruel muscle spasm side-effect of Obsidian.

His second foot moves, along with the calf attached to it. He groans in pain. Pain of muscles that have suddenly revived like Lazarus from the grave after years of shriveling from inactivity. He raises his knee into the air, sliding the sole of his shoe back with a grunt, hands-free, a burst of laughter erupts from his mouth, a wild cackle that grows in intensity as tears of joy flow like running brooks from his eyes.

48

"Mmm, these po boys are so good. Just what the doctor ordered. Where the hell did you *get* these?!" Jack munches through mouthfuls of fresh french bread, pickles, lettuce, and fried oysters, washing them down with fries and sweet tea, relishing the heavenly combination of flavors of a meal that screams *Louisiana*.

"I gave Ed a call this morning. Threw him a couple bucks. He got 'em from a place by my house in Gonzales. He lives like five minutes up airline from me apparently." Iris smiles and crunches into another flaky bite of the french bread, delighting in the flavor of the roast beef between.

"No shit? Come to think of it, I bet we're all pretty close in proximity. Mick and I live right there in Saint Amant." He says it like *san-a-mah*. "Wait, is this from Mike's?"

She nods, grinning.

"Yo! This is my favorite place! The little lady that works the front--"

"Tweet!"

"Yeah, Tweet! She remembers everyone!"

"I know, I just walk in there and she hollers out my order every time. I don't even have to tell her what I want. Just give her my card." She giggles and looks over at him.

His bandages are off and the blasting overhead sun reflects onto his face, illuminating it to a degree that Iris has never seen before. She can see the seams and lines on his face of various skin grafts. The odd push and pull in the corners of his eye, nose and mouth on the one side. But her eyes drift to his gorgeous set of straight, white teeth between two lips she wants to kiss. Her eyes drift to the defined jawline on the other side of his face, unmarred and unmangled. Strong and arched like a marble sculpture, sprinkled with mere hours of stubble.

Jack raises his lidded styrofoam cup in cheers. "First, let me say thank you for this. I've never had a woman buy me lunch before so this is *quite* a treat."

"Well, I'm happy to pop your cherry." She's trying to be playful but her cheeks immediately heat up. She can feel herself turning red at the remark as she taps her cup against his.

Jack tries to hide his smile and fails, which only makes Iris find him, *strangely,* more attractive.

"This blows the tuna sandwiches I was gonna to make outta the *water,*" he says, letting the opportunity for a retort on her comment pass with grace.

Iris pulls her cup away to take a sip. He stops her.

"*Bupbupbupbupbup!* I'm not finished with my toast yet." He smiles, using his drink to bring hers back until they are touching again.

"You best hurry up. This wind is getting chilly and I want the rest of this po boy while it's hot," she jests.

"Fair enough. A celebration is in order. To you." He stares at her, the nearby rushing water glinting in his hazel eyes. Ones that, she now notices, have a vast array of color in them, from rich browns, to greens, to flecks of stormy gray. She's never been close enough to see them, save for in the dim shed.

"Cheers to your new lease on life," he says, with a mix of genuine joy and selfish melancholy, joy winning the battle between the two. They clink cups again and she drinks, unable to pry her dazzling eyes from him.

His gaze darts down to the blanket beneath them when he notices her staring. Iris looks over, very seriously, at the pair of moss-green fishing rods near the water's edge, both propped against large rocks, sky-bound tips unmoving.

For many years, Jack was comfortable with that kind of attention and, after a while, expected it. Hell, at one point he even took it for granted. But now, the attention only reminds him of the man that he's become in the years since Kate's demise: pathetic and undeserving. The Elephant Man. Frankenstein's Monster. A hideous shut-in. A murderer who doesn't deserve to breathe the fresh, summer air when others can't, *thanks to him*. He chastises himself for sitting on the dirt, having a picnic, while *they're* beneath the surface, worms voraciously devouring their corpses for sustenance, chewing them up and shitting them out. All while weather erodes their shellacked caskets and time decays the cut flowers, severed offerings adorning meager headstones that he doesn't have the balls to visit. He can't show his face around there. Not even what's left of it...

"I think the medicine is just taking longer to work for you," Iris offers as an attempt to address the elephant in the room, piercing eyes locked on the bobbers floating in the water twenty feet or so from the grassy bank.

He laughs a little but there's venom in it. He's agitated that it even needed to be said. Frustrated that he ever believed the drug could work. Angry that Walsh is getting the satisfaction of watching his hopes dashed daily. "The pills aren't going to work," he finally says.

"If it can do all *this*," she motions to her exposed shoulder on full display from her pink, strappy camisole, "I have faith that it will for you, too. Yours just probably needs a little more time. But, Jack, even if it *never* works," she freezes for a moment, realizing that's probably the last thing he ever wanted to hear, even hypothetically, "I really think you're a good-looking guy already."

"You don't have to do that." There's a firm sadness in his tone now and he rolls his head a little on his shoulders, pinching his eyes tight.

"Do what?"

"You don't have to… be like that. You don't have to try to sugar-coat everything. It's like when a grandmother says *you'll always be my favorite* or when your mother says *those kids in school just don't know how wonderful you are yet.*" His tone grows quiet, annoyed. Not with her, but with himself, though it's impossible for her to discern that from his inflection. "I'm well-aware of how fucked up I look, Iris. You don't have to coddle me."

She faces him now, sitting up straighter, a little perturbed at how this has suddenly spun. "Excuse me, but I'm an adult with my own opinions. Yeah, you're burned, but its not the end of the world. You're not Freddy Krueger, alright. I can see enough of you to know that, to me, you're objectively attractive. But your *personality*, this whole *I'm convinced I'm hideous stuff*, it's getting frustrating. I'm telling you I think you're good-looking and you just keep talking about what a beast you are, ever since we took the walk that first night and I opened up to you. I don't just open up to people. I thought you would be… different. That you would get it, understand what it's like to feel broken and incomplete and not enough. And now I know that's *all* you see. Your flaws. Your scars. Your past. There's more to you than that. I've gotten to see more of that every day. I'm here because I like spending time with you. Do you think that has anything to do with your face?"

"It's not just my face, okay. There's a lot more of me that's fucked up."

The comment catches her off-guard. The thought never occurred to her before that the damage might be more extensive. But she shook it off and looked back at him. It didn't matter.

"You're so convinced you're hideous that it almost seems like there's no reaching you at this point. This," she motions to him and then to her, "feels like a losing battle." Her tone changes. She's getting choked up, fighting off tears now. "You're burned, Jack, but you're not *unattractive*. You are more than just a sum of your parts. *You're* not unattractive, but you are being a bit self-absorbed."

"Are you serious? I'm not *full of myself*. I'm a goddamn *shut-in*, Iris!" He stands up and walks in a circle in the grass, rubbing his burned hand on his neck inside his hood.

"Jack, I'm not *trying* to be *mean*, but you gotta take a step back and look at your life and see how all-consuming this is! You spend your time beating yourself up mentally and loathing yourself physically."

"You're one to talk, Iris. The whole reason you said you were here is because you were tired of looking in the mirror and seeing yourself that way."

"But I wasn't letting it ruin my whole life. I still met people. Had social interactions. Took a compliment once in a while. *This* is all day, every day, for you. You don't have to be in *love* with your image to be obsessed with the way you look. You think you're hideous and this dysmorphia is *consuming* you. You have so much self-hatred seething from you, it feels like there's no room for anyone else in your life. You're so obsessed with how you look that you don't even care that I'm looking *right at you*, telling you that I don't *care* about your burns and that *I* think you're cute. But you don't *hear* any of that. You *can't*."

A cold breeze brushes through the thick throng of cypress trees nearby, whooshing along the water's edge as if to punctuate the icy conversation with a burst of stinging air.

Iris rubs her bare arms and looks up at the summer storm brewing in the cloudy sky above. She imagines its only a few hours until it's full fledged.

"No one *gets it* more than I do." Her voice is calmer now, soothing even. "I've spent most of my adult life *hiding*. Not feeling safe around people. And with *you*, I thought things could be different. I felt like I could relate to you because we were going through something similar. But it turns out we're fighting totally different battles." She sighs, looking back at the ground, poking at an errant ladybug on the latticed beach towels they are using as picnic blankets. "If you want to keep punishing yourself for what you did to your wife for the next thirty or forty years, *fine*. Do what you gotta do."

The words hit him like a cinder block to the skull. He turns around, hoping he didn't hear her right, but as the words replay in his head, he knows he did.

"What did you just say?" There's frustration in his voice. *Betrayal*.

Iris looks up at him, trying to gauge whether he is just upset or whether this has become a situation where she will soon need to flee. But as she looks at his face, she sees someone who is genuinely hurt, not angry. Someone *wounded*, not *wild*.

"Who told you that?" He's baffled, clenching his jaw to fight the rush of emotions roiling within him. Her words have cut him like a fillet knife to the gut.

She crumples the wrapper of her po boy and stammers, "I-I shouldn't have said anything."

"Was it Mick? Did Mick *tell you* something?" He purses his lips, shakes his head.

"Don't be mad at him. I pried. You made the jail joke the other day and it got me all freaked out. Mick told me about your wife."

"Mick doesn't know shit." He folds his arms in front of him. "You should have asked me, Iris."

"I didn't think you would have told me. You're private." Iris stands up and folds her arms, too, but only to protect herself from another gust of cold air. "I should have come to you. I just… didn't want to end up carved up on the side of the road again." Her expression says: *are you happy now?*

Iris walks toward the water's edge and picks up one of the rods. She starts reeling in her line, clumsily. It's clear that she's never fished before. Once on shore, she sees that her worm is still intact and she fumbles around, trying to open the spool. She holds the line and swings the rod. It catches, stopping the line mid-cast, swinging the bait back at her. She squeals, drops the rod and crouches to protect herself from it.

Seeing this, Jack can't help but laugh a little, despite the pain burning inside of him. Her words cut deep but she wasn't wrong. His affliction has consumed him.

She picks up the rod and points it at him. "Stop laughing!"

Jack pretends to zip his lips and watches from afar as she casts again with the same results. She drops the rod again and looks up at the sky, groaning in frustration. Another blast of wind smacks her as Jack approaches.

She stares at him wordlessly, for a moment, as he stands by her side. He slowly unzips his hoodie and takes it off. She can see his whole face now, for the first time. She sees his curly brown hair, thick and full on one side, missing in patches on the right. His right ear is gnarled, resembling a shrunken version of a fighter's cauliflower-ear, trailing down in seams and divots to a neck that is wavy and thick with scar tissue, disappearing beneath the neckline of his shirt.

Beneath his plain t-shirt, his right arm is disfigured and slender with surgical scars running in various directions. The damage is much more severe than she anticipated.

He wraps the hoodie around her to protect her from the chilly wind of the impending storm. The depth of the gesture is not lost on her. She is awed by his willingness to not only hear her out, but to heed her words and offer up such an exposed view of himself. Something she's certain he hasn't done with anyone in years.

Touched, she looks at him and smiles. To let him know that it's okay. To let him know she still likes the whole package that is him.

He picks up the fishing rod, avoidant of further eye contact, feeling awkward and exposed even though only one person can see him.

"You're scaring all the fish." He says with a smile. "I'm gonna cast this back out for you because clearly you are a danger to yourself and others with this thing."

Iris stifles her laughter. He casts back out.

She zips up the jacket and lays her head on his burned shoulder, staring up at the bleary sky threatening thunder. The storm was coming.

49

Tate raps on the door. "Mick? Hello? Mick? You missed your scheduled exam this morning so I thought I would check--"

She hears movement in the room, along with the sound of a man sobbing. Fearing the patient has injured himself, she turns the handle and enters.

Mick stands before her, legs bowed and shaky like a newborn giraffe, one arm out for balance, the other clutched onto the mattress for stability. Tears pour down the bearded Cajun's face. He's an unwashed mess of sweat, matted hair, and bloodshot eyes, crying so hard he's dribbling a rope of drool from his quivering lips.

Tate's first instinct is to lunge at him, to stop him from falling. He manages a weak, clumsy footstep forward and throws himself at her, burying his sniveling face in her brunette curls, arms wrapped around her for dear life. He bawls uncontrollably, uttering something unintelligible on repeat.

After the sixth time, Tate realizes what he's saying.

"I can walk!"

50

On their way back to the compound, Jack's gaze meanders to the decrepit shack at the end of the row of buildings. It's shielded from the afternoon sun by two towering oaks. One has the tattered remains of an old, splintered swing hanging from one of the boughs, ravaged by the unapologetic hands of time and years of weather exposure. He recalls the shadowy figure lurking in the window upon arrival and shivers.

They pass the overgrown walkway, abundant with tufted patches of once-ornamental grass and the runaway vines of insidious Virginia Creepers. Above, hardened ropes of wisteria hang from higher offshoots of the gnarled oak like nooses from the gallows.

Perhaps it's what he *needs* to see. *Perhaps,* he thinks, *it's what he deserves.* A punishment befitting a crime that plagues him, as fresh in his mind now as the day it took place.

Iris's eyes are fixated, creased in the corners with the faint hint of budding wrinkles. She smiles over at the catahoula as it claws incessantly at the crackled red paint of the front door, nails lacerating deep grooves into the spongy wood. The door is probably an inch thinner in the corner from claw damage. His snout presses to the door, snorting puffs of swirling soot and spruce shavings into the air like smoke from a dragon's nostrils. His tail wags, desperate to gain entry.

"Whatcha lookin' at, boy?" Iris veers off the footpath, detouring up the off-kilter pavers buried in the detritus.

A pang of alarm shoots through Jack as she nears the building, feeling suddenly exposed without the protection of his hoodie.

Iris strokes the coat of spotted fur down the dog's back. Its hackles raise beneath her fingertips and he barks at the door, unperturbed by Iris's presence.

Jack won't leave the path, instead standing across an expansive sea of sun-dappled turf. Iris grins back at him mischievously. "Wanna check it out?"

Jack looks around, hoping to find a reason to say no, some excuse to retreat without sounding like a chicken-shit. Finally, he decides the simple truth would suffice. "Nah. I'm good."

"Aww, come on! This ol' boy's got my curiosity piqued."

"Curiosity *killed* the cat, you know."

"Yeah, but he's a dog, so I think we'll be fine." She jests, retorting quickly. With her canvas tennis shoes creaking on the squishy planks of the rotting porch, she twists the doorknob.

Locked.

Jack takes a deep, relieved breath. "Well, Velma and Shaggy'll have to try again another day, right, *Scoob*?" Jack jokes. The catahoula whips his head to look at him and cocks it sideways, almost as if to show his disapproval at the idiotic reference.

Jack takes a step toward the other buildings.

WHAM!

Iris shoulder-slams the door hard enough that the termite-chewed wood holding the locking mechanism cracks. The rusted metal hardware tumbles out of the door jamb with a muffled thud. She struggles to not fall, clinging to the loose door handle to keep from tumbling to the ground. The dog shoots in, nearly bowling her over. He's like a loosed arrow, launching himself through the room, sniffing around, tracking scents with a crazed look in his muti-colored eyes.

Jack is frozen in horror as Iris creeps into the darkened room, disappearing from sight. His feet are welded in place, as if wisteria has anchored him to the woods with their claustrophobic grasp.

"You coming or not," she hollers from inside.

Images of the massive, shaded figure flash before him again and he cannot quite find the courage to take a step.

Iris's beaming blue eyes peer out of the blackened entryway. "Jack, you gotta *see* this!"

Hearing his name from her honeyed mouth gives him the will to approach, albeit with trepidation. She's like a siren calling him to the depths of the ocean and he is unable to defy her request, trudging through the sod, closing the expanse to the condemned structure.

Inside, Iris splays her hands in front of her, offering the room as Vanna White would motion to lettered squares. "Check it out!"

The room is not quite what he expected. Instead of some spider-webbed dungeon adorned with candelabras, it's a small living room with a busted television atop a half-bookshelf, whose contents are spilled on the floor. The furniture is disheveled, and coated thinly in something charcoal gray and glistening like slime. The room is wall-to-wall faux wood paneling in vertical strips, from the rotten floorboards to the water-damaged popcorn ceiling. The filthy, drab carpet is stained all over in dark, strange-shaped spots like some sort of horrendous murder scene, years after-the-fact. Its worn down in footpaths like the outdoor trail they recently strayed from.

Clustered throughout the edges of the room, among stray piles of leaf litter and mildewed filth, are four-inch plastic tubes filled with a dull liquid. Jack doesn't want to get close enough to find out what they are.

A mangled couch with one shattered leg sits cock-eyed across from the TV with its cotton innards strewn all around it. More slime coats the brown flower design on it that was oh-so-common in the seventies. The room peers into a minuscule kitchen with a small, basic fridge. The door's been ripped off and is lying bent and banged-up against what used to be a countertop, water-damaged from the hole above, leading to the outside. The old linoleum squares on the floor are bubbled up from the rain, spotted with handfuls of dead leaves in the corners and edges. Dust swirls through the air, visible in the beams of light from the sky shining through the caved-in spots of the roof.

Iris pads down the carpeted hallway, dragging her fingers on the panelling, leaving parallel streaks in her wake. She passes a room the size of a closet. It used to be a bathroom, as evidenced by the sideways sink, upended with coffee-colored fissures webbing outward from the drain hole. It looks like it was ripped away from the floor and chucked at the claw-footed tub. The basin is full of something dark and wet. The swarm of flies on it are having a field day with the grotesque mound of decomposing, organic contents.

Jack holds his breath, afraid he might add his own vomit to the noxious lump in the bath. He wants to appear brave to Iris, but everything in him is telling him to run far and fast.

Two rooms are left in the hall. The catahoula incises the wood of the final door with ferocity. Iris and Jack enter the room before it. Gouges are etched in nearly every wall, scrawled through bunny rabbit wallpaper hanging in torn clumps.

Jack's eyes dart around the dusty space where fistfuls of dead glow sticks, long void of all phosphorescence, hang clustered from strings from tacks pinned to the ceiling. His stare continues past a child-sized craft table with gnawed crayons and piles of paper sketches, coated with a thin sheet of darkened mucous. A cluster of melted candles have dripped into a tumorous wax monstrosity down one of the table's legs. Beyond it sits a plastic vanity with a hairbrush on its flat top. Long hunks of blonde hair attached to withering, leathery pieces of scalp are snarled in its bristles.

"Oh, *Jesus*." Iris covers her mouth at the sight of a small girl's bed. The sheets are frilly with stained images of jumping rabbits. Goo-covered bunny stuffies sit in a neat row atop a shredded comforter and a moth-chewed bed skirt.

The stuffed animals remain in-tact, albeit slimy, lined along the back wall.

What shocks Iris is the hardware drilled into the wall studs. Long lengths of stout chains are attached, messily coiled like cobras on the floor. She hunches down to examine the generous length of chain and the steel shackle bolted to the end.

"Someone…" She hesitates to finish the sentence, afraid more of the conclusion she's drawing about the man whose care they are currently in. "Someone was chained up in here."

Jack is nauseated at the site of it all. Dizzy with fear, he leans against a wall, expecting to feel furrows made by frantic fingernails. A sharp pain pierces the meaty part of his palm.

"Ow, *what the--*" He hisses and pulls his hand away, clutching the bleeding extremity tight to his chest.

"You okay?" Iris asks, pausing her curious investigation.

"No! What the *hell*?"

Embedded in the wood are sharpened shards of glass. The grimy floor by his shoe is cluttered with smashed hunks of it. It crunches under his soles. The remains of a Catholic candle lays on its side, fragmented into smashed rubble. The expressionless, illustrated face of the patron St. Nicholas stares up at Jack from beneath a pointy hat.

Iris nears him to examine his wound and he can smell her perfume over the dankness and mold of the house, like a waft of something heavenly.

"That's gonna need a couple of stitches." Iris says, eyes flitting up to his. The way she looks at him, he feels like he might pass out. Her gaze is arresting. He needs to kiss her again. He's dying to savor the fruity flavor of her lipgloss, a delectable taste stuck in his mind for the hours since their lips first met but he knows this is *hardly* the right locale.

"I'll be fine. I'll see if Tate can throw a bandage on it."

"I don't know, it's deep--"

Her words are cut short as the catahoula barks in the hallway, scrambling to barrel through the door. He struggles to get traction on the slick linoleum as it gnaws at the decorative molding of the last room in the corridor. He whines, frantic, stopping only to listen to the sounds of something rustling on the other side.

"What's in there, bud?" Iris darts out of the girl's room and glances down the hall.

"Iris, please--" Jack's voice is begging her to leave this fucked-up place as she places her hand on the doorknob.

Vrrrrrrrrnnnnnnnn. It's the sound of furniture moving inside, followed by the *clickety-clack* of smaller objects skittering across the wooden floor.

They are not alone.

Iris yanks her hand from the knob with fear in her eyes, adrenaline making her carotid visibly pulse through the tender skin of her neck. "There's something in there!"

"I *told* y'all!" Jack growls through gritted teeth, backing away toward the door. "That first day, I saw something through the window. Something... *massive.*"

"With all these holes in the roof, it could be anything." Her alert brain runs through the gamut of possibilities, from squirrels to wildcats. Whatever it is, she doesn't want to chance pissing off something feral while in such tight quarters.

They hear chains tinkling and the burdensome groan of the floor planks, as if something hulking lurks nearby.

"I'm trying not to be *that guy*, but I am not sticking around to possibly be *mauled*." Jack walks backward down the passageway, tugging at Iris's hand, panicking a little as he brushes against another glow stick on a string.

"Yeah, let's go. This place is creeping me out." Iris follows Jack back through the mess someone once called *home*. She calls for the dog, but he stays put with only one thing on his mind: gaining entry into the room.

"C'mon, boy." She pats her jean-clad thighs from the doorway. He doesn't budge.

"Those dogs are hunters. He's not gonna stop until he gets it, or 'til he's bored. Leave the door cracked. He'll come out when he's ready." Jack is not sure he believes it, but he would say anything to pry her from this place. He doesn't want to stick around another minute.

Iris grabs a beefy baseball-sized rock from just beyond the rotten porch and props the door just enough for the catahoula to leave.

***

Moments after their voices disappear into the sprawling property, the catahoula scratches again, snorting the fine dust particles by the door like a line of cocaine. The doorknob twists and the door cracks open. Within a fraction of a second, the dog is inside, finally free of the barriers between him and his prey.

A moment later, he *becomes* the prey.

If Jack and Iris would've stayed, they would've bore witness to the single, pained squelch from the dog's mouth followed by a sharp silence as his life is snuffed out.

They would have heard the catahoula's bones crunching in the maw of something massive, his pelt separated from the viscera beneath with rows of razor-like fangs. Veins tearing. Steel links rattling with vibrancy through the cramped room. The gulping of a hungry throat, much too substantial to be human or animal.

If they would have stayed, they would've bore witness to the growing puddle of hot blood spreading below the cracked-open door, and the hours of chilling silence that followed.

51

"To Mick!" Fisher hoists a shot glass full of soda. Angie, Iris, Jack and Mick lift theirs, too, and cheer.

"Sorry it's not the real thing, man. If we could have booze in here, we'd be celebrating with the primo shit." Fisher beams for his fellow guinea pig.

"*Speech! Speech!*" Jack chants, once again shrouded in the shadows of his hoodie.

Mick rolls his eyes and hoists himself on trembling, spindly legs. Angie resists the reflexive urge to reach out to steady him, but doesn't, knowing how much he hates being coddled.

"Thank y'all. No applause necessary. I'm jus' doin' what little kids be learnin' to do all the time," a shit-eating grin spreads across his face and his voice grows loud, "an' 'dat's motherfuckin' *walk*!" His eyes lock on the security camera in the corner of the room, pinging its red signal every few seconds.

The eye in the sky.

"An' Walsh if you's watchin' this, cheers to you. To the brilliant motherfucker who gave me my life back. May you win a Nobel Prize fa' 'dis."

"*Salude!*" Angie lifts her cup to clink with his and tosses back her mouthful of seltzer water with a grimace.

"*Nostrovia!*" Fisher throws his back as well.

Jack glances to the camera and to the palm of his hand, expression sour, brows furrowing. He locks onto it, as if staring into the lens is a substitute for Walsh's own eyes. He drinks from his shot glass and puts it on the table, still eyeing the stitched, meaty part of his hand. Iris is fascinated and confused, following him with her eyes as he leaves through the front entrance of the house.

"Where 'da fuck's *he* goin'?" Mick asks Iris.

She shrugs in response. "I'll go, you know–" Concerned, Iris points to the door. Mick nods and Iris follows him out.

Mick grabs Angie and she hollers out, shocked and laughing. "What do you say later you make the head-pat up to me?"

"I'm not patting your *other head*, if that's what you're insinuating."

He pulls her close, grinning flirtatiously down at her from his new height. A view reminding him of old times. *Better* times. Back when he was always on the prowl for a decent lay. "How 'bout a dance, gorgeous?"

"I'll think about it." She smirks coolly, despite the fact the attention is making her melt. It's been years since her husband -- soon-to-be *ex*-husband -- looked at her the way Mick's steadfast brown eyes are looking at her now. Plus...

She's always had a thing for *tall* guys.

"Well, don' take *too* long." He says as she breaks away and retreats to the kitchen. "I gotta break 'ese puppies in!"

"Well," Fisher groans as he leans back into the sofa with the rest of the carbonated can, "what do we do now? You wanna hopscotch? Jump rope?" Mick laughs, disregarding the silly suggestion. "If it wann't 'bout to rain I'd say we could go for a dip." He motions to the water through the glass wall behind him, where threatening clouds hover like hands stretching out to strangle.

"There's alligator *gar* and shit in that bayou."

"So?"

Fisher cocks one of his dark eyebrows. Even being the adrenaline-junkie he is, he wouldn't dream of swimming in that murk. "Wow, they weren't kiddin'. You *are* fuckin' crazy."

52

Jack bolts through the door of the green building, which takes on a sickly hue against the bright security lights. Iris follows close behind, chasing Jack through the open door, closing it once inside.

"Hey, everything okay?"

"No." His answer is curt and she can tell by the frantic way he rips on the pull-cord of the shop light and rummages through containers that he's on-edge.

She approaches with caution. "What are you looking for?"

"Something sharp. I saw some little, like, tiny scissors in here the other day."

"For what?"

Jack doesn't answer. He's focused, scrambling through bins and boxes without any regard to how they are organized. He spills one and growls in frustration, fists balled. He bends down and whips the contents back into a messy heap in the box and kicks it out of his way. He rifles through a padded sewing bin with buttons and thread, swiping through the notions, plucking out a seam-ripper. He uncaps it and digs the sharpened end into the stitches on his palm.

Iris erupts in a frenzy of panicked noise. "Stop! What the hell are you *doing*?!"

Jack winces as the ripper tugs flesh and severs the threads through the wound.

"That's gonna get infected, Jack! Walsh just stitched that!"

"No, its not!" Jack holds up his hand to her. His forehead is a mess of wrinkles, eyes welling with a mixture of pain and horror behind tears.

She examines the laceration. The now-severed stitches reveal a pink line of sealed scar-tissue. Hours before, it was a meaty gash, cut clean by glass, deep in his flesh.

The wound is little more than a memory now, no longer in need of so much as a *band-aid*.

A tear threatens to fall from Jack's reddened eyes, but hangs like it's waiting for permission. "Do you know what this *means*?"

"Oh my *God*!" She's filled with excitement. "*Yes*! It means–"

"It means I'm *not* on the placebo." His voice wavers and all hope is lost.

"Yeah! It worked! The medicine--"

Jack rips the hood of his jacket down to expose his half-charred face and bare scalp. "No! It means it *DIDN'T* work! It means the burns…" Jack wants to die, wants to bury the seam ripper in his wrists and pull up. Instead, he smashes the blade into the worktable's top and snaps the metal in two. "If my hand is almost healed after slicing it open a few hours ago, these burns are never gonna heal!"

"Maybe it takes more time."

That's the last thing he wants to hear. He spins in place, wanting to punch a wall but they are all lined with shelves, so he holds the rage inside. He looks back at her, the tear finally making its way down the path of least resistance, travelling down one of the grafted seams on his face where the skin puckers inward, falling to its death on his hoodie.

She leans in, raises a hand to his face, and wipes away the remnants of the tear with her thumb, doing what no woman, *save for nurses*, have dared to do since Kate was alive:

Touch his face.

The anger in him dies off like the last rain band of a category 5 hurricane.

Her ice blue eyes are flooded with tears of their own now, filled with words unspoken. But the only ones he needs to hear are ones he already knows are true. Ones she would utter, if not for being overwrought with her own emotions right now.

She would say *she doesn't care*.

She would say his skin or the scars or the grafts don't matter to her.

She doesn't care that he doesn't sport a full head of hair like he used to. She didn't know him before, and yet here she is, unable to take her unblinking eyes off him.

He slides his hands up the sides of her face, burying his fingers in her blonde locks, smelling the sweet perfume on her skin. He kisses her and she kisses back, pressing her body against his and him pulling her into him as if he can't get enough of her. He spins her, pinning her back to the table, kissing her with a frantic energy he can no longer control. He feels the warm skin of her fingers beneath the hem of his shirt, sliding behind his back, tugging him close to her with both palms. She wraps her ankles around the back of his thighs like a constrictor.

He kisses her neck. Nibbles her earlobes as she fumbles for his belt, gasping. He yanks off her top, mussing her blonde locks. Her lips are on his again. He can taste the sugary lipgloss again as he peels the straps of her bra down in a frenzy. He takes one of her breasts in his mouth greedily as she moans, clawing at the waist of his pants and pulling off his hoodie, abandoning it on the floor with her camisole.

She grasps at the white t-shirt he now wears, tugging it, but he fights her to keep it in place. She presses into him, moving his mouth back up to hers and pulls at his shirt again, fighting to yank it over his head. He struggles, wanting to keep it on, but not wanting to stop kissing her for fear she'll change her mind and leave him with a throbbing cock and blue balls in a storage shed all alone.

Once the shirt comes off, she pulls back, holding it in her hands like she's about to check a basketball, taking in the sight of his torso, half-covered with burns like some DC villain. He retreats a little, arms at his side, slightly cowering with a rush of sudden embarrassment. She stares him in the eyes and throws his shirt over his shoulder, beckoning him to come back to her with a pale finger and a smile.

After a moment of hesitation, he does.

Her mouth is on his chest, kissing the seam from his neck to his ribs where original flesh meets repaired, trailing her lips and tongue downward, accepting every marred inch before slithering down the crack between him and the table to kiss lower. To follow it all down to the hidden depths below.

He presses his hands to the wood, squinting tight. The teeth of his zipper vibrate as her hand tugs it down, dragging his jeans down to the floor soon after. He forgets to breathe, listening to the heavy thrum of his heart slamming in his ears, feeling it pulse through the surging veins of his neck.

Her mouth wraps around him, enveloping him with her hot, glossed lips, unphased by the presence of long-healed scars made by molars that were not her own.

He moans, knees wanting to buckle. He pulls away, hoisting her to her feet again.

"What's wrong?" She whispers in his ear, nuzzling his lobe with her nose. Heat radiates off her beautiful face.

"Nothing's wrong," he says, unable to pry his eyes from hers. He smiles. Big and full, for the first time in years.

"Why'd you… stop me?"

He can hear his breath echo off the walls of the tiny, metallic room. "Because," he hesitates to elaborate, thinking about the story she shared the night they met. He swallows hard and presses his forehead to hers, feeling his heart bang like a rubber mallet against his ribs. "I want to be inside of you."

Before the shy smile can even form on his face, her lips are on his again, fingers tearing at his clothes.

53

Mick hobbles through the darkened living room on shaky legs, lit only by the moon and roll-off from the outdoor security lights. Everything is a murky silhouette of darkness, with muddled outlines, as he creeps to the landline, careful not to disturb the patients upstairs.

He lifts the receiver to his ear, hears a dial tone, and presses the numbers he's memorized by heart.

"Yo, Ed…" His voice is a harsh whisper. "I know it's late but you need to get your ass over here. I got somethin' to show ya. I promise, it'll be worth ya' while. You gotta see it to believe it, bruh." He listens to the groggy cadence of his best friend on the other end, grinning all the while.

"This Obsidian shit *works*. While Walsh was runnin' some tests tonight, I was able to cop some when he wann't lookin'. I think you could unload them fa' *way* more than $20 a fuckin' pill. How soon can you get here?"

54

An hour later, headlights make their way through the skeletal trunks of the twisty oaks lining the long drive. Mick fumbles his way to his feet from the porch steps like a child of divorce waiting for the good parent to come pick him up. The truck stops twenty yards away and he's so excited he doesn't notice it's not taupe rimmed with rust like Eddie's pickup. Its red as a barn and dabbed with fat raindrops glimmering in the garish security lights upon approach. The driver slithers out, raising the pickup a few inches with the release of the massive load.

"Eddie, dude, fuckin' took you long enough!"

Mick pauses in place as a second person slides coolly out of the passenger side, cowboy boots splashing into a thin puddle below.

"Ed, you bring a friend," Mick asks, squinting.

But he can tell from the rotund build of the driver and the sheer height of the passenger, neither are the bean pole with the sinewy frame he calls Eddie. These men are stout and beefy. The passenger is built like a barbarian.

It isn't until the security lights flash a slice of harsh light onto the man's weathered face and frizzed shoulder-length hair that he understands what's happening. The beard. The boots. The broad shoulders. The pudgy goon beside him…

It's someone he prayed he'd never lay eyes on again.

It's *Finn*.

Livid, Mick lurches forward in a moment of sheer insanity, lashing out for the years of pain and strife the Irishman caused. He decks Finn hard with a balled fist, still wearing his finger-less gloves out of habit, even though he's shed the filthy wheels he needed protection from.

He wishes he'd have had the foresight to carry his gun, the one tucked in his duffel bag inside.

As his knuckles connect with Finn's mouth, he wonders if he signed his own death warrant. As the man already displayed, he was dangerous and sadistic with no qualms about destroying a man.

Finn's flunkey leaps between them, smashing into Mick with his elbow, knocking him almost off his wobbly legs with the man's bulbous gut. Finn is large and menacing enough to not need his protection, but the lackey offers it, out of loyalty, anyway. The goon reaches into his holster and extends his fleshy arm, pointing a matte-black 9mm pistol at Mick's skull.

Mick stops in his tracks and backs up, gloved hands raising in the air. *He's a dead man.*

Finn grins with bloody teeth, touching his busted lip. He motions for the stooge to stand down. "Nice to see you *too*, Mickey." He looks down at Mick's legs and smirks. "Look at you. I must not'a drilled deep enough." He erupts in a fit of laughter, peppering Mick's face with aerosolized blood.

"Where's Eddie?!" Mick barks into the drizzly night air.

"He sends his regards." Finn tugs his phone out of the ass pocket of his pants, unlocks it with a massive thumb, and holds it up.

In the photo, Ed is zip-tied to the handle of his pickup truck, nose and lip smashed, bleeding down the curves of his pale face. Despite the presence of a blinding flash, he's blurred, as if captured in mid-thrash. He looks more infuriated than terrified. There's blood all over his American flag t-shirt, as though he's been badly maimed. Mick wants to puke.

Finn clicks the phone off and shoves the device back in his pocket. "You should know by now, Mick, I don't tolerate someone's *encroaching on my territory*. See, I'm onto your little game with the pharmaceuticals here. Word on the streets… *my streets*…is Ed's been peddling your medical-grade shit around town the last few days. Didn't take long to figure out how he got 'em. I got eyes and ears all around these parts."

"You don't learn lessons easily, do ya, Mickey?" The goon chimes in.

Mick never takes his eyes off Finn. "Is Ed…?"

The unasked question lingers between the three men for a moment until Finn flashes a bashful smile. "As you well know, it's not my style to kill for a first offense. He's down at the turnoff where you get off Airline. In the bushes. But he's, uh…" he laughs.

It's *cold. Heartless.*

"He's not *feelin'* so well."

Mick looks at the opening amid the damp trees, imagining Eddie down the squirreling dirt path, bleeding on the ground.

Finn steps closer, nearly nose-to-nose with Mick, face twisting into a look of fury. "When will you fucking *amateurs* realize, I *own* this parish? I *see* everything. I *hear* everything." Finn slams him backward with his thick forehead. Mick stumbles, his atrophied legs still as weak as a newborn foal.

"Now *that's* out of the way," Finn growls, eyes hard and unblinking, focused on the wavering Cajun before him, "we have a more *important* matter to discuss. Word in St. James is you got you somethin' special. A real *miracle* drug. Something that'll make a thieving *cripple walk again*."

Finn's lips jerk up into a wicked smile. In the harsh beams from the security lights, he looks like the devil. He holds a gigantic palm out, glaring expectantly at his foe.

The goon raises his gun again, pointing it at Mick's face, finger poised to shoot. Mick knows what the man wants and he'd give anything to ensure Eddie's safety. Petty profits aren't worth the life of his best friend.

He glances at the 9mm, staring down the barrel, and reaches in his pocket. He fishes out a sealed envelope full of black pills with reluctance. He slaps the stolen bundle of Obsidian in Finn's mammoth paw. The contents rattle against the paper.

Finn grins like the Cheshire cat and crimson saliva seeps into the crannies of his teeth. The sight of it makes Mick want to throw up.

"Pleasure doin' business with you." Finn shakes the envelope at him and starts back toward the idling pickup truck.

Mick kicks gravel at the man like a petulant child, wavering as he regains his wobbly stance. "Rot in hell, you *sumbitch*!" He screams, voice rising above the chorus of crickets and amphibians.

Finn hocks a loogie out the driver window and the goon u-turns, heading back down the winding footpath, hurtling pebbles and dust like a miniature explosion from the acceleration.

As the vehicle speeds off, and the brown dirt cloud settles, Mick hobbles down the path, hoping Eddie is still alive.

Mere hours after he learned he could walk, he learns he can run, too.

55

Iris writhes on top of Jack, both fully-engrossed by the naked flesh and intimate contact with another human, a first in years due to their traumas. Jack's scarred hand meanders up the curve of her hip, her waist, her side, until it is cupping her breast, thumbing her pink, responsive nipples.

She has her hands on his chest, thoughtlessly fingering the strange shapes of the grafts where original skin meets foreign, rising slow and sinking down hard and slow, savoring every moment of fullness. She breathes deep lungfuls of air when he bucks. He uses her hips to pull her down harder, to thrust deeper.

It is everything he can do not to cum, but he has an overwhelming desire to satisfy her. To leave her panting, gasping, *wanting more*. He tries to focus on the beams holding the corrugated tin roof in place above them, concentrating on the patter of the rain.

He sits up, scooping her back with his arm to bring her close. Their bodies meld, perspiration mingling, foreheads together. She cries out, body quivering in his arms, quaking against him, and he holds still, sensing the pulsing grip of her orgasm. Her legs lock and shiver.

But his focus is pulled from the act. As he runs his hands along her sweaty spine he swears something is not quite right. Something…

Beneath the flesh.

He palpates it with his fingers and it's like bone, in places where bone should *not* be. Subdermal pockets of flesh where human eyes might fit. A triangular divot shaped like an upside-down heart. And even lower... *jaws*. Pressing the dewy skin out in a horrific, skeletal smile.

He decides his mind must be playing tricks on him in the radiating heat of the metal box they're in. In the midst of his impending orgasm.

He slides his hand away, placing it tenderly on her jaw, kissing her as he thrusts again, speeding up like a freight train, aching to the release of pressure from his scarred cock.

But if Jack could see her back, he'd know he's not imagining things.

He would see the demonic looking face bulging from the back of her rib cage, tugging her sweat-drizzled skin taut. He'd see its wicked smile, emerging like a buoy in water before it retracts, undulating in retreat, back into the meat of her torso in a safe pouch of viscera obscured by heaving lungs.

56

Mick limps over to Eddie. The path is long. Too long for such atrophied muscles. His limbs sting. Eddie's face hangs low and Mick hopes to God he's only resting. He snatches up a thick stick from a nearby pile of brush and weaves it up between Eddie's zip-tied palms. He grabs both ends and puts a boot on the truck door, pulling backward with all of his might, using his foot to push away.

The zip-tie snaps and Mick is airborne, slamming back onto the wet gravel, rain drops whacking him in his face. Eddie's arms fall and his bloodied face looks up in a daze, grinning through the ruby shine.

He almost doesn't understand Mick is in front of him.

Standing.

"C'mon." Mick helps Eddie up. Eddie hisses in pain at the knife wound in his side, clotting his tank top to his waist.

Mick throws Eddie's weak arm around his shoulder and hoists him to his feet. The two men stagger up the long drive toward the compound.

***

"Walsh? Dr. Walsh?!" Mick sets Eddie down in Walsh's office chair near the desk safe and examines him closer in the light. Mick eyes the wounds on Eddie's torso, the numerous ones beneath his tattered shirt. "Don't look like he got you anywhere vital. Hang on, bruh, you' gonna be okay."

"This was my favorite shirt," Eddie moans, staring down at the sliced, bloody hem of it through his unswollen eye.

He fumbles the bobby pin out of his pocket and fidgets with the lock on the safe, an old pro at picking it by now. He opens it, plucks two pills out of the Obsidian bottle, and shoves them in Eddie's mouth. "Hea', bud, take 'ese."

Mick grabs a beveled glass of water from Walsh's desk and forces the stale contents into Eddie's mouth. Mick grasps the back of Eddie's neck and pulls the abused man toward him.

"I'm so sorry, Ed. I fucked up. I never shoulda asked you to–"

"Jesus… Reginald… Christ," Eddie interrupts. Blood trickles from the wound in his side, dabbing the floor in sanguine spatter, but he's more focused on Mick's feet. "When the fuck'd you start walking?"

57

DAY TEN OF TRIAL

Iris awakens in a cocoon of warm arms wrapped tight around her. Her sluggish eyes fixate on the window ledge above Jack's cot, overflowing with colorful origami creations. He's awake, planting soft kisses on the back of her head and nape of her neck. His scarred hand retracts from the embrace and brushes aside her blonde tresses. His lips plant on her neck, a spot that drove her wild the night before. He cups her bare breast, thumbing her nipple gently.

"*Mmmmm.* I don't know if I am up for round three yet. I need some Gatorade or something." She giggles and twists until she is facing him.

"Fair enough. Always wise to replenish."

She can sense his adoration as he caresses her shoulder and arm, struggling to find the courage to meet her gaze. "Good morning," he says, letting a warm grin wash over his grafted face.

"Mmmmmmmm, morning," she cooes.

"Want some breakfast?" He wants to kiss her but doesn't want to scare her off with too much affection. He worries she feels regret about the night prior, an anxiety racing through him.

"*Mmm-hmmm.* Yes, please." She props herself up on her palms, exposing her back to him.

Suddenly, her potential regrets are the furthest thing from his mind.

He bolts upright, distressed, unable to take his eyes off her shoulder blade where a once-healed expletive is now dark and pulsating. Its letters are alive, beating like a weak heart through open tears in her skin. They're blackened and starting to bulge through the cuts.

"Iris," his voice is almost not there.

"Yeah?" She demurely searches for her bra and shirt on his floor.

But he can't say more. He doesn't know a tactful way to tell a lover that a tar-like substance is oozing from the word SLUT, re-carved into her scapula.

58

Eddie limps into the doorway of Mick's room. His scabs and gashes from Finn's *warning* are prominent, but healing. He moves spryly through the hall with a paper plate of buttered toast. "Yo, there was no bacon left, but there was some bread–"

"Eddie!" There's fear in Mick's trembling voice.

As Mick comes into sight, Eddie drops the food. Mick is reaching out to him. His bearded face is awash with tears, quivering hand outstretched from the floor. Eddie's eyes travel down to the source of the pain. Black goo burbles out of two stigmata-like cavities in his impossibly-angled knees, pooling in a dark mess on the floorboards. Small, spiny protrusions jut out of the holes like horns in a demon's skull. He can swear one of them is moving.

"What the *fuck*?" Eddie cries out, weak on his own legs, struggling to stay atop them.

"Get Walsh!" Mick's pleading voice cracks like a prepubescent boy and he howls out in pain.

59

In the clinic, Jack paces by the closed office door for a moment before returning to Iris's side. She's hunched on the exam table with a dazed look in her worried eyes. Her fingernails pick at the sheet of paper beneath her.

Jack stares at his palm, where he injured himself the day prior. No trace of the injury remains, yet the back of his hand is still burn-scarred. He rubs at the marred flesh out of nervousness and wraps an arm around Iris's waist to comfort her. She leans her head into his chest and he plants a long kiss on the top of her head, marveling at how much he has already grown to care for her.

The front door slams open, startling them. Walsh rushes past the concerned patients and Jack reaches out, snatching up Walsh's frail bicep. "Hey! Where are you going? We've got a situation here."

Walsh's head whips and the old man, graceful and stately, gives Jack a look of fury sending a bolt of ice through his chest. "Get your hand off of me, LeBlanc," he growls, fuming, yanking his crisp, white lab coat free. He takes a moment to breathe and compose himself and starts again. "I'm busy dealing with Mick's crisis."

"I-It's her back," Jack stammers. "Wait, what's wrong with *Mick*?" He leans in as if it somehow will make Walsh answer quicker. It doesn't. There's something in Walsh's angered eyes that scares the living shit out of him. *Always has.*

The doctor pulls his chained glasses up and puts them on his face. He examines the wounds on Iris's exposed shoulders like an old man struggling with a crossword puzzle. He touches near the oozing area and she hisses. He glares at the back of her head.

"Helloooooo? I asked you a question. What's going on with Mick?" Jack asks again, feeling shitty for chasing skirt, as his father always called it, instead of being a friend.

"He appears to be having a," Walsh pauses for a moment, "*reaction* to the medication. He's resting. I've given him something for the pain." Walsh grinds his teeth, thinking about how few *Vicodin* and *Oxycontins* were left in the safe this morning. "I have to file a report." Walsh takes out a large square bandage, one barely big enough to cover the gooey word on her back.

Her wound is ink-black, puckering in spots, lumped in others. The surface is puffy and malformed and Walsh watches as something small and spiny undulates below her epidermis. He swallows hard, hiding that he wants to run away and never look back from this inadvertent nightmare of his own creation.

This isn't how it's supposed to go.

He wipes the area with a swab of iodine, leaving the rust-colored liquid melding with the goo on her back. He peels the backing off the bandage, places it over her wound, and tosses his disposable gloves.

"Both of you, go back to the main house. Once I file all of this, I'll send Tate to bring you back for individual exams."

Before Jack or Iris can protest, Walsh rushes off through the closed office door, locking it behind him.

60

"What the hell is going *on* out there, James?" Eileen asks, hands trembling as they touch down on his solid oak desk. Her scrub top tugs tight, straining against the well-endowed chest beneath as she leans in.

"This is all fucking wrong," Walsh flails his leg, smashing the unforgiving heel of his dress shoe into the wall with a thundering *boom*. It leaves a sharp-edged dent and black, rubber smear in its wake.

"How did this *happen*?!"

"Someone switched the *pills*, Eileen."

"How?! They were locked in a goddamned *safe*!"

"I'm aware!" Walsh pulls hard at his silver hair and looks back up at her, slinging his flattened hand in the direction of the safe in the other room. "He used a goddamned *bobby pin*!"

"*Who*?!"

"Mick!"

"What is he? Fucking *McGuyver*?!" She doesn't believe him.

"I watched him on the security camera footage, Eileen." Walsh picks up an amethyst paperweight and throws it, smashing it into the wall behind Eileen. She jumps and covers herself from a shower of shattered crystal rain. The tone in the room changes. She's underestimated his anger.

"What are you going to do?" She straightens up, calming her tone.

"I think you mean, what are *we* going to do."

"Oh no." She winces, shaking her head. "This wasn't what you asked of me. I am *not* going down for *this*. I have a *family*, James."

"I know," he roars with fury. "Thanks for that *jab*, by the way."

"Oh, come on! You know what I *mean*! James, I helped you do this *for Jessica*." She takes a deep breath. "You asked me to help and I told you that he deserves anything he's got comin' for what he did. But you promised this was *just* supposed to be *him*."

"Don't you think I fucking know that?!" Walsh stands and walks to the nurse.

She peers up into his crazed eyes, no longer seeing him as the frail old man in mourning he's been for years.The sad sap she pities. No, instead, he's a man with hatred burning inside of him. She turns around to stare out the window, contemplating their next move.

Outside, the sun is setting to a hazy yellow-orange glow, like a distant bonfire. Charcoal clouds roll in on the horizon.

Eileen twists back to face him, biting her lip, concerned. "We need to get ahead of this. Maybe if we go to the police and--"

"--And say *what*?"

"Well," she swallows hard, "we lie. We get creative. We say we were running this trial--"

"There's no fucking *trial*, Eileen. You *know* that. Police would know it, too, the *second* they started digging."

"Then *what*, huh?" She throws her hands up, voice distressed. "We just go down for manslaughter? Or-or-or *murder*? God *dammit*, James, how did I let you talk me into this?"

"Talk you *into* this?!" He steps to her. "You *volunteered*."

"Because that *bastard* had it coming! But *this*--" She starts to cry. "James... they're all going to be just like *that*..."

Don't call her that, he thinks.

Walsh's fingers grip the headset of the landline on his desk, wrapping around the hardened plastic handle, like a snake constricting prey.

Don't you dare...

"*Thing!*"

The moment the blasphemous word spews from her mouth, Walsh swings hard and fast, clubbing her in the skull with the telephone. She drops to the floor with the vicious hit, taken completely off-guard.

Before she understands what's happening, he is smashing her face again, arm tangling in the spiral cord. She screams at the top of her lungs, one eye wide with shock, the other swelling at the abuse. He slams it down again and again, striking her so hard she sees flashes of light with every devastating blow.

Tate feels the blood trickle down her forehead, tracing the curves around her nose and mouth. She can taste it, shocked at the pent-up rage in the old man.

She shrieks and tries to shield herself from the next blow. But he picks up the whole receiver and bashes it into the side of her skull like he's swinging a baseball bat, full-force. She feels the bone in her jaw crack, unhinging instantly from the sockets. She feels teeth loosen in her blood-filled mouth. All logical thought disappears out the window.

THWACK!

THWACK!

THWACK!

He rears up again, perspiring and out of breath, and brings it down one final time.

THWACK!

He tosses the receiver down on the floor next to her. Pieces of broken plastic scatter in a river of vital fluids. Walsh bends down to look closer at the soft, pinkish-gray hunks of brain matter escaping through the nasty crater he bashed into her head.

For a moment, he feels a pang of guilt. He knows her family. He did a residency with her husband. Watched her kids grow up over the years. Now, he's left two young adults without a mother…

But its all over now. Panic and adrenaline surges through his veins. There is nowhere for them to go, no way out of this mess.

Why did that crippled fuck have to break in to the safe, he thinks.

Of all the things he considered for the years leading up to this elaborate sham, things he put into place to feign the legitimacy of a drug trial, planning that went into making LeBlanc suffer just like Jessica did… he never once factored in the desperation of a devious thief trying to make a quick buck. Never imagined the pills would be tampered with inside a locked safe.

He never fathomed that he'd be standing over a friend of twenty-odd years, one whom he'd bludgeoned to death with a still-beeping landline, making all the noise in the world from a busted mouthpiece.

Sanguine blood slithers around the islands of slick, gray matter that was once in her body. It hugs the curves of the numerical buttons that lay scattered like scrabble letters.

Walsh, still trying to suck in air from his over-exertion and impending panic attack, looks over at the armoire with the ornate wooden doors where he keeps his lab coats and wonders how difficult it will be to get a placid, adult corpse inside of it.

61

Fisher relaxes with his head against the tile, letting the steamy water caress his rail-thin body. He runs a hand down his ribs, feeling the undulating curvature of every bone like fleshy speed bumps. It travels to a narrow waist, palpating the plate-shaped bones of his jutting hips. He pictures the skeleton inside of him, wishing he was little more than that.

He recalls the burger he had at dinner and considers purging again to get the last remnants of caloric content up, though he's gotten the bulk of it in time. He wants to taste the acid on his tongue and feel the heave of his tightening stomach as he hurls.

But he decides against it, knowing when Walsh takes his weight, his losses will be suspicious enough already. *He's pushing it.* He doesn't want to get ejected from the trial. Not with only eleven days to go. Or worse: checked into inpatient therapy involuntarily… again.

Still, his father's voice chants all the horrid names of his pudgy junior high years on a loop.

The one Dan liked the most was "Porker." Fisher recalled the way his father would *oink* at him as he passed in front of the television, hoping he'd be ignored like some ghostly spectre. Instead, he became the center of Dan's attention.

He remembered the first time he overate out of pure spite, wishing he could kill himself with food. Wishing he could explode his insides or shut his organs down. But all he felt was a malaise and sickness, a severe pain in his gut that wouldn't cease until he forced himself to throw up. The simple act of the evacuating purge was transformative. Though it hurt to feel stomach acids tearing at the lining of his throat, he felt something else, too.

Control.

For once, *he* was in control of something in his life.

Plus, if the calories didn't make it to his ass and thighs, he could enjoy the taste of things and lose weight, too. But after months of doing the same, it was impossible to stop.

Over time, the sweet feel of his bones became overshadowed by hair loss and thinning tooth enamel. He even started using a roll of lifesavers on a string to purge, to avoid further scar tissue on the back of his knuckles, and to coat the bile with sugar and flavoring.

Then the threats came.

Hecklers like Dan suddenly seemed worried, suddenly pretended to *give a shit*, threatening to throw him into treatment if he didn't keep food down. So he learned to eat enough to appease them. Or at least, to *act* like he did.

Now he looks at his bones behind the beads of water in the shower like they are old, secret friends. *Best* friends. Someone he could never bear to part with.

He turns off the faucet and stands there for a moment, watching droplets roll off his concave belly onto his dark thatch of pubes, smiling at what he sees. It's a body like sinew, whose only curves are made by the presence of the hardened calcium structure beneath.

He steps out of the tub and towels off in front of the mirror. There is something on his forearms and elbows. Black *smudges* of something…

He looks closer, realizing all of the spots are areas Walsh scored open days ago. All of which have healed since. He wipes his forearm with a white towel and twists his face in disgust when he sees dark, oily residue on the terry cloth. As he pulls it away, the gooey matter leaves nasty strings dripping from everything it touches and, just like that, he is out of love with the image reflected back at him once again.

62

"I want to go home. I want to opt out of the trial and see a doctor about this." With deep shame, Angie covers the gooey, horizontal scar below her stomach with the waistband of her skirt.

"*I'm* a doctor," Walsh says, eyeing the closed armoire behind the crying patient. He watches a drop of floor-bound blood make its way like dark molasses down the drawers.

"*Another* doctor. One who gives a *shit* that something's wrong with us." Her lip trembles. "I'm sorry. That was mean. I-I just came to find out if there were any exit forms or anything I needed to complete before you call a shuttle to take me back to my car. I want to leave tonight."

Walsh pauses, unable to peel his eyes away from the armoire.

He recalls glimpses of the attack, hours before. Especially the way Tate's brain matter looked as he toweled it up…

"I'm sorry you feel that way." He shifts back into the moment, flitting his wrinkled eyes to Angie. "I assure you, I am taking your conditions seriously. But I understand your concern. I can't keep you here if you don't want to be. Let me get them."

He stands, grabs a stack of papers out of the lower side-drawer of his desk, gaze drifting back to the huge, wooden cabinet.

Angie points to the framed picture of a little girl near a messy pile of patient journals. She softens, trying to remember that while she's scared and frustrated, the man *is* human, after all. "That your daughter?"

Walsh solemnly nods.

"She's pretty. How old is she?"

The question is like a box cutter in his gut. "Would've been thirteen."

Walsh hands her a pen and a stapled group of papers he photocopied from a past trial, a legitimate trial. He places the photo of the girl down on its face so his daughter's dishwater blonde braids, innocent eyes and bright smile are out of sight. He subtly wipes a dot of Tate's blood from the back of it with his thumb.

But Angie is focused on his answer, wishing she never asked.

Would've been.

Those words are heavy enough to be full of lead.

63

"I'm racing down the field, ball in my hand. I threw it to home plate and I shit you not, clocked the runner right in the face. Total accident." Chase is giggling his way through the ending. "Out-fuckin'-*cold*!"

"Lights out for that guy." Alan laughs. "Jesus, that's insane. I can't believe we both played for the fuckin' *Pelicans*, man. That's wild." He takes a sip of tequila straight out of the bottle, smile fading a little. "Did you ever have that asshole, Coach Pierce?"

"Yep." Chase tries to hide his shit-eating grin. A dusting of rose red creeps up on his dark cheeks. "In more ways than one. That's *Tim*. That's *my* Tim. The one I was dating when I came out."

Alan's jaw drops, recalling Chase's story during the storm front. "Coach *Pierce*? *That* was your… guy?"

"Yup!" He beams. "Tim Pierce. Oh, God, he *taught* me things."

Alan picks at the label on his booze bottle. There isn't much left. Not enough to drown out the feelings bubbling up inside of him at the mention of Pierce. His eyes drift to the darkened gashes that, in the last twenty-four hours, have crawled up his arms like fat, slick strikes of charcoal lightning.

"I hope that fuckin' prick *dies*," he says, turning the air of the room icy with his tone.

"Jesus Christ, what'd he do to *you*?" Chase leans back on his hands, shoulders scrunching by his ears, diamond stud twinkling in the overhead lights.

Alan's eyes are a mix of melancholy and hatred, deep lines framing them as he winces. He sucks back a huge swig of booze, chugging it down with a head-whip, and gasps at how much the cheap liquor burns.

He rises to his feet, holding the bottle like a bat. "He *assaulted* me." The disgusted look on his face paired with his vinegared tone make Chase understand the word *assaulted* is an understatement. "In the showers one day, after a game. Held me down so hard during..." he can't say the words. The room falls silent for a moment as Alan starts to pace, wiggling the bottle around with a nervous energy. "Actually tore my rotator cuff trying to get away. Didn't matter. As you know, hes a big ol' fucker and when he wanted something he *got* it. He was *strong*." He motions to Chase, feeling as if they have some sort of strange camaraderie now, both underage men having been taken advantage of by the same adult. "Hell, *you* know."

"Someone like that can just *take* something from you if he wants it." He continues with venom in his voice. "Whatever *feels* good to *him*. Whatever he *feels* like. And then, when he's done... He leaves you there on the tile like a dirty sock, all used and empty. And, of course, nobody listens. You say *rape*, they laugh and say *tenure*. You say sexual assault, they assume you're lying to get back at him for benching you half the season. Who was I? I was a dumb fuckin' kid. It was my word against his." Alan feigns a tight smile, teeth gritted.

He lifts the lip of the bottle back to his lips for a sip. "I've never told anybody that before." Tears rush out the sides of his eyes. "Not since it happened the first time. Shit, *second* time, I figured it was useless to try. I was still healing from the rotator surgery. I didn't even fight that time. He kept telling me that I wanted it."

"I'm so sorry." Chase's voice is almost a whisper. He looks up at Alan, follows him as he paces with sympathetic, espresso-colored eyes. "It wasn't the same kinda thing between him and I. He never did anything like that to me. I mean, he liked rough *sex*," he pauses, unsure if it's inappropriate, "but it was always consensual with us."

"Chase, you were a *child*."

"I was *seventeen*. I knew what I was doing." *Brrrrrmmmmmmm.*

The sound of everything electrical powering down fills the air around them, a noise they've heard a half a dozen times in the nights they've been there. Blackness swallows the room in an instant.

"Dammit, not *again*. Where do you keep your candles?"

"By the lamp over there." Alan mutters, although the sudden outage is a blessing. It couldn't have come at a better time. Now Chase can't see the pain-filled tears falling steadily from his bloodshot eyes.

64

Eddie lights the hurricane lamp next to Mick on the bedside table. Mick sulks in bed, devastated. He stares at his wheelchair.

That fucking chair…

A battered prison of metal and upholstery.

He can't stomach the idea of getting in it one more time. He wants to roll it out onto Airline to watch a Northbound semi smash through it.

He lets Eddie ramble on about some film he doesn't care anything about. Finally, he notices that he doesn't have a captive audience and says, "Wanna get outta here, man? Go see what everyone else is up to?"

"I can't go back in that chair, Ed."

"So you're just gonna sit 'ere and mope? The Mick I know doesn't throw a fuckin' *pity* party because he can't walk. He throws a *real* goddamn party 'cuz that motherfucker ain't never let no handicap hold his ass back. He's wild and he can do just about anything *anyone* else can do."

"'Cept *walk*!" His voice is full of pain. "Goddammit, Eddie! For the firs' time in five years, I had my *freedom* back."

Ed's never seen him this emotional before. Mick has always been a sarcastic clown, making light of the darkest situations.

"Look, I know this is devastating. I'll give you that, okay. But *damn* man, you're straight-up bummin' me out. How long you gonna sit here and feel sorry for yourself?"

Mick just glares at the chair. *His foe.*

"You can eye-fuck that thing all night if you want. You don't need an audience for that. I'm out. I'll catch you in the morning."

Mick nods, clutching his pillow tighter, wishing there was bourbon to numb the pain.

"Don't do anything fuckin' stupid while I'm gone." Ed orders with a pointed finger, like a stern, parental warning.

"Like what? *Get my hopes up*?" Mick scoffs.

After a pause, Eddie holds out his hand. "Gimme your piece."

"What?! No. Fuck off wit' all 'dat." He waves Eddie away.

"Motherfucker, I don't need you eatin' a *bullet* over this bullshit. You know how shitty'att'd be if I come in here tomorrow and find out you Jackson Pollock-ed your brains all over the goddamned walls?"

"Then at least my problems'd be ova'." He mutters.

"Mick!" Eddie is yelling now, hand splayed, wanting the gun.

"Goddamn! I won't do nothin', Ed, *Jesus Christ*," Mick groans. "*I'm not gonna kill myself,* jackass!" He raises his head from his pillow to argue. "But I'm sure as fuck not gonna be caught with my pants down if Finn shows his ugly ass back here again. It ain't like I can *run away* from the motherfucker, now can I?"

"*Swear?*"

"What are you, five yea's old? I gotta *pinky promise* you or somethin'? I swear, goddammit. I won't kill myself."

Eddie kicks one of the bed risers on the way out. "Better be here tomorrow when I come back."

"Where 'da fuck am I gon' go?"

"You *know* what I mean."

Angie appears in the darkness behind Eddie, lit dimly by the candle in her hand. Ed scoffs. As he leaves, he says, "Good luck, he's like a viper tonight."

Angie pokes her head into Mick's room, speaking meekly. "I'm heading out soon. Just wanted to see how you're holding up."

"Headed where? Where you goin'?" He manages to lift his head, but his voice is weak, like someone recovering from the flu.

"Home. I'm dropping out of the trial. This black shit is getting worse and Walsh doesn't care. I tried to get Tate to check it. Haven't been able to find her all day. I'm over it. I'm out."

The bearded Cajun rolls his eyes and stuffs his face back into the pillow. With a mixture of sarcasm and numbness, he moans, "This day just keeps gettin' betta' and betta'."

Angie props her suitcase by the wall and plops the candle by his lamp on the side table. She sits on the bed near his feet. "Can you...?"

"Not any more."

He forces himself to sit up. *It's a struggle, but so is everything.*

"I'm so sorry," she says, wanting to place a hand on his shoulder for comfort but stopping herself.

"Squandered my only chance. There was so much I wanted to do."

"Well…. You were taller than I thought you'd be." Her voice is shy. Coy, almost. It's unlike all of his other interactions with her. Pity has softened her.

"Yeah?" The comment makes him grin.

It's what he needed to hear.

She nods, her cheeks raising a little with the hint of a bashful smile. "I never *did* get to have that dance."

"Yeah, well, you snooze, you lose, I 'spose." Mick exhales and bops his head against the wall behind him a few times.

"I'm gonna miss whipping your ass at 5 card stud."

"You had *one* lucky night." He laughs, shaking his head at the ceiling. "I dare you to try 'at again."

"I beat you fair and square and you know it," she teases.

"I wish you weren't goin'." His smile goes lax and his expression turns melancholic. He stares up at the glimmer of the lantern as it casts strange, ethereal shadows on the ceiling, like blurred ghosts milling about.

She slides her hand along his thigh, commanding his full attention. "I wish there was something I could do to make you feel better."

Mick looks her in the eye. He's unsure what message she's trying to send, so he fishes, "I mean, I know a *few* things that would." He grins a little.

She sighs. "Walsh says I've got another hour or so until the shuttle gets here." Her smile is warm. *Inviting.* Eyes locked on his. He wonders if he's hallucinating again.

"What about mister MMA? I don't need him coming down here and kickin' my ass while I'm down if he finds out."

"Mister MMA," she drags her finger up the fabric of his pants, "moved out to be with a nineteen-year-old last month after he found out that I can't get pregnant any more."

He can't figure out what part of the confession turns him on more, but before he can say something insensitive, he leans in and kisses her, holding his lips against hers. He runs his gloved hands through the wavy locks of her long, red hair, shimmering in the light of the lamp. She kisses back, soft and teasing, tongue intertwining with his. He feels their excited breath mixing with the stuffy summer air.

She pulls away for a moment, the lower half of her face turning pink from his beard, and crawls on top of him, encouraging his hands to roam her body.

65

"Maybe you should slow down. I think you've had enough. You're gonna black out if you keep drinking." Chase lights the last candle, setting the spent match down by a used razor blade on Alan's bedside stand. It's caked in a thin veneer of dried blood, glimmering dully in the candlelight.

"Oh, you think so?" There's a nastiness to Alan's voice.

"Yeah, I do," Chase says firmly, agitated. He leans in to grab the bottle and Alan presses his lips hard against Chase's.

Chase pulls away, smiling. Not a smile of consensual enjoyment, but one of embarrassment for the drunken mess before him. Alan leans back in for another, unable to see the disappointment on the face right in front of him. Chase retreats further.

The mood changes. Alan is sexually charged and confused by the brush-off.

"Look, Alan, I'm... *flattered*, but–"

There it is. A 'but.'

A full-stop.

Alan stands, unable to process the rejection.

"Alan, I know what it's like to be in the closet. It's scary and SO confusing–"

"I'm not *in the closet*," his face is serious, angry, "because I'm not a faggot." He says the word plainly. Factually. Like he's saying *woman* or *dog*.

Chase sighs, too tired to fight with someone so drunk. He gets up to leave. "I get it. You're confused. You're drunk. You've got all these emotions–"

Alan interrupts with his aggressive mouth pressing to Chase's, as if being more forceful will change his mind.

"Get off!" Chase shoves him backward. Alan stumbles back into the dresser, rattling the mirror atop it against the wall with a repetitive thud.

Alan lunges, tackling Chase down on the bed with violence. Chase can smell Alan's boozy cloud of breath as he struggles. Alan tries to roll him onto his stomach with all the furious force he can muster. Chase resists, hollering out. Alan forces his head into the comforter, muffling his screams, wrenching Chase's arm behind his back.

Chase wriggles out, scrambles to his feet, placing distance between him and his attacker.

THUNK. THUNK. THUNK.

Alan punches himself in the side of the head, blocking the only exit with his body. He's completely unhinged, pacing like a pissed-off howler monkey. Growling in his intoxicated stupor.

"Alan, *move*!" Chase yells, eyeballing the blade on the bedside table.

Alan stops abusing himself, shouts out, "I-i-is it my *looks*? Am I not your type? What, am I not *hot* enough for you?"

"No, it's because you're a fucking *psycho*!"

"You think I'm *psycho*?"

Alan rushes Chase, choking him with brutal force, both hands on his throat. As he tackles Chase to the bed, Chase slaps a trembling hand out, fumbling for the blade.

"You wanna SEE fuckin' *psycho*?"

He feels it. Feels the razor. Glued to the wood by dried blood.

Alan tears Chase's basketball shorts down. The terrified man beneath flails. "I'll show you *psycho*…"

He punches Chase in the skull with his balled fists, stunning the man. "Help, please! Somebody!" It's all Chase can think of to scream, the raw, raspy tone clawing at the lining of his throat like ghastly fingers. "*Please!*"

Alan flicks the tuft of hair from his face with a swing of his head so he can see better. He tugs down his own sweatpants and spits in his hand, uses it to lube his cock, swirling it up and down the length of his shaft. He sinks inside the writhing man, burying himself deep.

Chase erupts in a guttural scream. Something primal. *Horrifying*. He digs deep within himself for a surge of physical strength in his disorienting inebriation. Tears trail down the sharpened features of Chase's face as he cries out, wondering why this man saw fit to bastardize such an intimate act.

The rape is violent. Alan pounds away as if Chase is just some squirrelly blow-up doll. Chase feels beads of sweat from Alan's forehead drop like cruel rain on his lower back. His tender skin shreds. He sees blazing white stars as he pinches his eyes tight, crying out to anyone who will listen.

But no one is.

Chase slaps his hand hard on the side table again, jarring the blade loose from its gory cradle. He feels it slide across the wood in his hand until the ultra-thin piece of metal is between his fingers.

Alan leans down, wrenching his arm around Chase's throat to stop the screaming. The booze and intermittent thoughts of coach Pierce and the legal consequences of this act, spread through his brain like rancid mold on cheese. He is having trouble finishing. But Chase still makes noises that ring out above the *slap-slap-slap* of skin making violent contact. His climax drifts like a rowboat from shore, despite the rhythm of his hips as they pound wild, despite how good it feels to be thrusting inside of someone.

Chase twists with a growl, like an ancient Greek racing into the front lines of a war, weapon-first. *Charging.* As Alan's grip loosens, he swipes blindly at his attacker and connects with something fleshy, slashing it with a force as merciless as the devastating act inflicted upon him.

The pounding stops, along with the searing pain. Chase bellows, slobbering on the bed, a mess of tears and spit as he claws his way out from under Alan. He yanks his shorts up with brainless automation, hands shaking.

Everything shaking.

He sees Alan now...

Clawing at his throat in the darkness. His maw wide open, gasping for air, only to produce a wet gurgle. Red rushes down his bare chest in rivulets, like garnet-colored water spilling over a full dam. The look on Alan's pale face is one of betrayal and confusion.

Chase realizes he still has the razor in his hand, coated with Alan's fresh blood.

66

Chase screams, cradling Alan's limp head in his blood-soaked lap. His pulsing fluid trickles out of the gash splitting his throat wide, wide enough to see the severed carotid artery itself. *Pumping. Pumping. Pumping.*

Wide enough to see *meat*. Split open, exposing the white trachea from which his final gasps seem to suck.

Iris and Jack approach the scene gingerly with a glass hurricane lamp, uncertain if the muffled screams they heard downstairs were of passion or torture. But the answer is clear as Chase bawls uncontrollably near Alan's bled-out body.

Jack and Iris are speechless, words feeling so insignificant in a moment like this.

"I just wanted him to stop." Chase is rocking, shaking. His tone is trance-like, as if he's already in a padded cell, chanting to himself. *But he isn't.* He's in a slow-pooling mess of ichor, covered in Alan's coppery perfume. "I wasn't trying to kill him. I just wanted him to *stop*. He--"

But Chase can't find the words. It all happened so fast. One minute they're sharing baseball stories.

The *next*...

"Is he...?" Iris steps in, her voice quaking with fear.

Chase rocks Alan's lifeless body. "*No*. No, no, no, no!" He's crying harder now, whipping his head in denial.

Fisher fills the door frame behind them, wide-eyed and breathing hard, stunned by the scene in front of him.

"Iris," Jack swallows. He can hear his heartbeat thumping in his ears. He clenches his teeth, flexing the muscles in his jaw. "Go call for help. Call 9-1-1."

Before he finishes saying the words, she's shooting down the hall like a bolt of lightning, scrambling down the stairs. Jack kneels down, placing his hands on Alan instinctively, wanting to give him chest compressions but knowing he's too far gone. His bloody hands tremble and he wipes them on his hoodie, unsure of what to say or do. A voice jolts him out of his own delirious mindset:

"HE'S DEAD! HE'S FUCKING DEAD!" Chase is screaming now, infuriated by the stilled sack of meat in front of him. He smashes a balled fist into the center of Alan's chest so hard it forces more blood out of the watery gorge in his neck.

"Chase... what did you *do*?" Fear cracks Fisher's voice from the doorway. It remains calm considering the wet, red carnage before him.

"I wasn't... trying to... kill him!" Chase wails. "I just wanted the fucker to stop!" He grabs his bald head with both glistening hands and holds it like his brain is going to explode, sticky fingers pressing wells deep into his temples.

But something is happening.

Something more horrific than Alan's demise.

From the sliced chasm in Alan's shorn throat, something *moves*, slithering out of the meaty crevasse into the muggy air. Chase scrambles backward, his feet clattering against the soaked wood floors, slipping around in the deluge. He points at Alan's throat just as a tar-black spike surfaces from the wound.

Jack stumbles toward the wall at the sight of the blackness protruding outward. *Reaching*. Crunching the bones and cartilage of Alan's sternum and throat as it emerges from the ripped, bloody flesh.

A second prong shoots out of the gory slit, sending Alan's jaw juddering in the opposing direction. The barb tugs hard until the neat perforation shreds further. Dark sludge gushes in an amniotic waterfall out of the wound like contaminated afterbirth.

Alan's gaping carcass is birthing something demonic.

Something... *Inhuman.*

Two gleaming rows of sharp teeth gnash through the shredded gully, biting its way outward to reveal additional, smaller sets behind it, like a shark. They stand in its gums like hundreds of white fork tines.

Fisher scuttles backward into the hall and catches himself on the door jamb before he can tumble to the floor. Chase's cries hitch, forcing him to gulp for oxygen.

The being inside of Alan skewers him through the open hole with another spike, extending and expanding as it mingles with the air. Shedding its meaty receptacle. Growing in size as it escapes its constrictive prison of bone and meat.

"Chase!" Jack throws out a hand to help. Chase clambers around the grotesque scene and accepts Jack's hand. He's yanked hard to his feet and Jack and Fisher take off down the hall.

Before he leaves, Chase looks back as the *thing* completes its hellish parturition process, unable to fully comprehend the reality of what he is seeing. Feet slick with viscous, mucosal fluids, Chase slips and falls racing out of the door. He scrambles to get up, creature looming high overhead. Now fully-birthed, it whips around with rapidity, hunching what appears to be its shoulders, clacking its hideous rows of teeth.

Chase scuttles backward through the thin corridor, but the beast has other plans for him. It heaves one of its pointed appendages straight through the hardened bones in Chase's chiseled face like an arrow.

Chase drops like an anchor. The thing retracts its barbed limb and Chase crumples to the floor like a tossed department store mannequin. His only brown eye that remains dangles limp and lazy from the socket by a thread of gore. There's a hole clean-through where his mouth and nose used to be, tongue severed cleanly by the force. Bloody molars lay scattered in a gruesome constellation on the floorboards like red-glazed, porcelain confetti.

His cavernous head no longer resembles anything *remotely* human.

From the gaping mineshaft through his cranium, something lifts from the viscera, squishy and loud, like galoshes coming unstuck from deep bog mud. The finger-like appendage feels around in the pungent night air. It slithers out of the wide gash above his broken jaw.

As the first creature leaves the scene, scrambling its gore-coated feet down the hall with force, a second being begins to birth out of Chase, crawling through his orifices, new and old, cracking his skull apart at the fissured seams. The beast slithers out of the gnarled mound of bone, mucus, and blood, growing exponentially as its curdled, clotting surface exposes to the acrid air, shedding its ungrateful host.

67

Iris holds the lamp close to the keypad on the phone to see the numbers. She yanks the handle out of the cradle and goes to dial.

Dead silence. No ringtone.

Iris mashes the telephone lever several times with her finger. She remembers the recent power outage and it all makes sense. She'd already forgotten about it in the midst of all the madness.

Jack and Fisher race for their lives down the stairs, Fisher stumbling down the last three, and taking off like a rocket through the living room.

"Jack!" Iris calls out, frantic, near the windows.

"Go! We have to go!" The panic in his voice alarms her.

"I can't get a dial tone! The power–"

"Forget about the phone! *It's coming!*" Fisher interjects, screaming. The comment couldn't sound more ominous.

"What do you mean? *What's* coming?" Iris's hands are shaking now as she slams the phone back in the cradle. Jack clasps a hand around hers and drags her toward the front door, stamping a cabernet-colored trail of footprints through the house.

"What's coming?" Her voice raises, child-like, frightened.

Jack shushes her, dragging a blood-smeared finger almost to his lips. She realizes his shirt and hands are covered with it.

Fisher points up the stairs as the black, pointed appendages come into view.

It staggers closer.

RAAAAAAAAAAWWWWWWWWGHHHHHHH NNNNKKK!

The snorting thing emits a gurgling roar with bass so low it vibrates the floorboards. Wet and abnormal. Like nothing they've ever heard before. *Like nothing they ever want to hear again.*

The creature takes another step toward the stairs, moving jaggy, like a film with a jittery frame rate. Flexing and tensing with irregular gesticulations.

The thing makes its way down the steps on slick extremities, baring something resembling a sick smile of nightmarish teeth. It leaps down the last few steps and takes off running.

The patients scramble to the glass doors leading to the bayou. The thing races toward them, hunched like a tarry apex predator atop anomalous feet loaded with jagged toenails, too many to count on each tarsus. They click like knives against the wood.

The beast charges, eager to catch them.

Fisher closes the sliding doors just in time to smash the creature between them. It shrieks in pain and frustration, squirming. *Writhing.* Trying to get out. It claws at them with a barbed spike, leaving a trail of mucus smeared across the glass.

"Go!" Fisher screams to Jack and Iris and they dart off to the right, toward the path in the woods. Iris struggles to keep the rattling dome of the lamp attached through the jostling.

A sickly green light emanates from a window of the decrepit structure at the treeline. *Lights that shouldn't be on in an outage...*

Iris runs in the direction of them, a gut instinct, even though she swore she'd never go back in that shack after seeing it in the daylight. Jack is close behind, on a mission to protect her from that... *thing*.

Fisher bows backward as the globule serving as the entity's face nears his, snapping gore-covered teeth like a sprung bear trap, missing him by *inches*. He looks in the other direction, knowing Jack and Iris will have a better chance if the thing follows him elsewhere. He sets his eyes on Walsh's clinic to his left. He lets the door go and hauls ass as fast as his thin legs will carry him, navigating by the dim light of the moon.

Fisher hears the beast slither out of the closed doors, but wastes no time looking back. He pads through the field, catching rocks and sticks in the soft underside of his feet. He doesn't slow. If he does, he won't make it. He skids to the door and yanks the handle, surprised to learn the building isn't locked. He rushes inside and slams it closed just in time.

The beast arrives, thrusting at the violently-vibrating glass like a battering ram.

WHAM!

WHAM!

WHAMMMMM!

68

"Did you hear that?" Angie asks, whipping her head around. Her massive, bare breasts bob with the movement. Mick can't focus on a word she is saying. A waterfall of ginger hair strokes Mick's tattooed chest. "Someone sounded--"

"Don't worry about *them*." He reaches up and drags her to him with a gripped hunk of her orange locks. His expression is almost a snarl. "You're being a bad," he pulls her down, thrusting himself deeper, "girl." His voice is a quiet growl, jaw clenched tight.

She rides him slower, panting, flexing her sweat-beaded thighs. Her eyes flutter with every languid stroke. Hissing with satisfaction. Feeling the hot flush on her face. Her weighty breasts bounce as she grinds on his girth. He marvels at her chilled nipples, hard, nearly blending into her skin in the candlelight.

His hand slides between their bodies, inches below her blackened C-section scar, rubbing the wet flesh beneath the skirt hiked to her tapered waist. Her lacy thong is wrapped around her calf like a loose anklet.

Behind her, something large and black brushes past the open doorway. Angie stops, mid-stroke, and whispers, *"who's that?"*

"Shut up." He pulls her to him and kisses her, biting her lower lip, yanking her down onto his cock with a muscular arm. "You gonna cum for me, baby?" He rubs her faster, rotating a skilled finger on her clit with one hand and thrusting her hips down on him with the other.

"Mmmhmm." She nods obediently. Angie throws her head back with a loud, breathy gasp, soaking his lap.

"Damn girl, you're so *wet*," he says with a proud smirk. But he can sense there's something *not quite right*. Something bizarre about the way Angie clenches around his cock. There's something strange about her silent mouth, open, gulping wildly for air. Pulsing eyes rolling into the back of her head. There's something *abnormal* about the way she shudders. He feels her jolt forward, lunging at his face with her own. Stopping inches from his beard.

That's when he sees it.

That's when he sees a black spike extruding through her mouth. He watches as the serrated point protrudes from her distending cheeks.

Then, he *hears* it.

It's the sickly *crunch* of skeletal *cracking*. A jawbone violently rearranged. Mick sees Angie's teeth, once rooted in firm gums, cascading in hunks out of her mouth. He realizes the sudden rush of fluid was from the brook of blood drooling down her spine. And urine, expelled as her skull crushed in.

The menacing, bone-white grin of the creature behind her shimmers like a waning moon. It whips her backward, yanking its extremity back out with a revolting slurp. The spike withdraws from the space between her cheeks. He sees the cavernous hole left behind. The severed brain stem.

The hole in the tunnel offers a fleeting glimpse of the wall beyond.

Angie slumps over, as limp as Mick's dick is. A hot gush of blood trickles from her lips into his screaming mouth. Onto his *tongue*.

But he doesn't care about that.

He only cares about the off-kilter gaze of the thing, black as a void, breathing down on him.

69

Against the vivid plum haze of the night sky, the gaping doorway makes the decrepit shack look like the structure is screaming. The cracked windows look like unblinking, bloodshot eyes. Eyes staring ahead in terror. Its crumbling steps look like cracked rows of hillbilly teeth.

CRACK! Crack-snap! Thump.

The noise is coming from inside, like bones snapped in half. A gentle toxic-green radiance follows the sound.

CRACK! Crack-crack-snap!

...Thu-thump

The neon-chartreuse light intensifies from within.

"The glow sticks," Iris whispers to Jack as they make their way through the overgrowth. Through the knee-high brush, they stalk like terrified soldiers in the jungles of Vietnam. "I remember seeing bunches of them when we were in there. Sounds like someones cracking them and throwing them on the floor."

They creep up the creaky porch. Jack pushes the door open. The shack is a pit of blackness, save for the ominous luminescence of the glow sticks.

Eeeeeeeeeeeeeeeeeee.

The door squeals. Jack widens his eyes to see in the green glow.

"Nurse Tate?" Iris calls quietly, hoping someone will answer back. *"Walsh?"*

Jack's bare foot sinks into a rotten hole on the porch outside the door, sending him crashing to the ground with a painful *smack*.

"You okay," she whispers, hunching to his aid. He hisses and nods, staggering to his feet.

Timid, Iris leads the way down the hallway, toward the origin of the illumination. Jack follows, limping.

They hear something...

Flies.

The gentle buzz increases and it doesn't take them long to find the source. She extends the lamp's globe into the room, alive with the sound of insects. The bedroom floor is now covered in wet piles of excrement. Iris covers her mouth at the putrid sight to keep from throwing up. Jack gags at the overpowering stench. The winged creatures feast on the mess of shit, while others buffet on the child's mattress, steeped in blood and bile.

Mired in the muck, they see something else. Something still and familiar, with scrawny, bent hind legs. Gnarled rib bones jut out of its carcass. It's the catahoula – *or rather,* what little *remains* of it. They can tell by the spots on the tuft of fur still tethered to its gnawed spinal column.

Iris lurches forward, unable to control her gag reflex, and launches more vile matter into the mix. She nearly drops the lamp into the befouled jumble of wet mush, handing it off to Jack instead. He takes it, using the illumination to examine their surroundings.

Dizzy from the smell, Iris holds the wall to steady herself. Her hand presses into deep, splintered grooves. *Claw marks.* From something larger than a grizzly, by the look of it. She pulls her hand away like they contain acid, stumbling back into the room across the hall, the room glowing with neon sticks.

There's a new noise now, quiet and steady. Something huge. *Gnawing* on slick viscera. Bones splintering between powerful masticating jaws…

"*Dr. Walsh?*" Her voice is mousy. She feels like she's suffocating in her fear. With a quick step inside, she trips over something substantial. She falls hard, landing on something lumpy and wet. "Jack!"

She's crying now, bawling on her knees. Feeling the lukewarm structure beneath her. She raises her hands to see if she's covered in blood or slime... or both. But it's so dark she can only see the silhouette of her palms against the glow sticks.

"Iris?" Jack makes his way in with the lamp in a flash, lighting up the room so they can see what she's fallen in, filling her with instant regret as her teraful eyes soak in what's before her.

The leg she tripped on leads to a torso, wrapped in a once-white lab coat, spattered in thick globules of gore. The wrists poking through the sleeves are gashed deep. Puddles of black-red glisten in the flickering light, pooled beneath them. In the crook of the body's left arm sits a soaked stuffed animal: a pink rabbit with a dopey look on its face, smiling merrily despite the horrors around it. As if it's expression says: *Just another day in paradise.*

The corpse has no head.

Just a gruesome void where a head *should be.*

From its gnashed throat hangs a jellyfish of severed arteries, shorn tendons, and wiry tendrils, along with a cranial bowl full of blood-slicked brain matter, covered in silver hair.

70

"WHERE THE FUCK IS HIS HEAD?!" Jack's bellow echoes through the hall.

"I don't know!" She cries, shrilly.

He pants feverishly at the sight of James Walsh's headless corpse. He shoves the lamp at Iris and topples to his knees in the hallway, dribbling drool onto the floor as he dry heaves. She peels herself out of the tacky puddle of cooling ichor, scrambling backward until she's seated next to Jack. They tremble like dogs in the snow.

She notices something propped beside Walsh's body:

TO WHOM IT MAY CONCERN, the sticky note on the front says.

Jack crouches by the corpse, past a fistful of unsnapped glow sticks tucked in Walsh's labcoat pocket. He plucks up the folder, holding it open toward the flame of the hurricane lamp.

It's a patient file labeled: *JESSICA WALSH.*

He reads the handwritten letter paper-clipped to the top of the folder, penned in shaky cursive.

"I've seen the devil himself. He lies not within a creature, but in the man responsible for Jessica's death."

Behind them, something emerges from the shadowed room at the end of the hall, silencing the chain around its neck with its mammoth hand. It slinks like a malevolent phantom.

"When he nearly killed my daughter, he tore my family and career to shreds. As the inner light

in Jessica extinguished, premature testing of Obsidian began. In an act of desperation, I administered the medication before fully understanding its subsequent atrocious deformities. In my haste to save her – to heal her – I destroyed the only thing that ever mattered. Jessica is the cursed product of my own creation. In the years since, I have become the monster. In her agony, I allowed rage to cloud my judgment. In my lust for revenge, I spread a malady meant for only one: Jack LeBlanc."

The confused look on Iris's face gives Jack pause. He's visibly ashamed, shaken by the letter. He continues,

"I needed LeBlanc to suffer like she did. The others were never supposed to become afflicted. One of the 'patients' broke in and, for whatever reason, switched the placebos with the medication intended for him. I promised him he wouldn't get the placebo and I intended to keep that promise. It's far too late for them now. They're cursed. Regrettable cannon fodder in a malicious scheme I've regretted since day one of this manufactured trial. They can't escape the inevitability of this metamorphosis. They're all marked for death. I can't bear to look at myself. I can't keep up this charade. For the victims of my crimes, words cannot express the depth of my regret.

Tonight, I came to be with my daughter one final time. To allow her to usher me from this life just as I ushered her into it. Whoever finds this, I beg of you this one last request: please, make her

death swift and painless. Just as I should've done all those years ago."

A huge, hellish beast inches toward the enthralled patients, so massive it dwarfs them with its size.

"I don't understand. Wh--what did he mean when he said you nearly killed his daughter?"

He solemnly croaks, "it was an *accident*." The words weigh as much as boulders, and yet, they don't explain anything.

"Wh--why's he talking about her like she's still *alive*?"

A long rope of slime dribbles down between them onto the letter, originating from the evil oral fissure hovering above them.

Iris's eyes bulge and she screams.

CCCCRAAAAAAAAAAAATTTT!

It lets loose a *horrid* noise from its widened mouth, flossed with goo and human hair. The smell it emits is the scent of concentrated death. *Of decay*.

It drops its chains to the floorboards with a ringy *thud* and rushes toward them.

They scream, almost in unison, and scramble back to the far wall.

CHING!

The chains pull taut, yanking the creature back by the throat, like a vicious, snarling dog on a leash. It swipes at them like a wild animal, hoping to lacerate them with its curly, calcified nails embedded in long, gooey fingers, but they're just out of reach.

The thing slams forward again and again, inches away. The chains hold steady, keeping the thing at bay. They eye the doorway, knowing they don't have enough clearance to make it unscathed. Quaking, they stay glued to the wall. Iris shields herself with the patient folder from rows of evil-looking teeth as they chomp like a junkyard doberman.

Eyes flitting for *anything* that will ensure his survival, Jack catches a glimpse of something small and colorful hung from a push-pin near a dusty framed picture of Jessica and Walsh, hugging in front of a mountain range.

It's all starting to click together in his fraying mind.

As Jack stares at the picture, he remembers the vile look of the catahoula soaking in the carnage, seated patiently, close enough to the wreckage to smell the coppery blood vacating his young owner.

He recalled the twitch of a young girl's hand, flinging droplets of rust-red liquid onto the tall grass. He remembered the beaded-letter bracelet she wore on her tremoring wrist. A bracelet that read:

JESSICA.

He saw it through the wafting plumes of smoke from the hood as he tried to crawl through the window, dick snared by crushed jaws full of forever-stilled teeth. He'd never been able to shake the image of her dangling hand and the horrific reality that he'd not only stolen his wife's life...

But an innocent little girl's too.

It was a moment he was forced to relive during the trial when Walsh begged the judge for the maximum sentences for Reckless Endangerment and Manslaughter. Jack could never forget the venomous look of hatred the little girl's father displayed when Jack was granted leniency for having a record clean of priors.

It was leniency they *both* felt he didn't deserve.

In the years since, through the painful burns and surgeries, through the bouts of physical therapy and reconstruction, through the nights spent crying himself to sleep on a threadbare cot in a prison cell, he carried one wish in his heart:

That he could trade places with Kate and the girl. That he could restore *their* lives by sacrificing his *own*.

It all starts to make sense to Jack as the chained beast gropes the dirty floor, seeking to latch its twisty claws onto their flesh.

The slick, black abomination before him is somehow... *Walsh's little girl.*

"Jessica?" His voice shakes.

The creature's head whips toward him, cocking sideways, like a dog's.

Like the goddamned catahoula, he thinks.

Iris trembles, more confused than ever at the reaction. At how Jack knew what to call it. At the familiarity in his tone.

The creature cranes its neck, jingling its chains. It takes a messy bite out of the hunk of tissue of Walsh's neck, pulling wormy veins out like a hyena feeding on a fresh kill.

Iris blurts out a nauseous cry. It whips its head back, splattering thick, clotting blood on their faces. Jack screams, unable to control himself. But the beast isn't looking at *him*.

No. Its entranced by the exposed flame of the hurricane lamp in Iris's pale palms.

"I-i-it's *this*." Jack sputters in a moment of realization. "It's the *fire*. " He takes it from Iris, watching the creature's softball-sized eyes follow with fascination.

71

"Walsh?" Fisher hollers as he makes his way through the clinic. He stumbles around the room, feeling through the darkness until he reaches the back wall. He pounds a fist on it, a sheen of sweat shimmering across him. He yells up at the ceiling, "Walsh! Wake the fuck up! We need you down here! There's…There's…" He doesn't know how to finish. Too many things are racing through his mind.

WHAM!

The brute outside throws itself at the glass door, smearing it with clots of black mucus. Moonlight bathes its clustered eyeballs, bathes the tumorous lumps along its body. It slams its calcified spike at the door and Fisher flinches at the thunderous noise.

Reeeeeeeeahhhhhhhh! The creature screeches, infuriated.

THWACK!

It whacks the door again, this time with the lump acting as a head, one full of slimy teeth. The impact cracks the door. Fisher feels the door frame and trails down to the knob. He opens it, rushes in, and promptly locks it. He shoves his back to the door, feeling the rapid thump of his heart pulse against the wood. Glass shatters and a guttural growl rings out.

Beep-beep.

The polite mechanical sound chirps. It's a battery backup, warning the owner about the lack of electrical power. The computer monitor is on, powered by the device, casting a passive glow on the room. He rifles through the contents of Walsh's desk, looking for the landline he's seen displayed during his morning exams. He takes a step forward to look elsewhere and howls out, nearly dropping to his knees from the searing pain in the arch of his foot. He braces on the desk and plucks a busted shard of plastic out of his meat with a hiss.

He examines it. The color and curvature are strange. He looks down at the debris to see numbered buttons scattered next to a gnarled pile of plastic. *It's the phone.*

WHAM!

Reeeeeeeeeaaaaaaaaaaaaaaahhhhhh!

The door to Walsh's office bulges inward with a thud, paired with another ear-shattering screech. Fisher touches along the walls feeling for the door leading to the upstairs.

He finds it! A sense of relief rushes through him until he tries the knob. Locked. "Fuck," he growls, yanking on it with all of his might, but it's thick and doesn't budge.

WHAM!

The creature at the door throws its clumsy, growing body against the wood again. The middle of the door, near the handle, starts to crack and splinter. Fisher can hear little bits of debris hitting the floor.

"Walsh, if you're up there, you had better come the fuck down NOW!" He orders, fighting the chatter of his teeth, looking for a place to hide. He recalls the room is modest, boasting only a few cabinets, a desk, a chair and the wall armoire.

He slides one of the weighty file cabinets to the door with a metallic groan. It topples against him and drawers come sliding out. He thrusts the clumsy weight of it toward the entrance. It careens onto its side with a clatter, blocking the base of the exit. *That'll have to do for now,* he thinks.

He rushes to the armoire, thinking maybe he can hide inside. He swings open the doors and topples backward over Walsh's chair at the sight of Eileen Tate, mangled. Full of rigor. He falls onto the overturned filing cabinet.

WHAM! Another beastly attack on the splintering door, cracking the grain of the wood. A shard of it goes flying, leaving a gap just wide enough for the beast to slither its drooling tongue into the room. It feels around, like a blind snake, tapping down on Fisher's shoulder.

He screams.

72

Jack and Iris watch as the beast's mouth opens wider than they ever thought possible. It is paired with the sound of bones breaking as it turns itself nearly inside out. The screech it emits is ear-piercing. With powerful alligator-like force, the two halves of its face snap back together with jaws large enough to sever a limb whole. Or a *head*…

Trembling, Jack eyes the decapitated remains of Dr. Walsh. The loosened meat draping out of the stump where there was once a cranium. The sliced-through trachea is like an off-white tunnel into nothingness.

"Here," Jack turns the knob on the side, raising the intensity of the flame inside the glass, brightening the room. He sets it on the floor close to that thing… to *Jessica*… like an offering. It's enthralled, mesmerized by the blinding core. He pushes it closer with his foot, careful not to knock it over. As the thing's repulsive, curled fingernails reach out to touch the globe of it, he snatches Iris by the hand.

"Go!" Clinging to the wall side, he yanks her out the door, folder in hand. His bleeding, bare feet pound through the grass, cracking sticks, tearing on bristled detritus beneath. But his need to survive overpowers the pain. He pulls Iris toward the far right edge of the property.

"Where are we going?!" She is screaming now.

"The storage shed!" His voice is more frantic and aggressive than he intends.

"Why? Why not the *road*? We could flag someone down!"

"It gotta be a half a mile to Airline at *least*. There are *tools* in the shed! *Weapons*! The chances of us outrunning these things on foot–"

CRAGGGGGGHHHHHHH!

Over his shoulder, he sees a ball of orange light woof through the open doorway, overpowering the green haze of the glow sticks. The thing screams. *It's hellish.* The fire morphs from a *crackle* to a *roar* in seconds as the shack catches fire like a pile of dry tinder.

Jack turns back to watch his path. He hears its painful, haunting screams as the orange light engulfs the building.

He experiences a strange pang of guilt. *Or is it empathy?* After all, he knows exactly how it feels to be engulfed in flames.

...To know you're going to die in them.

RAAHHHHHHHHH!

What remains of Jessica shrieks, tortured by searing agony as her gooey glaze sizzles. Chains clang with monstrous intensity, slapping the charcoal walls in its yellowed blaze. The derelict building smokes into the humid bayou air from all of the places the rotten building has fallen apart through years of nature's cruel, elemental abuse.

73

Fisher bellows from atop the overturned cabinet on the floor, the spiked creature's tongue lapping at him from the crevasse over his shoulder. He can feel pulsing in his arms, where Obsidian had once healed him. Where pink scars are now replaced by black, oozing scabs. They move and writhe, squirming beneath his dermis as if they're communicating with the tongue. *As if they are trying to join together.* As if they wish to become one horrific mass of goo and barbs and teeth.

The tongue retracts.

Silence. And then…

WHAM!

Fisher bolts to his feet, but he's too late. The last, powerful *whack* cracks up the whole length of the door. Before Fisher can run, there's a shooting pain in his abdomen, followed by the sound of his own panting breath in his ears. He opens his mouth to scream but, instead, hot blood burbles through his lips like spent motor oil, glistening down his chest. The pressure in his torso feels almost explosive, like he's being detonated from the inside with a grenade.

He looks down. A three-foot tapered spike is piercing his lungs and vital organs. The dark matter within him churns. The final thing he sees is the whip-fast removal of the serrated, skewering extremity and the sudden expulsion of his maimed entrails, once tucked safely within his fascia. They tumble toward the floor like dropped groceries.

The contents of his bowels and bladder follow suit. He clutches the hole as he drops.

As the blackness envelops him, something in him *undulates*, ready to void the shell that is Fisher. Ready to make its escape into the the darkness, into the open air. Ready to join its brethren.

74

Black clouds belch out of the gaps in the broken windows, staining the broken-down shack in soot. The roar of pain fills the night sky and the cacophony of the tumultuous wildlife on the bayou's edge is no contest for its volume.

Jack keeps his bloodshot eyes locked on the storage shed across the compound as they race through the field. Eerie moonlight reflects in the building's galvanized bends and waves. As they make their way to the door, Iris glances back at the flaming structure, collapsing in the middle from the burning, sagging roof. The front room crushes inward with a wooden groan. The entryway tumbles into a pile of charred rubble on the patio. The smoke has shifted into hues of deep violet as it bleeds up into the ether, now the color of an over-ripened concord grape.

The purple-tinted night sky used to be Iris's favorite thing about Louisiana. Now, it serves as an ominous symbol of lives lost, and more forever changed.

75

Awestruck, Mick looks at Angie's limp, bleeding carcass crumpled in the bed beside him. From the cavern bored in the back of her skull, something pointy protrudes, like a slick worm from the soil's surface, feeling its way around. It slithers from inside her, filling the cavity with its growing pieces and parts. *It wants out.* It gruffly parts the plates of her ossified skull with sounds like a melon being hammered.

Something stirs behind the creature that hovers over him, the one drooling greasy, black matter onto his chest in globular pitter-patters. It glowers at the blackened holes in Mick's knees, entranced by the grotesque transformation taking place there. It emits a gurgled screech, like a pterodactyl's dying shrieks as it flounders in the LaBrea Tar Pits.

"What... the... *fuck?!*" Mick feels his teeth chattering like a wind-up toy. They clack together, mimicking the jittery movements of his trembling hands.

The second being, nearly as tall as the first, nears the foot of the bed. It leaves a string of slime trailing from its limbs. It's littered with clots, sliding down the goo coating its exterior. It is not until they begin to blink that Mick realizes they are eyeballs, mired in pinguid matter. The interstitial material between them undulates like bubbling stew in a kettle.

Mick shoves Angie's bleeding corpse to the ground like a discarded rag doll. He rolls himself down, too, using her warm, wet body to break his fall. He scrambles beneath his cot, screaming.

The slimy beast kneels and bares its hideously-bunched layers of teeth. The squish of its legs sounds like sponges being wrung out. It slams a barbed spike into his exposed ankle, spearing it clean through. He screams, tears falling from his clenched eyes. The barb catches. Mick is yanked out. He grabs the frame, jiggling the structure on the plastic cup risers, struggling to stay under for protection.

The creature bites onto his left hand and Mick hollers again, wrist in searing pain. He lets go of the bed and the beast whips him out into the middle of the room, like a mastiff with a chew toy.

Mick grasps at anything he can with his uninjured hand, finding purchase on his dumped-over duffel bag. He catches the strap with his flailing fingers.

The thing bites down harder, nearly severing his hand completely, glove-and-all, grinding down chunks of bone and muscle and swallowing them greedily,

He caterwauls, viewing the mangled remnants of his irreparable wrist. It looks like ground chuck. His palm is held on by only a few remaining tendons garnished with jagged shards of crushed ulna. His other hand reaches the bag and he finally touches the ridged design of his 9mm pistol. He grasps it tightly.

The drooling being watches Mick through its thousands of blinking, gelatinous eyes. Mick feels the pressure in his knees now. The wormy things inside of him are moving his kneecaps and nerves and tendons. They gash open like fault lines. Something dark is clawing its way out of him, widening holes Finn once drilled in his patellas as some sort of an entry portal into the putrid air beyond.

BOOM!

Mick fires off a bullet in the first beast's chest. It screeches and jolts backward but recovers, unfazed.

BOOM! BOOM!

He unloads two more bullets. The creature is unperturbed, not alarmed in the slightest. Tentacle-like extremities worm their way out of the holes made by the bullets giving the thing new, baby extremities that seem to expand in the air.

The eyeball-covered creature shoves its thorny, spinuled limb into the meaty tissue of his calf and tugs him across the floor.

As he's dragged, he sees something hideous. Another... *thing*... is crawling out of Angie's discarded corpse. Something mired in her jellied brain matter. Its tiny flippers slap onto the ground near her ears, smearing bloody mucus in her rust-colored locks.

Mick raises a fingerless-gloved middle finger at the staring, tumorous beast glowering beside him. The one unperturbed by the three bullets he put inside of it.

"Fuck... you!" He turns the gun toward himself.

...And pulls the trigger.

76

BOOM!

The gunshot echoes across the lawn.

Jack skitters to a halt, u-turning. Iris's blue eyes bulge as she scrambles to pull him back toward the storage building. "What are you doing?! Don't go back there!"

"*Mick!*" He pants his friend's name in a fear-filled breath like it's an entire explanation. "He's my friend, Iris! I can't just leave him there!"

"Jack!"

"Go see if you can find something in the shed. A weapon! I'll be right behind you, I promise!"

She growls in frustration and stamps her foot in the grass. She scrambles up the steps of the windowless shed, catching a glimpse of two creatures, one large, one small, lumbering clumsily out of Walsh's clinic onto the grass. The towering, gangly one whips its head at her, gifting her with a clear, nightmarish view of its wide rows of blood-drenched fangs.

77

All is quiet when he gets to Mick's room. *Too quiet.* Jack steps quietly around the corner, struggling to keep weight on his injured foot.

"God, Mick," he whispers, as he notices Mick's fingerless-gloved hand. Then he sees the rest of him. Lifeless. Naked on the ground. Covered in black slime and injuries from head to cock. As the words escape his mouth, one of the beasts whips its lumpy head at him from the darkened corner where it is feasting on another. It bares its gore-caked teeth.

Jack spots another by it, a separate entity, birthing from a nude female on the floor. He thinks the corpse might be Angie, but in the dark, *with all that blood*, it's too difficult to tell. The thing cracks her sternum in half, tearing her breasts into ragged flaps of shorn fat.

Snaking extrusions ease their way out of the raven-black cavities in Mick's bare knees.

Two seconds to soak in the visual before him feels like a *lifetime* to Jack. He scrambles backward, slipping in the clotted blood and slime on the wooden floor, smashing back through the narrow hallway with his shoulders like an out-of-control pinball.

78

THUD-THUD-THUD!

Someone is bashing the side of the storage shed door, and it scares Iris half to death until she hears a familiar voice behind it.

"Let me in! Please, Iris!" Jack sounds panicked. She can hear the faint screeches beyond him.

Iris unlatches the door and presses it open just a crack. Jack, panting, presses her through the door. As he turns to shut it behind them, he catches one last glance at the burning building across the way. Jessica's massive, clawed hand slides down the broken window, leaving a smear of black tar down the busted glass.

Guilt swells. He feels like he's killing her all over again.

Without any pleasantries, he slams the door shut, locks it, and wipes his crying eyes with the spattered sleeve of his hoodie. He stumbles through the darkness to the far wall, feeling his way through in the pitch-black.

"Did you find anything," he asks in a hope-tinged tone.

"No," she sobs, "it's too dark! I don't know what the fuck is *what*!"

He stumbles over to her, using the workbench as a familiar north star to guide him back. Jack feels around. As soon as his skin makes contact with hers, he wraps her in a tight hug and kisses her head. He feels her tear-streaked face and plants a kiss on her lips. Though he can't see her, he whispers with compassion. "We're going to get through this, Iris, okay?"

"Okay," she cries, sucking in a wet sniff of air.

He releases her and feels his way back to the wall. "There's gotta be… something we can use in here." He's out of breath, rummaging blindly through boxes and shelves, feeling for a flashlight or a weapon.

"This is... *insane*!" Iris touches around in the dark, finding a medium-sized box half-full of circular objects. Touching them with her fingertips, she realizes they are waxy, with wicks. Her heart leaps with excitement. *It's a bulk box of tea lights!*

She feels around in the bin, clumsily digging through the items when her hands find something plastic and rod-like with a trigger. She depresses it and a flame spurts out of the tip of the long-necked lighter. She gasps, relieved. "Yes!"

As she ignites some tiny candles, they're now able to see vague shapes of what's in front of them. He grabs at a broomstick and cracks it over a corner of the sturdy table. He uses one of the pieces to prop the door's locking mechanism, jamming it tight against the lever.

Just then…

BAM!

Something slams hard on the other side of the door, denting a pointed cone right into the galvanized sheet metal. Iris shrieks.

BAM! It bashes again, screeching that horrid screech that no human could ever make. It shakes the wood beneath them, rattling it like a subwoofer.

They can hear the *click-clack-click-clack* of the bony, spiked appendages dragging along the waves of the aluminum like knives across a washboard. After lighting more candles, Iris collapses into the corner, overwhelmed. Her head bobs forward with every slam of the beast outside. She presses her back against crisscrossed studs on the door, clutching the broken broomstick with one arm so it can't jiggle loose. She guards the only entrance with the fleeting bit of courage remaining in her.

The pounding stops for a moment and they can hear noises. *Chittering*. Two voices. As if they are communicating with each other, beyond the door, in a vibrato gurgle unlike anything they've ever heard.

Iris blinks hard, squeezing tears from her puffy eyes. Jack fumbles through more boxes, dumping contents on the floor in pursuit of something useful. He turns back toward Iris and slips on something slick, catching himself on a shelf, ripping it off the wall.

"You okay?"

"Yeah," he grumbles, examining the source of the liquid. He'd slipped on his own blackened blood, oozing from the wound on his foot when he sank through the porch. The adrenaline and shock of the situation nearly made him forget about the injury's severity. It's gashed open wide, exposing meat and tendons.

Iris tosses down the stained file and peers at the photos that are sliding out of the back of the folder. She fans them across the floor. They're gory, featuring a little blonde girl in a bed, hooked up to IV's.

The noises Iris makes concern him. Her heavy sobs turn into moans. He knows she's emotionally unraveling. He kneels beside her, unsure what to say to comfort her, yet wanting to. He wraps an arm around her.

"Why didn't you *tell* me about Walsh's daughter?" She asks shrugging him away.

He's taken aback by the question. "I was ashamed. It's not something I go around advertising. It was an *accident*. A *horrible* fucking accident. That… goodamned *dog* ran out in front of me. I swerved so I wouldn't hit it. I went off the road. Kate, my wife, died on impact. But *Jessica*…" The tears are falling now, steady like jungle rain. "I didn't see her there! And… She suffered. Horribly! I was sure she died! Not a day goes by that I don't *hate myself* for what happened! Believe me, Iris, if I could trade places with *either* of them, I would. In a *second!*" His voice is cracking now, strained from all the night's screaming.

A creature smashes into the door. She yelps, heart slamming around the walls of her chest like a racquetball.

BAM! Another hit.

BAM-BAM! Two are pounding now, bashing the door in tandem like linebackers.

WHAM!

"W-what does the file say?" He stutters, pointing down at the folder, hoping to distract her from the dangers outside.

Iris examines it, wiping her reddened eyes raw. "I-I-it's a patient log. It's notes about Jessica taking Obsidian. It says..." she reads from the page, "the accident required her to be put into a medically-induced coma. After two weeks on a ventilator, the hospital released her to Walsh for hospice care at home. He started giving her the drug there." She ruffles through more pages, trying her best to block out the banging overhead. "A week into the course of treatment, her surgical wounds and accident injuries healed. Everything but the burns. Day eight... looks like... she... came out of the coma."

Jack stands and resumes rifling through boxes searching for something. *Anything*. Ideally, a tool to bludgeon or cut with.

Iris studies the paper-clipped photo of Jessica healing, rampant injuries at bay. "Then it says, on day ten she started experiencing *severe* side effects."

"What do you mean?"

"I'm looking." She flips to the next photo. It features youthful Jessica, holding a stuffed rabbit on her bed, crying. Blackened spikes jut out of her outstretched hand, reaching for the camera.

The beasts outside claw and hiss. One sounds like it's climbing atop the other. It clamors up to the tin roof of the building and stomps overhead. Soon, a third joins their ranks, its voice higher than the rest.

"It looks like on day ten, it says she got a paper-cut. Within hours, she developed black, spindly *protrusions*. Walsh terminated Obsidian, but–"

The next photos she flips through show the process of the blackness tearing through the little girl, molting her epidermis like a snake's old skin. Sloughing bones out of perforations in the new orifices. There's a blurry photo of her from the shoulders up, the girl's terrified face is peeling back like the thing beneath is shedding a silicone Halloween mask. The transformation looks excruciating, judging by Jessica's silent screams.

Jack finds a pair of hedge-clippers and hands them to Iris as a possible weapon. She nods as if she's in a bad dream and puts them across her lap. "Oh my God," she says in a hushed tone, eyes darting across the pages. "It says after seeing what she'd become, Walsh tried to 'terminate her' with lethal doses of pain meds."

"*Jesus.*"

"It didn't work, obviously." She points over her shoulder in the direction of the shack they vacated. "He restrained her. He–" She gasps at something on the next page.

"*What?*"

She lowers the hand covering her mouth. "He tried to shoot her. She was in excruciating pain. But he said 'the bullet hole only exposed the inner affliction to more air, expediting the metamorphosis.' There's a sticky note on the page that says 'oxygenation initiates the transformation. Fuels it.'"

The creature above body-slams the roof, sagging in the corrugated tin over Jack's head, scaring the shit out of him. He screams up at the ceiling and punches the metal wall in front of him. He takes a deep breath, holding his pained fist.

"Does it say anything about him working on a cure? A--a-an antidote? *Something*?!"

The way he screams the last word, she can tell he's unraveling. "Um, it says he did a round of testing on lab rats afterward." She shuffles through, eyes scanning the pages. "The same thing happened to them. He says here… 'with the rodents, *fire* is the only thing that seems to kill the transformative tissue for good.'"

"I don't get it." He dumps another box onto the floor after sifting through the contents. "Why keep that *thing* around?"

"I guess maybe… its because," she is grasping at straws, "it was still his *daughter*."

"*Daughter*? That *creature* back there, that wasn't *human*."

"Yeah, *now*. But maybe he still *saw* it as Jessica. Like she was *in there* somewhere. I don't know. Probably lost his nerve. If she's like this, all these years later, I think it's obvious he didn't find a cure."

"Goddammit!" He squats on his haunches, a lost look in his eyes, feeling his heart flutter in his throat.

She presses the folder shut, tosses it to the floor, picking up the hedge trimmers. She pries the jaws of the cumbersome tool open.

He scans the room again, spots a chainsaw. His laugh rings in the metal box they're trapped in. "Yes!" But his celebration is short-lived. As he pulls it out of the pile of clutter, his smile dissipates.

No pull-cord. Only two prongs where an extension cord should plug. It's *electric.*

He hurls the chainsaw down violently and screams, feeling the sting of it in his throat, his gut.

WHAMMMM! Another resounding slam at the door, bowing the entrance inward permanently with the impact, pressing Iris forward. She rises to her feet, furiously staring through the half-inch gap in the warped door frame. She sees glimpses of them thrashing like black sludge in a garbage disposal.

"Leave us alooooooone!" She buries her face in her hands to scream.

Jack looks at the scar on her scapula dribbling runny tendrils of black sludge down her back from each carved letter: *S.L.U.T.*

It's like a nightmare he'd give anything to wake from. The reality of the situation sinks in...

They're going to die.

Slowly. *Surely.*

He stops searching, shoulders slumping. "Maybe Walsh was right in his letter. Maybe this *has* to stop here! If we leave, we could unleash whatever *this* is. *We could spread it.* Those things are coming out of us. I *saw* it, Iris, I *swear.* I watched what it did to Alan, just... breaking him open... and *Mick.*" He's crying now, sobbing. He doesn't know when the shaking of his voice started or when the faucet of tears started. "Jesus Christ... *Mick.*"

She turns to him, waving her hands like an infuriated football referee. "Maybe they can quarantine us till they find the answer. There's got to be *someone* out there who can *fix us!*"

"Who, Iris?! *Who's* going to *fix* us?"

"I don't know! But even if it takes a while, we've still got to *try*!"

"*Do* we? And what if they *can't*? People still die of cancer. Or the flu. Things that have been around for *ages*. You think they're going to be able to just somehow fix this? You're insane to think that! They're going to *dissect* us… *both*. Iris, they'll cut us open and poke and fuckin' *prod* us like *lab rats*! That is, if they don't just straight-up *kill* us on sight! I mean, seeing *this* shit, they won't *give* us the chance to explain. This thing births through wounded skin—"

The thought stops him cold.

He looks down at the shredded flesh on the top of his foot, glistening in the light of the candle. The blood encrusted on it in veiny webs is not red, like he assumed.

It's black as *pitch*.

A tethered clump of it writhes across the open wound like gooey spider legs. But Iris can't see what he does. She's listening to the furious *click-clack-click-clack* of spiny spikes as the beings try to pry their way through the bent-metal crevasse they've dented into the door.

Jack examines his palm where he removed stitches days before. It is seeping now, too. Gray slime seethes from the cut. His voice is quiet now. *Grim*. "I won't spend what's left of my life like some animal in a cage."

"We have to *try*, Jack."

"I can't, Iris! I can't go back to that. I've already done it! I spent five years in a concrete box. I wouldn't wish that hell on *anyone*. It's not a *life*!" He hollers. "These things… they're *in* us! We're not getting out of here alive."

"You just told me we are going to be okay!" There's fury in her voice now.

There's a lengthy silence between them where the screeching bastards outside are making the only noise at all. He speaks again, with an unrivaled bleakness. "I know, but… We have to make sure this thing never spreads."

The words are ominous. Iris doesn't like what he's getting at. "*How*?"

Jack walks to the corner and picks up a gallon jug of lamp oil. He picks up the long-necked lighter with the other hand and looks at her. His suggestion makes her rush to the far corner to vomit, heaving and sobbing with everything left in her.

His voice is quiet again. "We could end this right here and now. Go out on *our* terms. *You and me*. And we could take those things down with us."

She doesn't reply. She wipes the bile from her lips and stares at him with eyes as innocent as a child's.

"You read that stuff he wrote about the lab rats." He points to the file with the lighter. "You saw how that *thing* reacted to the fire. You saw how this shit healed everything in us *except* my burns. That is *not* a coincidence."

BAM! A beast blasts the door, rattling it almost off its hinges.

After a moment of thought, she tearfully mumbles, "This'll die with us?"

"Yeah, I really think it would. Look," a tear falls from his eye, "I can't stop you. If you want to take your chances out there..." He trails off because what he's saying is pointless. With the creatures at the only entrance, there is nowhere for either of them to go. If they leave, every scenario ends with them dead. Jack hands her the lighter and removes the cap from the lamp oil. The pungent scent of kerosene fills the air. He yanks down his hood, baring his full face to her once more. He looks up at her with tears in his eyes, one of them malformed, pulled tight from healed tissue grafts. He turns away and upends the jug of clear, potent liquid, drizzling its noxious contents all over the shed. He finishes by pouring the remnants on himself, dolloping some on his scalp, letting it dribble down his sweat-matted mop of hair. He doesn't want to chance surviving the burns a second time.

Iris, shuddering as she cries, triggers the lighter. A flame shoots out of the tip, high and bright. Jack holds up the patient folder between them and Iris lights it ablaze. Once lit, he tosses it into the pile of clutter in the back of the shed. It erupts with a woof, fueled by the accelerant.

"Jack…" It's all Iris can muster to say.

Jack grabs Iris and kisses her, hard and long, as the flames engulf the room, leaving no ounce of love unexpressed.

He tugs out the shard of broom handle keeping the door locked and the malformed hunk of metal creaks open. Gray smoke wafts through the only exit, fueling the fire with fresh oxygen.

It feels like the end of the world.

But it's only the end of *theirs*.

Jack stares, one last time, at those shimmering azure eyes of hers. He runs a scarred kerosene-soaked thumb along the dimples in her cheeks. He loves her already. He knows it. He's felt it for days. Not for her body. Or for having a smile that could stop traffic. He loves her for her kind soul. And for the willingness to accept him as he is, flaws and all.

Those monstrous feelings about his hideous exterior and heinous actions suddenly don't seem so horrific now that he's choking on black clouds, feeling spindly protrusions retract behind the wounded skin of his foot at the growing heat.

In another life, things could have been different, he thinks.

In another life, things could have been good.

The pounding creatures rush through the dented door, gnashing them with viscous fangs, piercing their malleable bodies with powerful, bony extremities.

However, the smattering of beings soon realize their deadly mistake, screeching their wails of horror and pain, clods of eyeballs wide with terror. Wide with the understanding that they're ablaze.

In his fleeting moments of life, the sick humor of it all is not lost on Jack. Because in this life, this world, things *aren't* different. *Or* good.

No, in this life…

The world is on fucking fire.

79

Several onlookers stand against a canary-yellow line of caution tape tied to the oak trunks at the edge of the drive. The stripe funnels them back into the overgrown mud road. They gawk at sinister plumes poisoning the air as the fire torches the buildings in the distance. Eddie whizzes past a stunning field reporter as she adjusts her tight blazer, and tries to duck under the tape.

"Sir, no one is allowed past the line!" A female officer stops him with a firm hand on his recently-bruised chest, shoving the scrawny man backwards. He steps back.

"Did they make it out? Did *Mick* make it out? What 'da fuck happened?"

"Sir, I'm gonna have to ask you to calm down and stay back behind the line." The cop glowers at him.

"My fuckin' *friend* is in there! Can you 'least tell me if he's alive?!"

She crosses her arms. Eddie stares angrily from the tape. He absentmindedly touches one of the cuts on his arm. *Wounds that are markedly better a day later.* As he looks at it, he remembers that it's time for more medication. He digs in his filthy jeans and pops another of the black pills Mick gave him in Walsh's office into his mouth, using his saliva to dry-swallow it.

The reporter watches the cameraman in front of her countdown with his fingers.

3…2…1… She springs to life, reminding herself to hold her grave expression. "We're back now," she states, serious eyes glittering in the luminescence of the onboard light. She sweeps a tuft of clean hair behind her ear, "There's been a fire at the St. James Infirmary here on this private compound in rural Paulina. Officials received a call from a trucker passing by on Airline Highway, just after four a.m., who reported that he saw smoke rising above the treeline."

Two paramedics pull a sheet-covered body out of the clinic on a stretcher, loading it into the van with solemn expressions. "The St. James Fire Department is currently trying to control the fires however, as you can see behind me, there *do* appear to be multiple fatalities."

She takes a step to the side so the cameraman can get a shot of the second charred building.

"This sprawling property belongs to noted pharmacologist, Dr. James Walsh, who was allegedly running a private clinical trial despite the revocation of his medical license five years ago. Police officials have not yet been able to locate Walsh for questioning."

80

Officer Griffin snaps photographs in Walsh's clinic office. First, the surveillance monitor. Then the gruesome remains of Fisher's corpse. He doubles back to the yellow evidence flag. He clicks off another photo and uses the butt of a pen to open the armoire doors to take some of Eileen Tate's battered body, noting the brain sludge visible through the crater bashed into her temple.

The shattered phone is coated in dried fluids, shards shimmering in the light of his external flash. What's left of the landline chirps through a smashed reciever, "*We're sorry. Your call did not go through. Please hang up and dial again.*"

Officer Pierce surveys the scene, watching the multi-camera monitor on the desk with folded arms. His eyes sweep across the room, settling on the safe full of pills. "You already photograph the monitor?" Pierce points over his shoulder.

Griffin nods. Another man enters the room, a higher-up judging by their suddenly-improved posture.

Pierce bounces his brows at him. "There's a minimized video player."

The higher-up inches his way to the desk, careful to avoid stepping in any of the dark blood in his cloth booties. "Click it."

Pierce taps the mouse with a gloved finger and the colorless security feed comes up. *Prerecorded.* It stars a little girl, tied to the four posters of a bed atop a bunny comforter. Pierce's eyes bulge thinking he is about to see something sexually graphic.

"Pederast?" The higher-up gurgles, clearing his throat.

Pierce shakes his head. "I hope to Christ not."

"Daddy! Please!" She struggles against her restraints.

A man off screen is talking to her. "Jessica, I can't let you go, baby. You're... you're not well." His voice cracks.

"Daddy... it *hurts*!"

Pierce leans forward, face close to the screen. It's hard to tell in black-and-white but it looks like something dark is inching its way out of a wound on the girl's neck. It looks like a squirming millipede.

"What the fuck..." Pierce chews his gum so fast and hard it tenses his jaw like chiseled marble.

"I know monkey, I know it hurts. But it won't hurt any more." His promise is ominous.

Jessica struggles, going berserk, chewing at the ropes with her teeth, flashing a wicked look back up toward the camera. Her tone is evil now. *Changing.* "*What did you do to me, daddy?!*"

From the lower edge of the frame emerges a glock handgun, its squared edges catching the overhead lights. The barrel is pointed right at her forehead from a few feet away. She shrieks.

BAM!

The gun fires. Pierce and the higher-up wince in unison. Griffin has turned around now, standing with his Nikon flaccid around his neck.

The bullet hit dead-on, right between her eyes. Walsh sobs loudly.

All of the men in the room are riveted, eyes wide at the video evidence, unprepared for what they are about to see next...

Though her body goes limp, seeping inky fluids onto the stuffed bunny in her lax arms, something *gruesome* emerges from the hole...

81

The sun's rays reach like fingers over the manicured grass, tickling the land and brushing through the Spanish moss like bristles of a hairbrush. Finn pulls up to a luxurious antebellum, freshly-painted white. Two sets of stairs lead out from the raised porch, craning in either direction like wooden arms reaching for a hug. A reporter speaks through a radio on a table near the patio's bench swing. The voice coming through it drones on, narrating the sensational aspects of the prior night's events, a topic the whole parish will be abuzz about soon enough.

"The blaze has been contained by the Paulina fire department. Multiple fatalities have been reported. We are going to stay with this story here on WNLA--"

A pair of filthy cowboy boots waltzes with confidence across the tidy, expansive front yard, edged with careful precision. The brown shit-kickers shuffle their way up the steps to the wraparound porch and stop before the woman seated in the swing. The woman is in her sixties. Her haircut is expensive, nails freshly-manicured. She lifts her made-up eyes to greet her visitor, adorned in the corners with crow's feet. She raises a sweating glass of foggy, yellow liquid, with slices of real lemon swimming between the ice cubes to toast him. Her rings shimmer, recently polished.

"Only *twenty* minutes late this time." She smiles, twisting two lips full of collagen upward, tugged unnaturally by a several-year-old fading facelift.

"Yeah, well, 'at girl don't run quite like she used to." The behemoth points to his old, red pickup, beyond the large black-clad man waiting in front of it, hands clasped in front of his belly.

He turns back to her and a flirtatious grin forms above his wily, graying beard.

It's Finn.

"Think it's the alternator this time. Here's to hoping it starts when I leave." He chuckles in his gravelly voice.

"It's time to put that old thing out of its misery." She scoffs and leans back into the chain swing, rocking lazily as she sips.

"No, ma'am, 'at there's a classic. She may have some extra miles and some wear-n-tear on her," he leans down, palms on his knees to get eye-level with her, "but that don't mean she ain't the *hottest* little ride this side a' Texas."

She forces a weak smile across her filled lips. "You can slap a new coat of paint and some seat covers on her all you want, but that won't make her any younger. She's still gonna be just an aging hunk of metal with duct tape and string holding everything in place til you eventually get bored of her and toss her in the junkyard with the others. With the money you make doing what you do, I'd imagine you have plenty in the bank to trade her in for a younger model."

"I don't *like* younger models. Not my style. I prefer a *classic*. One that's curvy and already broken in. A work of art to parade around and show off. Something that inspires envy in other men."

She clears her throat nervously, slightly tempted by his veiled offer, though ready to cut to the chase and move beyond the metaphor. The man in front of her is from a different world. Yet, she'd be lying if she said she didn't want someone to desire her in that fashion.

"I'm intrigued by your alleged little *miracle* pills. They're for my niece. Fell off a horse, poor thing. Left a nasty scar up the side of her face. But," she smiles again, genuinely this time, "if they work as well as you claim they do, I might take a few myself. Who doesn't need a little rejuvenation at my age?"

"I've seen what they can do. You'll be amazed." He taps his back pocket, feeling for them. "I have fifteen of 'em left. Though, I gotta advise against you taking them yourself. You don't need these. You're a stunner, Kelly."

She scoffs and waves him away like cigarette smoke. "Flattery will get you everywhere, sir."

Finn doesn't take his eyes off of her, allowing his intense gaze to stay fixed on her.

"What's the damage?" She pulls her checkbook and pen from her purse, spinning it on the little table toward him.

Finn waits for a moment, unblinking, then brazenly writes an amount on the check. He spins it back. The number is severe, far higher than she estimated.

"You've *got* to be kidding."

By the time the words leave her mouth, Finn is nodding politely and turning away. "Well, it's been good seein' ya. You have a good one now."

"Wait!" Kelly ponders for a moment, taken off-guard by his reaction. "How do you spell your name, Finn? One *N* or two?"

He turns. A grin creeps onto his grizzled face. "I spell it C-A-S-H."

Kelly shakes her head and chuckles, signs the check, and hands it to him.

He tugs out a small manilla envelope rattling with loose pills. "*Always* a pleasure, Kelly." Finn nods to his hired hand and they both start back across the grass.

Finn puts a hand on the red hood of his pickup, rubbing it. "You ever wanna go for a ride some time, you let me know. I'll show you first-hand that something new and shiny ain't got nothin' on a classic. They don't need fresh paint or bondo. They don't need fancy rims or wax jobs or constant tune-ups. They're perfect... just as they are."

Kelly holds up the sleeve of pills, thinking about the real implications of his words. She smiles. "Thank you for the house call."

Finn nods and hops in the driver's seat. His goon seats himself in the passenger side and Finn turns the key. The vehicle struggles for a moment and then starts up with a roar. He leans out the window and slaps the side of the door with joy. "See? You can't improve on perfection."

Kelly can't help but laugh a little as Finn makes his way back down the long driveway. In the privacy of her wraparound porch, on the tidy plot of land, she pours the pills into her cupped palm, studying the black capsules, hope glimmering in her aging eyes. She rolls them in her palm carefully, as if they contain a miraculous formula, one that's life-altering.

Unfortunately, they *do*.

<u>A NOTE FROM THE AUTHOR</u>

First, I would like to thank you all for reading my book. I'm sure some of you were either involved with the making of the film (*Obsidian*, formerly known as *The Black Pills*) or were fans of it due to word of mouth. Maybe you just stumbled upon it on a streaming site and thought it was cool despite the limited budget. Or maybe you have never even heard about *Obsidian* and you don't know what the fuck I'm talking about.

I just want to say that if you WERE a part of the making of the film, down there in Louisiana with me, even if in the smallest of ways, I thank you from the bottom of my heart. We couldn't have made the film without you. Even though it's no blockbuster, I'm so proud of what we all did despite the hurdles (and there were many!)

In many ways, I think this book is superior to the film because the lack of budget, seams in the scar makeup, actor's schedules and comfortablity, and nightmarish Covid-19 re-shoots weren't a factor in its conception. It's pure *story*. It's an amalgamation of the original tale before it was perverted by any producers (who backed me into creative corners constantly.)

But I just want to take a second and explain (with brevity, I promise!) the idea behind the original concept and thank a few people who made the BOOK part of this possible.

First, I need to tell you that the late Nic Wilder was one of my best friends from my mid twenties to my mid thirties when he died. Nic was wild. I met him at a party for our mutual friend Darcee where I was seated next to him at a round reception table. I looked down at his wheelchair and looked up at him (he was absolutely gorgeous. Black hair, mischievous smile, tattoos.) and he says "Yes, my dick still works." I laughed and said, "I didn't ask," to which he replied, "You were thinking it."

I *was* thinking it.

That blunt humor became the basis for our long-standing bullshit-free friendship. From that point on, he was in my next two films and would have been in Obsidian had he still been alive. Our group of friends also included Eddie Sampson (who inspired Eddie in Vanity Kills) who was another real character. But it was Nic who inspired the plot.

After I moved away, I came back to Florida for a visit and stayed with him. He rolled out the red carpet for me in every way possible, despite everything being a more-difficult, taxing chore while in a chair. As I made the long trek home, I thought to myself that I'd give anything, any amount of money or worldly possession in that moment, if there were just a pill to make him able to walk again. (He'd dived head-first into a too-shallow lake years before I knew him and became a quadriplegic. He'd later re-developed the use of his arms, changing his unofficial status to paraplegic.)

I thought to myself that with *my* luck, being as terrible as it is, any pill like that would probably have dire consequences and fuck him up worse than it would help. I thought about what a pill like that would do and by the time I finished the 11-hour drive, I had the plot all worked out. I couldn't write fast enough! I consulted with him for advice in the early drafts and he was so touched about the whole thing.

The monsters (in the movie *and* book) being black and tumorous were inspired by my cancer. At 19, I was diagnosed with Hodgkin's Lymphoma and by the time I got on chemo I had 72 tumors from my ears to my groin. Literally nothing in the world scares me like my own body. When you've had to plan your own funeral (literally), it strikes a fear in you that is hard to rival. So these monsters are my little homage to them. Each is my version of some form of the body turning monstrous and attacking its host from the inside.

Finally, I would also like to thank a few people who made *Vanity Kills* what it is throughout the last ten years, since the story's initial inception: Nic Wilder, Eddie Sampson, Tom Proctor, Heather Wohl, Dave Sikora, Mark Anthony, Amanda Jean Ruzsa, Chisto Healy, Otis Bateman/Travis Davis, Ash Ericmore, Mia Faller, Henry & Mary Frost, Hick Cheramie, Ashley Barton, Mattie Rojas Kupper, Nat Whiston, Jay Costigan, John Ryland, Justin Boote, Uncomfortably Dark, Olivia Peck, Amber Upson, Becky Sinn, Grace Ferguson, the supporting actors and crew of the film *Obsidian*, Milt Theodossiou, Travis Davis, Leeanne Wright, Corrina Morse, and, finally, to the two producers I eventually was legally able to fire after they put me through a 106 re-writes of the script and tried to fire me and take over my film because I wouldn't, quote, "play ball."

To you, I say: I hope this story is *finally* enjoyed by audiences the way it was always meant to be written.

<u>ABOUT THE AUTHOR</u>

Erica Summers is an independent filmmaker, writer, film industry grip, and artist with an unwavering passion for horror. Several of her award-winning feature films have screened worldwide including Obsidian, Mister White, & Loverboy (on Amazon Prime and most streaming services.) Though born and raised in Wyoming, Erica spent most of her life in the swampy American South. She now resides in Connecticut where she works in film and writes horror fiction. In her downtime, the bizarre, bisexual, cancer-survivor is typically slathered in garden dirt, fishing, or devouring horror movies with her boyfriend and two jack russell *terrors*.

Publications include, "The Mother" (*Their Ghoulish Reputation*), "Tines" (*It Calls From Below*), "Painted in Vermilion" (*Air: Elemental Series*), "All the Same Color on the Inside" (*Year Five Anthology*), "Take a Breath" (*Anthology of*

Splatterpunk), as well as her novel, *Mantis* and western-horror novelette, *Bad God's Tower.*

She recently finished a co-written shared-character anthology with horror authors, Chisto Healy and Mick Collins, scheduled to release in the fall of 2023. She is currently co-writing worm-related horror with her sister, and fellow author, Heather Wohl, that will be released by Rusty Ogre Publishing near the end of 2023.

BAD GOD'S TOWER:

A WESTERN HORROR NOVELETTE

Vicious criminals, Eugene Dempsey and Chester Craven, escape Wyoming Territorial Prison armed with nothing but striped prisoner pajamas and a Lakota's hand-drawn map that, according to legend, will lead them to the unfathomable riches in a secret tunnel burrowed into the base of Devil's Tower. Seeking their golden fortune, the fugitives head north, leaving their dusty trail stained in the blood of innocents.

With two determined buffalo soldiers nipping their heels, the sadistic escapees will soon realize all the gold in the land isn't worth what lies in wait for them in the claustrophobic underground beneath.

Obsidian (Feature Film)

The award-winning independent feature film version of *Vanity Kills*. (Streaming on most services including Prime. Also available on Bluray at www.rustyogrepublishing.com)